Who are the Royle sisters? All of London is gossiping about the beautiful triplets who've taken the ton by storm. Their slightly scandalous behavior is the subject of gossip and it's whispered that they may be the "secret" daughters of the highest prince in the land . . . As for the oldest, Mary, she certainly has learned . . .

HOW TO SEDUCE A DUKE

Why is the notorious Duke of Blackstone ruining Mary's well-laid plans to marry his brother, the handsome Viscount Wetherly? Every time she turns a corner, he is there—tantalizing her, teasing her . . . and the more she tries to ignore him, the more insistent he becomes. Mary knows she must make an advantageous marriage, but surely Blackstone is the wrong man for her. Isn't he?

Blackstone is not about to let his brother become bewitched by some wily blueblood pretender . . . even one as deliciously tempting as Mary. But until she came along, no woman has ever resisted his smooth, well-practiced seductions. Could it be that he's actually fallen in love with this infuriating chit?

If You've Enjoyed This Book,
Be Sure to Read These Other
AVON ROMANTIC TREASURES

KATHRYN CASKIE

How To
Seduce A Duke

An Avon Romantic Treasure

AVON BOOKS
An Imprint of HarperCollinsPublishers

This is a work of fiction. Names, characters, places, and incidents are products of the author's imagination or are used fictitiously and are not to be construed as real. Any resemblance to actual events, locales, organizations, or persons, living or dead, is entirely coincidental.

AVON BOOKS
An Imprint of HarperCollins*Publishers*
10 East 53rd Street
New York, New York 10022-5299

Copyright © 2006 by Kathryn Caskie
ISBN-13: 978-0-06-112456-3
ISBN-10: 0-06-112456-7
www.avonromance.com

First Avon Books paperback printing: October 2006

Avon Trademark Reg. U.S. Pat. Off. and in Other Countries, Marca Registrada, Hecho en U.S.A.
HarperCollins® is a registered trademark of HarperCollins Publishers Inc.

Printed in the U.S.A.

10 9 8 7 6 5 4 3 2 1

To Jenny Bent,
who believed in me all along.

Acknowledgments

There are several people to whom I owe a great debt of gratitude for helping me bring this story to life:

My wonderful editor at Avon Books, Lucia Macro, who probably has no idea how her hilarious daily e-mails spurred me on when the finish line seemed miles away.

Jenny Bent, my incredible agent, who went above and beyond the call of duty to help me deliver this book on time.

My amazing research assistant, Franzeca Drouin, who was always one step ahead of me.

Regency expert, Nancy Mayer, and also the learned ladies of the Beau Monde, especially authors Diane Perkins, Dee Hendrickson, Gaelen Foley and Tonda Fuller, who were always willing and able to answer any and all last-minute questions I had about complex period details.

My friend and fellow author, Sophia Nash, who encouraged me throughout the course of writing this book—including making arrangements for a very important revitalizing day at a spa as my deadline loomed.

My sisters, Lisa Sellers and Jenny Byers, and also my own two princesses (when they are old enough to read my books!), who might see glimpses of themselves between these pages.

And to my husband, for proving to me that everyday heroes really do exist.

Thank you all.

Chapter 1

In the blue veil of night, three human statues stood clustered behind a prickly screen of holly bushes, their voices carefully held to mere whispers.

"He's just *there*." Mary, the eldest of the Royle sisters, poked her white, heavily powdered index finger through a gap in the branches. "Do you see him? He's the blond gentleman before the fountain. Is he not exquisite?"

"I cannot see anything other than the back of your head." Her younger sister Anne did not find tonight's adventure nearly as diverting as Mary

1

did. Since the moment they'd left their great-aunt Prudence's house, she'd done nothing but complain about the nonsensical nature of their invasion of the garden rout next door.

But standing hidden along the hedge was perfectly logical to Mary's way of thinking. They weren't invited to the rout this eve . . . but he *was*.

What else was she supposed to do? Sit in her bedchamber while he was walking through the gardens only yards away? No, she was not about to miss an opportunity like this.

Until this night, Mary had only seen the viscount five times in passing. And though she was an excellent judge of character—everyone said so—she had had to concede that she needed more time to gather a better sense of him . . . to be sure. For she was nothing if not decisive. And once she made a decision, she never changed her mind. Ever.

Being able to watch him from the holly bushes, undetected as she was, would allow her to confirm her initial opinion of him, even though in her heart she already knew her perception was correct. He was exactly as he appeared—positively *perfect*.

Anne huffed and tugged hard on Mary's shoulder to move her out of the way.

Snapping her head around, Mary grimaced at her sister. It had taken her a full two hours to achieve the correct marbled effect. "You needn't be so impatient. I shall step aside if you'll lift your hand *carefully*."

Obliging her, Anne raised each finger in turn,

then lifted her damp palm from Mary's powdered skin.

Mary twisted to peer at the damage to her white finish. "I knew it! You've smudged the powder. Your fingers have left prints all over me."

"Will both of you please lower your shrieks?" Elizabeth, the youngest of the triplets by almost ten minutes, according to their father, blinked her powdered white lashes angrily. "What if we're caught? Our family will be ruined. Am I alone in considering this?"

"It's *dark*, Lizzie. No one can see us here." As she stood, Anne tripped on the hem of her Grecian gown, sending a puff of white powder into the air.

"Anne is right." Mary edged around the thick bush. "But we can't see or hear what's going on either. I daresay we *have* to move closer." She turned and signaled for her sisters.

It was then that she saw Anne and Elizabeth exchange loaded glances. *Oh no.* They weren't backing out now. They *were* going through with this. They were. After all, they'd promised her. "Do not even consider leaving. This was the plan, or have you forgotten? We dress in white and powder ourselves, then invade the rout, posing as garden statuary."

Elizabeth huffed at that. "And as I said at the house, your scheme is madness. Though I have to admit, in the moonlight, our marbling looks flawless. The effect is really quite amazing."

Anne flinched as she gazed down at her gleaming white arm. "What else is in this powder anyway? I feel as though ants are crawling all over me. Lud, Mary, I don't know how you convinced us to do this. And why—because you're smitten with some dashing soldier? I agree with Lizzie, this *is* madness."

"There is an ocean of difference between a simple soldier and a war hero. Did I mention that a viscountcy was newly bestowed on him, by the Regent himself? It was a grand reward for his valor in battle." Movement caught Mary's notice. "Blast, he's leaving. Come along, we have to catch him up. He's probably headed for the lawn."

Elizabeth shook her head vehemently. "The only place I am headed is back over the wall, and into a bath to wash this coating of white powder from my person." She came to her feet, then lent Anne a hand to help her stand.

"*Please.* Not until you've at least seen him. I am going to marry him, you know." Mary finished her sentence with a firm single nod.

"So you've said." Anne brushed the crumpled, dried holly leaves from the knees of her snowy gown. "But you don't need to marry the man just to secure your future. We've got the entire season . . . and more to find the proof we need."

Mary huffed at that. "I am not about to bank my life on such a slim possibility. I am being realistic about our prospects—and so should you." She watched the viscount lift a glass to his mouth, saw the crystal sparkle in the moonlight, and a sigh fell from her lips. "Beginning with *that* gentleman . . . that beautiful gentleman."

"Oh, very well, show me." Anne stood on the toes of her slippers and peered over the top of the hedge. "Which one is he?"

Mary looked closer and saw that there were two men now. But while *her* viscount—because indeed she already thought of him that way: *her* viscount— had golden hair, the other man's hair was as dark as jet, and he stood at least a head taller.

"Well, certainly not that hulking giant. My tastes are much more refined." Mary trotted a few steps along the hedgerow and beckoned for her sisters to follow, which they reluctantly did.

She paused only twenty paces from the two gentlemen. "*There*. The one with the cane," she whispered when her sisters drew alongside of her as she peered over the holly. "What did I tell you? Such fine, aristocratic features. Shows good breeding."

"Oh, good heavens! *Mary*—" Elizabeth sputtered, and her eyes rounded.

But Mary was too preoccupied with admiring the viscount to pay her nervous sister much mind. "Such grace in his gestures—oh, and, not that it matters, but he's got plump pockets too—ten thousand per annum."

"Mary!" This time it was Anne. "He's heard us. He's . . . he's coming this way—the *large* gentleman."

"Never mind her, Anne," Elizabeth whispered, "just *run*."

From the corner of her eye, Mary saw Elizabeth dart off into the darkness, with Anne right behind her, clumsily stumbling over vines and fallen branches as she ran.

Mary whirled around and looked back toward the two men.

Oh, no. Now there was only *one.* And indeed, a huge, dark, shadowy figure was pushing through a break in the hedge and heading toward her.

There was no time to run.

Lord above, no time to hide.

So, being a piece of slightly smudged garden statuary, she turned her back to the hedge, then simply folded her hands before her and tried her best to appear a slab of elegantly carved marble.

No sooner had she closed her eyes than she heard his footfalls nearby, and in the next moment, Mary knew he was standing right before her.

Do not move. Do not breathe.

She heard him exhale a quick, deep chuckle.

"Damned odd place for a statue," he muttered to himself. "Quinn, there's a statue behind the hedge," he called out. "Have you seen it? Quite lovely, actually. You should examine its profile. Extraordinary detail. Very realistic."

She heard the viscount's smooth voice coming from a distance. "Haven't. Must be one of Lord Underwood's recent acquisitions."

"No, this statue does not have . . . um . . . the

patina of antiquity. Come here and have a look for yourself."

The gentleman before her didn't move again, and Mary had the distinct impression that he was studying her . . . very closely. In fact, he was so near that she could feel the warmth of his breath upon her skin, and it made her tremble inwardly.

Oh perdition. She couldn't endure this any longer. Why wouldn't he just go away?

She knew that although it was fairly dark behind the hedge aside from a few fingers of moonlight breaking through from above, it was more than possible that her disguise had failed.

She had to see what was happening. Had to risk it.

Slowly she raised her eyelids ever so slightly, peered through her powdered lashes and saw—a large hand stretching outward as if to cup her breast.

Good heavens. He's not going to . . . oh Lord, he actually intends to touch my—

"How *dare* you, sirrah!" Mary's eyes snapped fully open, and she drew back her hand and landed a stinging slap on the man's cheek.

She'd never seen such a look of shock and utter surprise on anyone's face before. His mouth fell wide open as he yanked back his own hand and hurried it to the powdered print she'd left on his left cheek.

"I beg your pardon, miss. . . . I thought you were a—"

"No, you didn't. You *knew*. You were toying with me. You, you . . . scoundrel!"

Then from behind her came a hail of laughter. The viscount had obviously caned his way through the hedge as well. Mary froze in place.

"Even the garden statuary knows you're a rake, Rogan. I vow it should be very clear to you by now that there's no escaping your reputation, brother, no matter how hard you try."

Oh God. The viscount was directly behind her.

There was no way this eve could have turned out any more disastrous. None at all.

Mary angled her face away. She could not let the viscount see her features, for indeed, he might recognize her.

Her heart thudded impossibly hard in her chest, and with no other choice, no possible explanation to give for her outlandish appearance, Mary gave a shove to the ebony-haired man and, with her path of escape clear, raced past him and into the night.

"Damn me." The viscount's gaze trailed after the ghostly female figure until she disappeared in the darkness. "Who was that?"

His brother lifted an amused eyebrow as he rubbed his sore, powdery cheek. "On my honor, I swear I have not the faintest notion. But rest assured, I intend to find out."

The direction Mary dashed, unfortunately, was the exact opposite way from that in which she needed to go, which was only next door. Instead, she was forced through the back gardens, stables, and over the ivy-draped walls of no less than six town houses before she could slip down a narrow alleyway leading back to Berkeley Square and her great-aunt's town house, where she and her sisters were lodging for the season.

As Mary pressed the front door closed behind her, she emptied her lungs of breath in a grand sigh of relief. She was home at last and, thankfully, fairly certain the viscount had not glimpsed her face.

Even if he had for the briefest of moments, with her body and sable hair coated with a thick layer of flour paste and powder, he could not have recognized her as the woman he tipped his hat to in Hyde Park each Tuesday while riding during the fashionable hour.

At least she hoped not.

The glow of a flickering fire illuminated the open doorway to the parlor, and she started for it, knowing she would find at least one of her sisters inside.

"*There* you are." Elizabeth sat hearthside on a stool, combing the dampness from her newly washed, bright copper locks.

Mary's gaze searched the shadowy room. "Aunt Prudence is still asleep, is she not?" she whispered.

"You know the answer to that. What else would our ancient aunt be doing at such a late hour . . . or in the morn . . . or in the afternoon?" Elizabeth flipped her long wet hair over her shoulder, sending droplets sizzling into the fire. "Anne and I were ever so worried that you'd been nabbed."

"Evidently not *that* worried. You abandoned me."

Elizabeth lowered her gaze to the floor. "Yes . . . well, we are dreadfully sorry about that." She raised her eyes then, and smiled. "But all is well. You have come home. No harm was done."

Mary crossed her arms over her chest and did not reply.

"Y-you were not . . . apprehended?"

"No, but nearly. The large one almost had me." Mary remembered the stunned look on the oaf's face as she slapped him, and she chuckled to herself. He deserved it, though. Had she not stopped him, he would have . . .

"Oh, Mary, thank heavens you are safe!" Anne, wearing a dressing gown and appearing fresh from her bath, rushed into the parlor and made to hug her marbleized sister. But at the last moment, noting the powder all over Mary, she changed her mind. "Why are you so late returning? What happened?"

"Nothing at all. I simply ran in the wrong direction and had a devil of a time making my way home." It was then that Mary noticed that Anne's face, throat and hands—indeed, every exposed bit of skin—were as red as a heated brand. "The question should be, what happened to you?"

Anne snatched the comb from Elizabeth and

passed it through her damp golden hair. *"The powder."* She flicked her eyebrow upward in annoyance. "I told you that it itched. Why I let you persuade me to disguise myself as a statue, I will never know."

"I only wanted you both to see the man I have decided to marry by the end of the season—and he was right next door this eve." Mary smiled broadly. "You agree with me, don't you? He *is* perfect in every way that matters." Mary bent to sit upon the settee, but Elizabeth waved her off before her powdered gown could mar the silk cushion. "I haven't much time, so naturally I shall need my sisters' help to bring about the match."

Anne shook her head. "I dare not even ask what your idea of *help* might entail." She thrust the comb back in Elizabeth's hand, then crossed the room and opened their late father's leather document box. From it, she withdrew several large folds of foolscap. "Besides, once we prove the information held in these letters—"

Mary raised a palm. "Stop. We do not even know where to begin. Proving anything will be impossible, given the time and financial restraints we have."

Elizabeth joined Anne before the document box. "There is plenty of information here and a number of sound clues to follow. Papa saved these letters for us for this very reason—to prove who we are."

Huffing her frustration, Mary stalked across

the parlor and slammed the lid of the box closed. "Papa wasn't saving these documents *for* us, he was hiding them *from* us. *From everyone.* Had he had any notion that his death was so imminent, I feel certain he would have destroyed this box and its contents."

"I completely disagree. He could have burned every scrap if that was his intent, but he didn't, did he? This was his assurance that someday the babes he rescued would meet their destiny." Anne lifted the hem of her dressing gown and, appearing more than a little annoyed, dusted Mary's white powder prints from the leather box with her swollen, red fingers.

Mary pinned her sister with a hard gaze. "For the sake of argument, let us say that we are the girls mentioned in these letters . . . and let us further assume that every letter inside that box is true—do you think those who worked so hard to erase our existence would simply allow us to suddenly appear in London society with diamond tiaras on our heads?"

"Do not be daft, Mary." Elizabeth shook her head at the ridiculousness of her sister's words. "We would not wear tiaras. What a silly thought. One must be married to wear a tiara. Isn't that so, Anne?"

Mary growled her frustration. "You missed my point entirely. This endeavor of yours could be very dangerous if the letters are genuine. Very dangerous. If not, uncovering the truth of our births will be naught but a colossal waste of time *and* coin."

Anne raised her delicate chin, and, with an all-knowing smirk curving her lips, she addressed Elizabeth. "Now here it is, Lizzie. The truth of Mary's resistance."

Elizabeth peered blankly back at her sister.

"Do you not see it?" Anne expelled a deep breath. "Our penny-pinching, ever-frugal Mary doesn't wish to spend a single farthing on investigating the circumstances of our birth."

Elizabeth lowered her gaze to her laced fingers, which were twisted as surely as the twigs of a nest. " 'Tis a Herculean task to be sure, Mary." She turned her wide green eyes upward again. "But we owe it to Papa . . . and to ourselves to try."

"Very well, so be it." Mary tossed her hands into the air, then let them fall firmly to her sides, coaxing twin clouds of powder from her gown. "The two of you can do as you wish, but I plan to use my resources logically."

Anne scoffed. "We are rich, Mary."

"No we are not rich, not even close to it. It only seems that way to you because we lived so simply in Cornwall." Mary shook her head. "I do not know how Papa managed it, likely by doing without and saving his pennies for years, but he bequeathed us each with great gifts—adequate portions to live on—and dowries large enough to allow us to attract gentlemen of standing and consequence. If we are careful with our spending, and practical in the matches we make, we have the means to assure comfortable lives for ourselves, instead of scraping together every halfpenny to buy flour for bread. But only *if* we are not wasteful and set aside this fanciful notion of our supposed lineage."

Mary started for the doorway but, realizing that her sisters had not replied and were likely ignoring her pragmatic advice, turned back. "We must be realistic. We are just three sisters from Cornwall who happen to have been left large dowries. *That is all.*"

"No, Mary." Elizabeth lifted the box and held it with reverence before her. "We are the hidden daughters of the Prince Regent and his Catholic wife, Mrs. Fitzherbert."

"We'll never prove it." Mary gestured to the old leather box. "Don't you understand? This notion is but a faery tale, and we'd be mad to believe otherwise."

"Deny it all you like, Mary," Anne countered, "but you know as well as I that it's true—by blood at least we are . . . *princesses.*"

The next afternoon, as Mary sat curled in the window seat, immersed in the pages of a thick book, there came a solid rap at the front door. Her gaze shot to Aunt Prudence, who had fallen asleep in the wing-backed chair beside the hearth with an empty cordial goblet in her withered hand. Prudence snorted once but did not awaken.

Instead of rising to answer, Mary pinched the curtain between her thumb and index finger, parting the two panels no more than a nose's width, then peeked through.

Aunt Prudence's advanced age had curtailed social calls many years before. Mary and her sisters had not yet made any formal acquaintances in London, so she knew that a friend coming to call was not a reasonable possibility.

Her only thought that moment was one of dread.

What if she had not escaped the garden last evening as cleanly as she believed? And now someone had come to discuss the serious matter of her trespassing.

Oh God. She didn't have the faintest idea what to do.

Mary centered her eye on the gap in the curtains, but the angle was too sharp, and no matter how she positioned herself, she simply could not see who stood before the door.

There was a second knock.

Mary jerked her head back from the window. Good heavens. What if *he* was the caller? Her viscount . . . or worse, the giant ogre of a man he called his brother?

Mary's heart drummed against her ribs.

Suddenly, there were footsteps in the passage, and Mary turned in time to see MacTavish, the lean, elderly butler recently engaged to manage the household pass the parlor doorway.

"*No*, please, do not open it!" Mary leapt from the

window seat and hurried across the parlor toward the passage.

Thankfully, he heard her. MacTavish reappeared in the doorway riding a backward step.

"Might I ask why not, Miss Royle?"

Mary gave her head a frustrated shake. Was it not obvious? "Because . . . we do not know who it is."

"Beggin' yer pardon, but I can remedy that problem by simply openin' the door."

Mary steepled her fingers and turned her gaze downward as she tapped her thumbs together.

There was a third succession of knocks.

"Miss Royle? I should open the door."

Mary looked up and replied in the softest whisper she could manage. "All right. But if anyone should inquire, my sisters and I are not at home."

"Verra weel, Miss Royle. I understand . . . a bit."

As MacTavish headed for the entry, Mary raced on her toes down the passage and slipped into the library, where she found her sisters taking tea.

Flattening herself against the wall of books nearest the door, she strained her ear to discern exactly who had come to call.

"Drat! Can't hear a word they are saying," Mary mumbled to herself. Still, the voices were both low, indicating at least that the caller was male. This, however, did not bode well for her.

Elizabeth, whose red hair gleamed in the ribbons of dust-mote-speckled sunlight streaming through the back window, narrowed her eyes at Mary. She slammed closed the red leather-spined book balanced on her lap. "I know that look. What have you done now?"

Mary shoved an errant lock of dark hair from her eye and scowled back. "Hush! Do you wish for someone to hear you? We are not supposed to be at home, you know. Read . . . whatever it is that you have there, Lizzie."

"It is a book on maladies and remedies. I found it in Papa's document box."

Anne twisted around in her chair. The redness and swelling on her hands and face had subsided, leaving her skin as light and luminous as her flaxen hair. "Why must we be quiet? You're not making any sense." Her eyes widened then. "Good God, Mary. Is something amiss? Why, you're as white as a—"

"Marble statue," Elizabeth interjected, then both she and Anne exchanged a shoulder-bobbing chuckle at Mary's expense.

Mary opened her mouth to reply when she heard the metallic click of the front door being pressed closed.

A moment later, MacTavish was standing in the doorway of the library with a square of wax-sealed vellum centered on his sterling salver.

" 'Tis for you, Miss Royle." He raised the tray before Mary.

"For me?" She blinked at it but did not reach for it. "Why, I can't imagine—"

Both of her sisters were on their feet in an instant.

"Who is it from, Mary?" Elizabeth's emerald eyes sparkled with excitement.

"I am sure I don't know." Mary glanced up at the butler.

" 'Twas left by a liveried footman." MacTavish cleared his throat. "If I may, Miss Royle. Much as openin' the door will reveal the identity of a caller . . . the sender may be divulged by simply . . . openin' the bloody letter."

Anne gasped loudly. "MacTavish, your language!"

Her sister's reaction was a bit overdone, to Mary's way of thinking, but MacTavish's language had served its purpose. Mary had gotten the intended message quite clearly.

"Beggin' yer pardon, miss." The Scottish butler tipped his bald pate. "If ye'll excuse me please, I'll just be poppin' down to see if Cook needs any help setting the roast to the spit."

As MacTavish quit the room, Anne leveled a superior gaze on Mary.

Oh no. Here it comes again.

"Why you could not bring yourself to pay a little more per annum to engage a proper butler I will never understand." Anne crossed her arms over her chest and plopped back down in her chair. "MacTavish is little more than a street thug, and you well know it."

"I know nothing of the sort." Mary shook the

letter at her sister. "What I do know is that by being thrifty with wages, I was able to engage a butler and a cook, and I have just placed a notice in *Bell's Weekly Messenger* for a maid. So unless you would rather handle the cooking, shopping, and emptying of the chamber pots for the duration of our stay in London, you would do well not to mention MacTavish's minor shortcomings again!"

"Minor shortcomings? The butler and our cook are completely unsuitable. This house would have been far better served if you had kept Aunt Prudence's existing staff."

"Please stop, Anne. We've had this discussion too many times. The old staff took complete advantage of Aunt Prudence's age and poor memory. They were robbing her blind, and you well know it."

Elizabeth turned then, caught Mary's arm, and guided the letter before her eyes. "Come now, tell us who it is from."

Mary swallowed deeply, then, her composure regained, broke the crimson wax wafer and opened the letter. She scanned the heavily inked words quickly, then stared for a clutch of seconds as the name of the sender met her eyes.

"Oh my heavens." The letter slipped through Mary's fingers to the bare wooden floor.

"Please do not make us wait any longer, Mary—may I read it?" When Mary didn't answer but simply stared down at it on the floor, Elizabeth snatched the letter up and began to read. When she finished, she backed stiffly to her chair and collapsed into it.

Anne's mouth fell open. "Will one of you please reveal the contents of the letter? My patience with your drama is growing ever thin. Who is the letter from?"

"Lord Lotharian of Cavendish Square, Marylebone Park. Our guardian." Elizabeth turned her gaze to Mary. "We must go to him, Mary, we must!"

Mary huffed at that. "Are you mad? Pay a call to a gentleman we do not know? A man we haven't heard from *ever*."

"He claims to be an old acquaintance of Papa's. I see no reason he would make such a claim if he were not."

When Mary shook her head, Elizabeth then reached across the small tea table and took Anne's hand into her own. She peered into Anne's gold-flecked eyes until she nodded.

"Yes, I'll go, Lizzie."

Elizabeth turned her gaze to Mary. "We all *must* go."

"Aunt Prudence must be informed of your plan," Mary noted. Of course, even if she told their dear great-aunt that her sisters were off to call upon a gentleman, their supposed guardian, she wouldn't remember within an hour's time. But that wasn't why she'd mentioned it. She was hoping to appeal to Anne's great sense of propriety.

Only her ploy did not work.

"Aunt Prudence is napping," Anne replied matter-of-factly. "I shouldn't wish to wake her."

Suddenly Elizabeth rose and raced from the room. She returned with the shiny brass key extracted from the document box's keyhole. Her cheeks were flushed with excitement.

"According to this letter," she told them, "this key has a dual purpose—one that may assist us in our quest."

Mary raised her eyebrows. "How does this gentleman know of our 'quest,' I ask you?"

"He was a friend of Papa's." Anne's eyes glittered with excitement. "He may know all about our true parents."

"I think you both suppose too much." Mary sighed as she walked over to Elizabeth and pulled the key from her fingers. "You both actually believe that this simple brass twist of metal may in actuality be . . . the key to the mystery of our births."

Anne and Elizabeth's eyes locked, then in an instant, they shot out of the library. The thunder of boots echoed down the passageway floor.

"Mary, do come. We must away—this instant!"

"This is naught but a lark, I tell you—though I *will* come along, only so I can be there to remind you that I told you so." Resignedly, Mary turned and started for the passageway.

When she neared the door, her excited sisters flung a woolen shawl around her shoulders and shoved a straw bonnet down upon her head.

"But I will not waste good coin on a hackney for this useless sojourn." Mary gave her head a hard nod to emphasize her point. "Cavendish Square is not so far away, and the air is mild enough this day. We shall walk."

Anne opened the front door and stared up at the heavy gray clouds above. "But Mary, it is about to rain."

Mary turned a concerned gaze to the skies. "Oh dear. That *does* make a difference. Wait just a few moments for me, please." Turning, she hurried back inside the house.

Anne and Elizabeth stood in stunned silence for several seconds.

Finally, Anne turned to her sister. "Good heavens. Our frugal Mary is actually going to spend a coin to hire a hackney. Why, I can't believe it."

"Nor can I, so let us find a hackney cab before she changes her mind." At once, Elizabeth rushed into the street and waved her hand madly, finally catching the notice of a hackney driver who stood puffing on his pipe at the corner of the square and Davies Street.

"Elizabeth, we are in London!" Anne rushed into the square and dragged her sister back to the steps. "Your hoydenish ways must end. We are ladies, no longer coarse country misses. Remember that."

When Mary came back out the door, she was dismayed to find her sisters about to board a hackney.

"No, no! I do apologize, my dear sir," Mary called out to the driver. "But my sisters shan't require your services after all."

Anne and Elizabeth jerked their heads around and stared at Mary, their mouths fully agape.

Mary smiled pleasantly and handed each of her sisters an umbrella. "Since we're walking, we'll most certainly need *these*."

Chapter 2

◦◦◦◦

The scent of coming rain permeated the damp air as Rogan Wetherly, the Duke of Blackstone, and his brother, Quinn, the newly belted Viscount Wetherly, reined their gleaming bays down Oxford Street in the direction of Hyde Park.

A single chill droplet struck Rogan's cheek, and he turned his eyes upward to the darkening sky.

The clouds were black and heavy with moisture. They were bloody insane to venture even a few short miles from Marylebone—for the sake of a woman.

But the lady in question, according to Quinn, who was set on making her acquaintance, visited the park every Tuesday at this hour. And who was Rogan to dash his brother's hopes of meeting her?

"Good God, Rogan—*halt*!" Without warning, Quinn unsteadily rose up in his stirrups, reached out, and caught Rogan's right rein. He yanked back hard, driving Rogan's horse straight into his own, stopping the beast's forward progression.

Rogan's heart lurched in his chest. "Bloody hell, Quinn! If you were trying to unseat me, you very nearly succeeded."

Quinn cleared his throat. He removed his hat and tipped his head forward, turning Rogan's attention to the trio of wide-eyed, stunned misses.

Fools. They must have crossed from Davies Street without paying any heed to oncoming riders. And now they were standing in the middle of the crowded street, still as statues, less than a foot before them.

The tallest of the three women glared up at Rogan from beneath the faded silk brim of a most ridiculous beribboned hat. Her amber eyes flashed angrily.

For the briefest moment, her mouth twisted, then opened, as if to give him a suitable dressing down. Then her expression suddenly changed—to one of distress. Abruptly, she looked away.

Rogan was about to call out to her when she caught up the gloved hand of the copper-haired beauty closest to her and guided her small party quickly from the center of Oxford Street down the flagway in the direction the two men had come from.

"Where was your mind? You might have

trampled them." Quinn turned in his saddle and watched the three women make their way through the bustling crowds and down the street.

"They obviously walked straight into the road without paying any attention to oncoming horses. Even had my horse trod upon one of them, I daresay the fault would not have been solely my own." Rogan turned his skittish mount in a circle and joined Quinn in gazing upon the women's retreat. "Did you see the way the tall one looked at me? Like she bloody well thought I had the pox, or worse."

"No, I did not notice. I was far too occupied with stilling your damned horse."

Rogan tightened his reins and stood in the stirrups for a better look as the young women stalked past the shops lining Oxford Street. "There was something familiar about her look, don't you agree?" He dropped back into the saddle.

Quinn exhaled. "No doubt. I know you have adopted a respectable mode of living since assuming Father's title, but after years of roguish adventure, it is not inconceivable that you somehow wronged the woman in the past."

Rogan huffed at that. "Not that one. Oh, she's comely enough to be sure, but did you see her clothing—and good God—that hat? Straight from the country with nary two shillings in her palm, I'd say."

Quinn grunted at the comment but didn't reply.

He nudged his horse and started again toward Hyde Park.

"Come now, you cannot seriously wish to continue on," Rogan called out, but his brother did not stop. "Look at the sky."

Quinn settled his beaver hat and pushed it lower upon his head. "You can come along, or return to the house, Rogan, but I will continue on. She *will* be there, I know it, and this time, we will meet."

Rogan shook his head and turned his mount around. He drove his heels into his horse and drew alongside his brother a moment later. "So, this woman you seek in the park . . . you think she is the future Viscountess Wetherly?"

"I do not know. We have not properly met. But she may be."

"Why the race to the altar? You're certainly not a wrinkled maid withering on the vine. You're a hero, awarded a grand title for your valor. You're handsome, young, and moneyed. You have everything to live for—and yet you wish for shackles?"

Quinn's expression grew solemn. He jerked his horse to a halt and did not speak until Rogan did the same. "I wish it because I do not want to wait to be happy, to have the life I desire. At Toulouse, I learned how position and rank can suddenly mean nothing. How I could clink glasses with a friend one night, then dig his grave the next."

Quinn gave a long sigh as he lifted his lame right leg and withdrew his foot from the stirrup, allowing the leg to hang limp. "If war taught me anything, it was that life is to be lived, Rogan. And for me, that means a wife and children. And I don't intend to put it off any longer."

Rogan nodded resignedly. How could he argue with that logic? His younger brother had seen more death during his years on the Peninsula than he himself would in a lifetime. He didn't begrudge Quinn the idyllic life he dreamed of. Lord knows, after all Quinn had endured on the Peninsula, he deserved it.

Only the blissful married life he sought didn't really exist, no matter what Quinn believed.

But that was a discussion for another day.

Rogan straightened his back and smiled. "Well then, Quinn, we shall find your lady—as long as we get back to Portman Square before the sky opens upon us."

Quinn hooked his hand beneath his knee and maneuvered his boot back securely into the stirrup. A mischievous smile curved the edges of his lips. "We best make haste then." He leaned low over his mount's neck and brought down his heels hard. "I'll see you at the gate, old man."

Rogan chuckled, then drove his steed hard toward Cumberland Gate. How pleasingly diverting it was that Quinn, injured as he was, actually thought he could reach the park before he would.

The wind rose up as Rogan spurred his horse

down Oxford Street, catching the lip of his new beaver hat and flipping it from his head. He heard the splash as the topper likely landed in a muddy puddle, but he never bothered to look back.

He had a race to win.

A damp breeze raked through his thick hair, and his coattails rode the wind behind him.

Within a short minute, his horse charged past Quinn's. Rogan whooped in triumph. He turned to look at Quinn. "No one ever gets the better of the Black Duke!"

Quinn drove his mount harder until the two horses were nearly neck and neck. He laughed as his bay galloped past Rogan's. "No one?" the fair-haired brother shouted back.

Rogan grinned and snapped his short whip against the horse's right haunch. The bay shot into the lead once more. "No one—and that includes *you*, dear brother."

Fat drops of rain splattered the ground around the Royle sisters as they reached Cavendish Square in Marylebone Park. A raw, mossy scent rose up into the air as the earth soaked in the droplets.

Elizabeth excitedly positioned the missive before Mary's eyes. "We've arrived. There it is, do you see? Number Two, straight ahead."

"So I see." Mary did not move from her place on the flagway, even though the tempo of the rain had increased twofold within the past minute.

"You may dawdle here if you like, Mary, but I do not wish to see my new morning frock ruined by the rain." Anne charged up the narrow walk to the steps that led up to the grand house. As she reached the first step, she turned and looked back at her sisters. "At least you are coming, Lizzie, aren't you?"

Elizabeth turned her gaze to Mary, then reached out and pushed a damp sable lock from Mary's cheek. "Please, sister. I know you believe this may be naught but a lark, but I have to know if this Lord Lotharian can tell us anything about our births. Please come with us. You are most clever and will divine the truth faster than Anne or I ever could. *Please.*"

Mary gazed up at Anne, who now stood with her hand menacingly poised about the brass door-knocker.

"I'm going to do it—I am going to knock this very instant." Anne lifted the heavy ring. "You two are going to look quite the ninnies when the door is opened and you are still standing in the street, wet as river carp."

Elizabeth turned a pleading gaze upon Mary.

She had walked all the way here, had nearly been killed doing so. Might as well go inside. "Very well," Mary said, "but if this little adventure yields nothing to support your fanciful story of our births, you must promise me you will give up your investigation and concentrate on your futures."

"Oh, what a goose you can be sometimes," Elizabeth laughed. "You know we can never agree to that." She grabbed Mary's hand and hurried to the door, arriving just as Anne slammed the brass hammer down twice upon its base.

Before Mary could offer even a syllable of reply, the door swung open and a portly manservant ushered them inside and out of the rain.

The house appeared quite grand from the outside, but it was only once they were inside that its true enormity could be realized.

The entryway walls soared three stories, following the sweep of a staircase edged with gilded balustrades. The polished marble entry floor glistened like a mirror, which pleased Mary's eyes, at first—until she realized that the marble reflected the white of her underskirts.

Best to walk with knees pressed firmly together.

A trio of young footmen suddenly surrounded the sisters, startling them. The servants' gloved hands quickly plucked off all wraps and snatched away the girls' dripping umbrellas. Then the footmen disappeared as quickly as they had come.

"My lady will receive you in the library," the manservant said as he tipped his head and turned, as though he expected them to follow. "She is about to take tea."

Mary stretched her hand outward and tapped his shoulder before he could leave the foyer. "I beg your pardon, but I believe we might have been given the wrong direction."

The manservant turned to face her, appearing more than a little perturbed that she had had the audacity to touch him. But Mary was not about to be put off.

Elizabeth handed the card to Mary, who took it and pointed out the address to the manservant. "Two, Cavendish Square."

The man blinked his lizardlike eyes and peered at the vellum, then turned his gaze back to Mary. "No, you have the right of it, miss. You are the Royle family, are you not?"

"Why yes, we are," Mary began. "But we—"

The manservant broke in as if he did not hear her. "As I said, Miss Royle, if you will all please follow me, I will take you to my lady."

"Stop, please! We have not come to see a *lady*." Anne, who was clearly growing impatient, folded her arms over her chest.

"We have come to call upon our guardian, a gentleman . . . um . . . Lord Lotharian." In her confusion, Elizabeth's brilliant green eyes had grown as large and round as the manservant's.

"Quite right." The manservant nodded his head. "And you shall see his lordship soon. Right this way, if you please."

Elizabeth and Anne each clutched one of Mary's arms—for support, or to ensure she wouldn't turn on her heels and escape, Mary wasn't sure—and they followed the squat little man down a long passage and into an expansive library.

Leather-bound books filled the shelves to the gold-framed mural painted on the ceiling. A mingling of leather polish, candle wax, and mustiness permeated the cool air of the room.

In the center of the rectangular chamber, a diminutive, elderly, onion-shaped woman sat upon a silk-sheathed settee blinking up at them.

So startlingly small was she, other than in girth, that her dainty slippers did not come close to reaching the Turkish carpet stretched across the floor.

The manservant walked into the middle of the room and promptly announced them. "My lady, the Misses Royle." Then he quickly quit the room.

The old woman on the settee grew noticeably excited. "Oh, oh, at last I can see you with my own eyes. I am so glad that you have come—we weren't sure that you would, you know. But here you are and every bit as beautiful as I imagined. I have heard so much about you three gels, so much!" Her little feet, shod in silk slippers with surprisingly high heels, kicked merrily.

Her hand dropped down below the curved arm of the settee and pulled a wooden lever. At once a tufted footstool shot out from beneath the settee. The round lady hopped down upon it, then stepped lightly to the carpet.

"Stand up straight and let me see you properly. So lithe you all are. Tall, too, all of you!" The old woman's gaze fixed on Mary. "Which are you, dear?"

"I-I am Mary." Her cheeks began to heat, especially when the old woman raised a lorgnette and studied her. She did not like one bit being the subject of scrutiny, especially by someone she did not know.

"Since you are triplets, I had expected you to greatly resemble one another, but you don't. The color of your hair is completely different. Even the shape of your faces—not at all alike."

The old woman turned her lorgnette upon each of the sisters.

"No, you are as different as morn, noon, and eve. Only your commanding height and your eyes give your kinship away."

She turned back to Mary. "Look at you, gel, such long, dark hair, and why, you are nearly the height of a man." The short woman chuckled with delight. "You have the blood for certain. Spectacular height often reveals itself in women of royal lineage."

"Really?" Elizabeth was clearly enthralled.

"Oh, indeed." The lady turned her gaze upon Elizabeth. She waddled close, then stood on the tips of her toes to finger Elizabeth's bright copper hair. "You must be Elizabeth. Look at that fiery crown of yours. Queen Elizabeth had hair like yours, dear—and she stood nearly six feet in height."

Elizabeth gave Mary a smug look.

Oh, good Lord. Mary fought the urge to roll her

eyes. *As if any of these inane observations mean any-thing.*

The lady followed Elizabeth's gaze, then added, "Her cousin, Mary, Queen of Scots, quite matched her height, you know."

Then the woman's pale gray eyes sought out Anne. "Ah, such delicate features, and hair like spun gold. Beautiful, so, so beautiful."

Anne colored becomingly.

"I vow, when the *ton* gazes upon the three of you, there will be no question—for it is clear you have the blood of kings and queens surging in your veins."

Mary could endure this prattle no longer. The woman, whoever she might be, had offered no support for her words. And no good could come out of exciting her sisters this way. The tale of their births was naught but a faery story.

"I beg your pardon, madam, but I fear you have the advantage." Mary smiled at the old woman. "We have yet to make your acquaintance."

"Oh, mercy." The elderly lady clapped her hand to her bountiful bosom. "I do apologize. I thought Lord Lotharian would have mentioned me in his missive. I am Lady Upperton."

Though evidently Lady Upperton believed that this revelation would hold some meaning for them, it did not. The three Royle sisters stared mutely back at the frosty-haired old woman.

"Then, you have not heard?" Lady Upperton

smiled broadly and filled her lungs with a deep breath before speaking. "Lotharian has asked me to be your *sponsor*—your entrée into London society."

"Our sponsor? I-I do not understand." Mary struggled to comprehend how such a claim could possibly be true. "Lady Upperton, I do not wish to appear ungrateful, but until three minutes ago, my sisters and I had not even gazed upon you—had not heard your name."

"Dear me, I suppose I can understand how an offer from a complete stranger to launch you into society might seem rather unbelievable. But it's all true, I assure you." Lady Upperton took Mary's hand into her own. "I promised your father I would do it when the time came. Promised Lotharian as well. And I shall. Once I give my word, I keep it."

Promised their father?

"When?" Mary blurted. "I mean . . . when did you make our father this promise?"

The elderly lady grew very quiet and thrummed her small fingers upon her painted lips. "I suppose it must be almost twenty years ago. After the rakes and I heard the circumstances of your birth, how could I deny your father anything? Of course, the three of you were but babes, but he was concerned, even then, about the course of your futures."

Surely her ears deceived her. This could not be happening. Why, their father had never mentioned anything of this. And would have. Certainly.

"You mentioned having heard the circumstances of our births." Anne stepped forward and stole the old woman's hand from Mary. "You . . . and the *rakes*?"

"Oh, yes. He told us all—my husband, sadly, he departed some years ago, and his fellow members of the Old Rakes of Marylebone."

Anne's eyebrows drew close in her apparent confusion. "Father was a member of a gentlemen's club? I cannot imagine such a thing."

"Indeed he was. As was . . . *is* Lord Lotharian." Lady Upperton gave herself a mental shake, then withdrew her hand from Anne's. "In fact, I think it is time you gels should meet him."

Lady Upperton spun around on her teetering heels and shuffled her way to the bookcase situated to the left of the cold hearth.

She flashed the sisters a mischievous smile, then positioned the flat of her hand over the face of a goddess column and pushed. The masterful carving of the goddess's nose depressed beneath her hand, and suddenly, from somewhere behind the bookcase, came a loud metallic click.

Lady Upperton turned back to the young ladies and raised her brows nonchalantly. "Are you ready?"

The Royle sisters exchanged nervous glances, then, as if cued, they nodded their heads as one.

All except Mary.

"Very well then, in you go." Lady Upperton gave the bookcase a firm nudge, and at once the lowermost six feet of the shelves opened like a door to reveal a dark passage.

Anne started forward without hesitation, with Elizabeth at her heels. When they reached the opening, they stopped and looked back at Mary, who had not taken even a single step.

Good heavens.

Suddenly, Mary felt rather light in the head. When she had agreed to call on Lord Lotharian with her sisters, she had been fairly certain that nothing more would come to pass than her sisters coming home with another useless packet of letters or the like.

This turn of events, however, was unimaginable. She could not have prepared for this.

Not for a grand lady prepared to install them in to London society.

Not for a secret membership of old rakes.

Certainly not for doorways hidden within walls of old books.

"Hurry now, Mary." The old woman beckoned her forward. "The gentlemen will be waiting."

"G-gentlemen?" Mary swallowed deeply. "I thought we were to meet Lord Lotharian?"

"Oh yes, dear, but there are two others who heard the story of your birth that night. You will wish to make their acquaintance as well. Come now. Do not tarry."

Mary moved her feet slowly toward the open bookcase. At that very moment, Anne and Elizabeth disappeared into the darkness beyond.

A cool draft from the secret passage lifted the fine loose tendrils of Mary's hair, making her shiver. Still, she stepped forward.

The moment the thick darkness of the secret passage enveloped her, Mary heard the bookcase begin to move closed again. She whirled around.

In the waning light of the library, she could just see Lady Upperton's smiling face. "You are not joining us, Lady Upperton?" she asked.

Lady Upperton grinned at that. "Oh goodness no, child. It is a gentlemen's club, after all. I am but the gatekeeper. It would not do for you three to be seen entering the club, so Lotharian sent you to my house. Go on with your sisters, gel. Follow the small circle of light you will see in a moment. Follow it until you reach the passage. Then knock twice. Hard. I daresay Lotharian's hearing is not what it once was." Without another word, Lady Upperton closed the bookcase behind Mary.

"Are you coming, Mary?" came Elizabeth's whisper a short distance down the passage.

Mary dragged a breath of musty air through her nose. "I am."

No more than a clutch of moments had passed before Mary felt the presence of her sisters beside her. As Lady Upperton had said, a thin wand of candlelight sliced through an eye-shaped hole at the end of the passage. The sisters, hands instinctively clasped, moved together toward the end of the passage.

Mary released Anne's hand and made to rap twice upon the wall, as Lady Upperton had instructed. But her sister stopped her.

"Look through the peephole first and tell us what you can see."

Mary tilted her head and gazed up at the oval. "I am not nearly tall enough," she whispered.

"I will do it." Elizabeth began moving about in the darkness. "Come now, Mary, give me your knee and help me onto Anne's shoulders—like we used to do in Mr. Smythe's orchard."

"This is madness." Mary braced a leg behind her, then bent her forward knee for Elizabeth.

A great wheezing sound burst from Anne's lips as Elizabeth's legs came down upon her shoulders and her feet pressed at the sides of her sister's back for balance.

Anne took a shaky step forward. "Go on, look through. What do you see?"

Elizabeth bent a bit at the waist and peered through the peephole. "It's . . . a library. Why, it appears to be Lady Upperton's library—except in reverse . . . it is like viewing her library in a mirror's reflection! I'd swear to it."

In that instant, Mary heard the sound of metal moving against metal. Suddenly, the wall moved, depositing Anne and Elizabeth in a tumbled heap onto a Turkish carpet, leaving Mary standing alone in the shadowy passage.

A rail-thin man with a full head of thick gray hair looked amusedly from Mary's sisters to two men who stood near the tea table. "What did I tell you, gents?"

He leaned forward to settle his pipe in a burled wood tray, then raised his quizzing glass to his eye and peered down at the two young women sprawled near the hearth. He lifted one wayward eyebrow and chuckled softly. "Are the gels not the epitome of grace and royalty?"

Mary swallowed deeply. She ought to have revealed her presence and spoken for her headstrong sisters, who, embarrassingly, had not yet even attempted to right themselves. Instead, they lay there in a tangle of skirts, legs, and arms and stared dumbly at the three men.

In truth, Mary could scarcely blame them. Though the gentlemen were at least as deep in their years as their father had been when he passed away, there was something different about these fellows. They had a quality about them, a vitality. Whatever it was, Mary couldn't quite identify it. But even standing here in the darkness, she could feel it.

"Darling, please come in from the passage. You've naught to fear." The thin gentleman rose from the settee and beckoned, though Mary was certain he could not see her.

Blast. Her momentary reprieve had evaporated. And so, Mary fashioned the most confident smile she could manage and stepped out from behind the bookcase and into the candlelight.

At once her sisters scrambled to their feet and came to stand beside her near the glowing hearth.

"I am Earl of Lotharian." Then, with an agility Mary could not have believed a man of his advanced years could possess, the lord eased his fine coat from one hip, swept back his leg, raised one arm to his side, and honored her with the most rakish of bows.

Mary and her sisters dropped serviceable, if not elegant, curtsies in return.

But Lord Lotharian held his bow.

Confused, the Royle sisters exchanged glances. Then, not knowing what else to do, they obligingly curtsied again.

Still, the old man didn't move and surprisingly continued to honor them.

Elizabeth stepped slightly behind Mary and whispered in her ear. "I believe he means for us to curtsy lower, as must be proper in London society. Do try harder this time, Mary, or we may be curtsying all afternoon."

"Very well." Mary nodded to her sisters, and the three lowered their heads and dropped the deepest curtsies of their lives.

When they rose, Lord Lotharian still had not moved, but he was snapping his fingers madly now. "Good heavens, Lilywhite, a hand—a hand, if you will!"

"Do apologize, old man. Hadn't realized your situation." Lilywhite, a good head shorter than Lotharian, hurried to the lord's side and bent to heave his shoulder into his friend's armpit. He helped him straighten and stand. "Good bow though, Lotharian. Best you've achieved in years."

Lord Lotharian grinned. "Do you really think so?"

"Oh, without question."

"Wasn't a proper bow." The third man, who wore an absurd auburn wig upon his head, tilted a bulbed glass of brandy to his lips.

Lord Lotharian grimaced. "What do you mean, Gallantine? I thought my bow was more than proper—it was . . . magnificent."

"Hardly. Half of a truly magnificently crafted bow is sweeping upright again. Observe." With that, the wigged gentleman bowed gracefully to the Royle sisters. Then, with hardly any popping or crackling of bones, he drew up again and clicked his heels together in triumph. "That, gentlemen, is a proper bow."

For the fourth time, because it was the correct response to Gallantine's bow, the Royle sisters curtsied.

Then, they curtsied twice more for propriety's sake when Sir Lumley Lilywhite and the Chancey Chumley, Viscount Gallantine introduced themselves.

To Mary's way of thinking, it was now time to finish their mission. "My dear gentlemen, my sisters and I are standing in what I believe to be a private gentleman's club—*a rakes' club*."

Mary straightened her spine and continued,

"Despite our entering through Lady Upperton's home, which for some reason looks to be a mirror image of this club, I am sure you realize that our presence in the club is quite unseemly, as we are unmarried young women." Mary pursed her lips, as she'd seen Anne do so many times before when wishing to impart the seriousness of any given situation.

"Therefore, I wonder if you might share with us the meaning of your rather cryptic missive so that we may depart as soon as possible and protect our family name. We have brought along the key, as you requested." Mary nudged Elizabeth, who wore the key on a blue satin ribbon around her neck.

"Yes, we are keen to learn its dual purpose. But, before we do, sir, might I ask your opinion?" Elizabeth asked as she stepped toward Gallantine. "Was my curtsy properly executed?"

When the gentleman merely stared at her, she stammered on. "I-I do wish to know. We were raised in the country and I believe largely unschooled in the ways of polite society."

Lord Lotharian laughed and answered in Gallantine's stead. "Your curtsy—*curtsies*, rather—were splendid, my dear. And I seriously doubt your social schooling was lacking in any way, because your father traveled in the most select circles of London's Quality."

"He did?" Anne blurted. "Lady Upperton hinted

as much. But . . . but he was an ordinary country physician."

"Oh, a physician he was, dear. But hardly ordinary. He was the Prince of Wales' *personal* physician . . . as well as one of his boon companions— his drinking mates—and a founding member of the Old Rakes of Marylebone . . . though we were just the Rakes of Marylebone then. Handsome lot, we were. Not quite as wrinkled as we are now."

Lord Lotharian grinned for a moment, then took in a deep breath and exhaled hard through his nose. "Do not misunderstand. I am no longer proud of the nature of our association, but I cannot deny that at one time, before the three of you were born, we were all intimates of His Majesty the Prince Regent."

Father was an intimate of Prinny?

Mary felt the blood racing from her head, and she made to the settee and collapsed upon it.

Lord Lotharian's hand shook almost imperceptibly as he lifted a decanter of brandy from the tantalus and splashed full a crystal glass for Mary. "Please take this, Miss Royle. It will ease your senses."

"I-I'm sorry. This is all too much information for one day." She looked up at the crystal he held before her. "Oh, no thank you, Lord Lotharian."

"Dear gel, I highly recommend some Dutch courage." He lowered the drink into her hands.

"For your visit is not yet at an end, and there is more I must tell you."

More? Lud, maybe she ought to take it.

She accepted the brandy from him and quickly raised the glass to her mouth.

True, she had no tolerance for spirits, none at all, but she drank down the nerve-bracing amber liquid without hesitation.

Lord Lotharian shoved his hand through his thick hair. "Damn me," she heard him mutter beneath his breath. "Please forgive me, ladies. I should not have tossed your father's past into the air as I did."

Anne hurried to Mary and sat beside her. She looked up at Lord Lotharian. "We needed to know, my lord. You did nothing wrong by telling us."

"Our Mary was simply not prepared to hear it." Elizabeth crossed to Mary and patted her shoulder. "You see, while Anne and I believed what my father's documents suggested, enough to investigate the story of our births further, Mary did not."

Mary's head was already spinning a bit, and the conversation at hand was too fantastic to be believed.

Feeling more than a little uneasy, she lowered her gaze and set herself to the mindless task of straightening the wrist lacing on the underside of each of her kid gloves.

When she glanced up again, she was immediately pinned by Anne's all-knowing gaze.

The edges of Anne's lips lifted in that superior way of hers as she curled her fingers around Mary's wrist. "Though I daresay, she cannot ignore the possibility of the story's truth now. Can you, Mary?"

Chapter 3

Mary primly folded her hands in her lap and looked around at the five people gazing upon her.

"Father was educated and well mannered. It is not such a leap to imagine him well regarded in London society." Mary paused then.

No one said a word. She was compelled to explain herself further. "Picturing him as a member of Prinny's retinue, however, is a lump of information not as easily swallowed, but still not outside the realm of believability."

"So you *do* believe." Elizabeth's countenance brightened radiantly.

Mary shook her head. *"No."*

Anne's body seemed to stiffen. Her brow furrowed, and whether intentionally or not, she tightened her fingers around Mary's wrist enough to make it smart. "But you just said—"

"No, I did not." Frustrated, Mary shook her head. "Even if I take the story of Father's past as gospel—and I have no reason not to believe what the gentlemen here have shared with us—I have yet to hear anything that would lead me to consider that our blood is the slightest bit blue."

"That is precisely why I asked the three of you here this day, darling." Lord Lotharian nodded his head at the other two gentlemen, summoning them. Silently, they came to stand behind the settee where Mary and Anne sat.

"*We* are convinced of your lineage," Lord Lotharian said firmly.

"What proof have you?" Mary raised her right eyebrow. "Any at all? My lords, I do not mean to be rude, but this claim you make, if true and bolstered by evidence, would not be inconsequential—our lives would be changed forever. And Lord above, I dare not even consider what stand the Crown would take, though I should think it reasonable to say the position would not be one of support."

"Mary!" Elizabeth turned away and turned a pleading gaze upon Lord Lotharian. "My lord, please forgive my sister's brusque words. She is simply overcome."

Lord Lotharian waved his age-spotted hand in the air dismissively. "Were I in her place, my words would be much the same." He paused for a moment then and lifted a thick gray eyebrow. "Though, I might have waited for a reply after asking for proof."

"Is there proof then?" For an instant, Mary almost believed that there might be, for Lord Lotharian seemed quite assured.

She *almost* believed. *Almost.* But not entirely.

The idea that she and her sisters were the issue of the Prince of Wales and Mrs. Fitzherbert was more than a bit preposterous. The notion was completely mad.

"The key!" Elizabeth blurted. "The key is the proof!"

Lord Lotharian shook his head slowly.

"But you lured us here by hinting that *this*"—Elizabeth revealed the brass key—"was the key to more than Papa's document box."

"And it may be, but I do not know for certain," Lotharian admitted. "May I?" He reached out for the key, and Elizabeth handed it to him. "The key has a dual purpose, as I mentioned. Watch." The tall, lean lord turned the oval grip at the head of the key and removed it, revealing a hexagonal tip. "Your father told me that if anything should happen to him, this hidden key would open the trapdoor."

"What trapdoor?" Anne demanded. "In our house in Cornwall?"

Lotharian shrugged. "I fear he shared no more with me than I have with you. I got the distinct impression that he was apprehensive about telling me about the key at all. But, yes, I would assume the secret key is for a trapdoor in his country home. I admit, I had held out some hope that you gels would know better what his cryptic words truly meant."

"We know nothing of any trapdoor." Mary cast a knowing glance at each of her sisters. "Our trip here is for naught."

"On the contrary, Miss Royle. We had a very good reason for requesting your presence this day," Gallantine broke in before Mary could utter another word.

The door from the passage opened then, and a petite, doe-eyed maid entered the room with a tray of tea and biscuits.

Given the nature of the preceding conversation, Mary expected that Lotharian would raise his hand to Gallantine and silence him until the privacy of the library was restored.

But he did not.

"Allow me to share another story from our past. Something you three must hear." He slid his crystal over his lower lip and swallowed a few sips of brandy with an audible gulp. "The year was 1795. A full month had passed since the prince had dispatched your father to Margate to tend to Maria . . . Mrs. Fitzherbert."

Mary's gaze followed the maid as she laid the tea service on the small table before them. She did not speak, nor look directly at anyone, despite the extraordinary tale Lotharian was beginning to share; she merely finished her business and silently left the room.

"At the time," Lotharian noted, his thick eyebrows twitching excitedly, "it was rumored Mrs. Fitzherbert had fallen ill after the prince had abruptly severed their union and agreed to marry Princess Caroline."

Mary found herself holding her breath, waiting for the piece of the story that would prove the story naught but a fantasy.

She slid a glance at Anne, the more evenminded of her sisters. But even she was staring moon-eyed at Lotharian, much as she had done when Papa had read them faery stories when they were children.

Lotharian continued the tale, pausing only for a breath or another sip of brandy. "It was clear to all of us that George still cared deeply for Maria, his wife of the heart—that's what he oft called her, you know—so it did not seem out of character for the prince to send his trusted personal physician, your father, to tend to her."

Lilywhite nodded his head vigorously. "But a month was a damned long while for your father to be out of Town without so much as sending a letter to anyone. Not like him in the least. I began to wonder if something was wrong. Finally, I decided to send a missive to Margate, the house in the country to which Mrs. Fitzherbert had retired, to inquire about his plans to return to London."

Gallantine nodded his auburn-wigged head in

agreement. "Your father always was the responsible sort. We knew something was not as it should be."

Lilywhite slapped his hand to his thigh. "Well, you can imagine my surprise when the letter was returned, unopened. We soon learned that your father was no longer at Margate. Hadn't been for weeks. He had, in fact, retired to his family cottage in Cornwall and had expressed to no one any intent to return to London—ever."

"Bah, there could be many reasons he retired to Cornwall." Mary twisted her wrist and wrenched it from Anne's painful grasp. She rubbed it as she shuffled through her mind for the correct words. "The most likely being that Mrs. Frasier, the housekeeper, found a basket of three babies on the doorstep and he needed to attend to them . . . or us, rather."

Lotharian's wild eyebrows arched, giving Mary the impression of a frost-covered grassy hillock. "My, my. Is that what you were told?"

"Yes, it was. It was never a secret in our house." Mary peered through narrowed eyes at each of the three gentlemen in turn. "And you all must admit that the idea of some pinch-penny country unfortunate leaving her babies on the doorstep to be taken in by someone more able to care for them is *far* more likely."

Gallantine nodded his head. "She has you there, Lotharian." He headed for the tantalus. "More brandy, anyone?" His offer was greeted by the other two gentlemen raising their empty glasses in the air.

Clutching the decanter in his delicate, long-fingered hands, Gallantine crossed back to his friends and filled their crystal goblets half full.

"My thanks, old chap." Lotharian tilted the short-stemmed goblet to his lips and drank deeply. When he finished, he dabbed his lips together, then ran his tongue over his lips, as if ensuring he recovered every last drop.

He looked pointedly at Mary. "Oh yes, I do agree. The abandoned babies story is infinitely believable—but sadly, that retelling of your delivery into your father's care is far from the truth." He tapped his hand twice upon his knee for emphasis.

Elizabeth reached out and laid her hand atop Lord Lotharian's. "Then will you share the true story?" She shot an uneasy glance at Mary, then added, "The true story . . . as *you* know it, my lord."

"Oh, do allow me." Lilywhite circled around from behind the settee, catching up a small cherrywood chair near the hearth as he moved closer to the sisters. "It's such a dramatic tale, and I vow neither of you gents will do it justice."

He slowly lowered himself into the chair, sucked in a deep breath, and glanced at Lotharian as if first seeking permission to speak.

Only when the taller lord nodded his consent did Lilywhite begin.

"With no explanation for Royle's disappearance, Lord Upperton, God rest his soul, Lady Upperton, and the three of us decided we had no recourse but to venture to lower Cornwall ourselves and learn the fate of our friend."

"And what did you learn, my lord?" Anne's fingers absently clutched her skirts, wrinkling them for certain.

"*Everything.* We arrived unannounced, late one night, but Royle welcomed us inside the cottage and offered us brandy. He was clearly distraught with our sudden appearance. I remember hearing it in the low tone of his voice and seeing it in his eyes—the way they kept darting toward the staircase every minute or so. Most certainly, we could not have known that there were three babies, the three of you, sleeping soundly inside one of the upper bedchambers. He obviously meant to keep it a secret. But his nerves grew ever more shredded as the minutes passed, and he turned to the brandy again and again."

"Oh, good heavens, Lilywhite." Lotharian threw back his head in clear frustration. "You are taking far too long with the telling!" Lotharian returned Elizabeth's gloved hand to her own knee, then he rose and moved to the hearth, leaning an elbow upon the white-veined green marble. "Get on with it, man."

Lilywhite began speaking very quickly, as though, Mary decided, if he were to pause, Lotharian would seize the story for his own. "Within an hour, the brandy had loosened his tongue, and Royle, the man who raised you, revealed a series of events like no other." He cast a wary glance at Lotharian.

"Good God, man, go on." Lotharian lifted his goblet to his mouth but did not drink. Mary could see he was peering intently at her over the lip of the crystal. He was watching for her reaction, waiting for it.

Lilywhite took another deep, calming breath before speaking again. The story was certainly about to take a dramatic turn.

"He told us that Prinny had called upon him late one eve, demanding he hurry to Margate to tend to his wife. Yes, he used that term—*his wife*. Your father was given no indication of what necessitated his urgent dispatch to Margate, but he left at once. When he arrived, he found Mrs. Fitzherbert, barely coherent, and in the midst of a difficult birth."

Lilywhite feigned a cough, raised his goblet, and gestured for Gallantine to refill it, which he begrudgingly did.

The portly Old Rake tilted the glass to his mouth and gulped down its contents completely, cuing Mary to gird herself for more.

"Her confinement was a surprise to Royle, since the prince had not mentioned it to him. But her condition was not as jolting as what he saw next."

"What did he see? Tell us, *please*," Elizabeth pleaded.

Lilywhite's eyes widened. The tension in the

library grew very heavy. "In the shadows of the room stood Lady Jersey—and Queen Charlotte."

"The queen?" Elizabeth's feet tapped excitedly on the carpet.

"Indeed. In fact, when your father inquired about Mrs. Fitzherbert's altered faculties, it was the queen herself who confessed that Mrs. Fitzherbert had dosed herself with a goodly amount of laudanum at first pain and that she had been unable to stop her. Royle lifted her lids, and indeed her pupils were black and large, but when he asked for the bottle of laudanum she had used, hoping to ascertain how much she had taken, it was not produced."

Anne's brow wrinkled with concern. "Someone else drugged her?"

Lilywhite sighed and shrugged. "Royle suspected as much but was in no position to question the queen's account. Two long hours later, though Mrs. Fitzherbert was barely conscious, she delivered three stillborn babies."

"*Stillborn?*" Elizabeth gasped for air, as if it seemed her faery tale dream of being a princess had just been torn away from her. "Then . . . then we could not be those babies."

"That's enough, Lilywhite. I shall finish." Lotharian strode back to the settee and slowly, in three attempts, managed to kneel on one bony knee before Elizabeth.

"Dear, they *appeared* stillborn, but your father, even though known as London's finest physician, was not permitted to examine the babies, even for a moment. He begged for a chance to revive them, but the queen would not hear of it. She proclaimed the children dead. If they were not yet, they soon would be, and that was the way it must be."

Anne cupped her hand to her mouth. There were tears in her eyes.

"Though she expected Royle to follow her edict, she took no responsibility for it," Gallantine broke in. "Instead, she tasked Royle with penning a missive to the prince, informing him that Mrs. Fitzherbert would soon be well and would harbor no traces of her earlier illness."

"Her . . . illness? Oh my word, she meant—*the babies*." Elizabeth's jewel-green eyes sparkled with unshed tears.

Lotharian gazed down at the Turkish carpet for several seconds before continuing. "Then, at the queen's direction, Lady Jersey wrapped the bluish babies in her own shawl and deposited the still bodies in a lidded basket, which she hurriedly pushed into your father's arms. He was to remove the bodies to the country, bury them, and never tell of their existence. *Ever*. The future of the Prince of Wales depended on it."

"But the babies weren't dead," Gallantine added excitedly. "Not yet."

"Devil take you, Gallantine. You are ruining the drama of the story!" Lilywhite balled his hand into a chubby fist and thumped it on his own knee.

Lotharian extended his arm backwards toward

Lilywhite and snapped his fingers. "Assistance, please."

"Oh, certainly." Lilywhite helped Lotharian stand. When the tall gentleman sat down in Lilywhite's chair, Lilywhite was left standing, mouth agape.

"Do stand at the opposite end of the settee, my friend, so I may see the gels' lovely faces as I put a period to the story of their birth and second chance at life."

Gallantine grumbled but did as Lotharian, the obvious commander of the Old Rakes, had asked.

"Royle was nothing if not loyal to the Crown, and so he left Margate to do as the queen had commanded. But as the carriage rolled off into the night, he heard a weak mewl coming from inside the basket."

"The babies!" The tears in Anne's eyes breached her lashes and spilled down her cheeks.

"Yes," Lotharian told her. "Royle lifted the lid to see three sets of blinking eyes peering up at him. He ripped open his shirt and held the three shivering babes to his bare chest for warmth, then wrapped his coat around them all. They were not dead, but if he returned the infants to Margate, and the queen, he was certain they would not survive the night."

Gallantine clutched his brandy crystal tightly in his hands, as though gathering up his courage, as he usurped the role of historian. "Your father knew what must be done, so he whisked the babies to his family's cottage, where he immediately engaged two wet nurses." He smiled at each of the women. "And, well, you know the rest of the story. He raised them as his own into three fine young ladies."

"In the morning, Royle—likely after realizing the danger of what he had opened himself and the babies to by sharing the story—recanted everything. Blamed it on the brandy and his penchant for storytelling," Lilywhite sighed. "But we had only to look in his eyes to know his poignant words the night before had been the truth. So then, when he asked us that if anything were to happen to him, we would see to your future, we vowed we would."

"And so we shall." Gallantine swallowed the last few drops of his brandy and settled the goblet on the tea table. "So we shall."

Lord Lotharian leaned forward, took Mary's hand in his, and curled his fingers around it. "And there you have it, Miss Royle, the *true* story of your birth."

Mary felt numb.

No, it is impossible. The story cannot be true. It cannot!

It is far too outlandish. Far too grand.

And yet, she had to admit to herself, there was a part of her that did believe.

Wanted to believe.

Oh, not the bit about being daughters of the prince.

From everything she'd heard, Prinny was a spoiled, loathsome oaf, and good heavens, being found to be his child would be naught but an embarrassment to her—even if the same could hardly be said for her sisters.

No, the part Mary longed to believe was her father's heroic actions—even when it meant refusing to do as the queen commanded. Saving the babies, despite the very real threat of reprisal from the Crown, was in precise keeping with the character of her father. He was exactly the sort who would do whatever he could to save innocent lives.

As Mary sat silently, considering these amazing revelations, she belatedly noticed that her sisters had her pinned with expectant gazes.

"So, what say you, Mary?" Anne seemed very impatient with her for some reason.

Had she missed a bit of conversation while mulling over her thoughts?

"I can see that you are still not fully convinced." Lord Lotharian pressed down on the chair's wooden arms and hoisted himself up from its seat. "No matter."

The tall lean gentleman returned to his place beside the hearth and gestured for the other two elderly gentlemen to join him.

For nearly a full minute, the Royle sisters sat quietly, their ears straining to overhear the low buzz of conversation taking place before the mantel.

To her surprise, Mary caught her name mentioned, twice, but she could not understand any other part of what seemed to her to be a most serious conversation. At last the three old rakes rejoined the sisters.

Lotharian smiled at each young lady in turn, then fixed his eyes upon Mary. "We shall begin with you, my dear, if that is acceptable."

What is this?

"Er . . . begin what with me, my lord?"

"Why, see to your future, gel. Promised Royle, I did, and despite my reputation . . . in other areas, I assure you, I always keep my word."

My future? No, no, no—

Lord Lotharian took Mary's gloved hand and drew her up from the settee. "Mrs. Upperton has seen to the preparations. Everything should have been delivered to your lodgings by now."

His eyes twinkled excitedly, making Mary wonder exactly what sort of readying Mrs. Upperton had done.

"My town carriage will fetch you and your sisters from Berkeley Square at nine o'clock this eve for Lady Brower's rout —where you and your sisters will be launched into London society."

Good heavens. Mary's tongue felt thick in her mouth, but she somehow managed to lace together a few words of protest. "My lords, you are very kind, but we are not acquainted with Lady Brower."

Lord Lotharian waved his free hand dismissively. "My darling, you know no one in London. So you must trust my guidance."

He gestured to her sisters, then patted Mary's hand and led her to the turning bookcase. "Your father bequeathed each of you a reasonable portion and sizeable dowry. You have the gentlemen of the Old Rakes of Marylebone to see to the rest. Yes, Miss Royle, by season's end, as your guardian I vow to see you properly matched to a gentleman of supreme standing. Then Lilywhite and Gallantine shall do the same for each of your sisters. Such a diverting challenge this will be for us all."

"Are you referring to finding matches for the gels, Lotharian?" Gallantine busied himself by making minute adjustments in the position of his wig.

To Mary, he seemed more than a little ill at ease at the moment.

"Or . . . perhaps you are referring to proving the gels' lineage?" Gallantine asked. "For you have yet to mention the latter, and I daresay that task will be far more of a challenge to accomplish."

For the briefest instant, worry cinched Lotharian's ample brows, but in the next, his expression relaxed and his characteristic rakish grin made its appearance on his lips.

"Why, *both*, my man! For the only way to secure the Royle sisters' futures is to secure their past as well."

"Did you hear, sisters? They mean to help us—in *all* things!" Elizabeth, unable to restrain her excitement, let forth a high-pitched giggle before stifling it by clapping her hand to her mouth.

Lotharian chuckled softly, then set himself to the task of turning the bookcase, opening it wider.

Taking this as a cue to leave, Mary made to step into the secret passage, but the ancient rake held her firmly in place for a moment more.

"I do not jest, Miss Royle," he told her with all seriousness. "There will be no settling for a simple mister or even a sir for you."

Once again, Mary did not know how to respond.

Certainly, she didn't need anyone's help selecting a husband. She was more than capable of managing her own life. Why, she had already set her cap for a very worthy man—and a titled war hero at that.

She was about to admit as much when she happened to glance at her two sisters.

If there was even a chance that the Old Rakes of Marylebone could see to her sisters' *marital* futures, well, she would have to go along with the plan, at least for a while.

It was true that Anne's and Elizabeth's charms were many, but they were completely distracted by this tale of the blue-blooded babes.

Unlike she herself, they lacked the focus needed to set their futures on the proper path—by finding husbands.

Because of this, Lady Upperton's guidance and direction in making proper matches was truly a godsend.

Why, with Lady Upperton as their sponsor,

surely their minds would be too occupied with the hunt for husbands to allow them to waste their time and meager resources investigating the farcical tale of their supposed royal birth.

Lotharian raised a brow. "Do you doubt my connections, miss?"

"Oh, no, my lord," Mary blurted.

"Very well then. We shall focus our matchmaking attentions on dukes, marquises and earls . . . though we might consider a viscount or even a baron—but only if the family is very old and prominent."

Mary squinted at him. "Why is a title so important?"

"Why indeed," he said, winking at her playfully as he released her to follow her sisters into the hollow blackness behind the bookcase, "because, my dear, you are the daughter of the future king of England."

Chapter 4

⌒⌒∽◯∽⌒⌒

Rogan and Quinn were soaked to the skin, but this was no great surprise. They should not have raced like mindless schoolboys to Hyde Park when the rain was so clearly poised to fall.

Still, Rogan had never been able to turn his back on a challenge, especially one from his brother, Quinn.

Just as he'd known all along, Quinn's mystery chit was nowhere to be seen when they finally arrived at the park.

At least, Rogan mused, *she* had been wise enough to stay at home on a wet day like this. Showed she had a brain in her pretty little head. That was something to recommend her.

66

Not wishing to slosh water up the stair treads to their chambers, Rogan and Quinn headed straight for the glowing hearth in the parlor and began to shed their clothing there.

Rogan dried his thick hair, then handed his valet the wet towel in exchange for a warm dressing gown. "All I am saying, Quinn, is do not marry in haste."

"Why not, if she is the one for me?"

"This gel who's got your blood heated may well be your perfect match," Rogan exhaled, passing his hand through his damp hair. "Only promise me you'll get to know her, truly know her, and her family, before speaking of a ring ... *and children*, for God's sake."

Quinn tossed his sodden coat over the back of a chair before the fire, then sat down and allowed the footman to tug off his wet boots. "Haven't you ever seen something from afar, a fowling-piece, or horseflesh perhaps, and known instantly that it was perfect for you?"

"A gun is a far cry from a woman, Quinn. If I became less than enamored with a fowling-piece, I could sell it, or stash it away in the bowels of the house. Can't do that with a woman. Against the law, you know. At least I think so." Rogan rubbed his chin. "Might be worth looking into though ... for future reference."

Quinn laughed as he rose and peeled his sodden lawn shirt from his upper torso. "You know what I mean. She's beautiful, quiet, and shy. Definitely of the Quality—I can tell by the graceful way she holds her back."

"You can tell all of that from riding past her each Tuesday?"

"Her beauty is not up for debate, Rogan. You will see soon enough. And as for her nature, well, that is quite evident as well. When we pass in the park, she always glances up at me through her lashes. Gives me a shy smile, then blushes the most delicate rose hue and turns her face away."

"Oh, a *delicate* rose hue, well, that changes matters, doesn't it? Of course, I amend my stand. You *should* marry her at once. A delicate rose hue, imagine that."

Quinn tied his dressing gown closed. "How can I make you understand?"

"Doubt you can. In my mind, marriage is not about infatuation. 'Tis a business arrangement between families." Rogan lifted two glasses of port from the footman's salver and handed one to his brother. "Proceed with caution, that's all I ask. Wouldn't want to end up with a common mushroom interested only in your purse."

"Why is it that when you, or I, meet a woman, you immediately suspect her of having her eye on our fortunes?"

"Because I am a realist, Quinn. I have seen too many gentlemen give their hearts to women who love only their money. You want to live in misery the rest of your days, go ahead, marry a commoner."

"Marrying a commoner is not always the wrong decision, Rogan. When our father married my mother, she was a simple miss with nary a guinea to her name. Until the day Father died, theirs was the most successful of marriages."

Rogan turned around and faced the fire so that Quinn could not see the blood rise into his cheeks.

Good God. That statement was at least ten furlongs from the truth.

How could Quinn have been so blind to his mother's greed? She was a guinea-grabber, and nothing less!

Less than a year after Rogan's mother had died giving birth to him, Miss Molly Hamish, a fresh-faced commoner from Lincolnshire, had sunk her talons deep into his grieving father. He'd been smitten, and so in need of affection that he'd married her the very moment his grieving period had been at an end.

From what his father had told him in later years, once she'd become a duchess and borne her husband a son—Quinn—she'd closed her bedchamber door to him for good. She no longer even pretended to love the duke, or to tolerate Rogan. She lavished gifts upon Quinn, bought baubles and gowns for herself, and traveled to fashionable spas with her vulgar friends.

The old duke was left in despair, lamenting

his rash decision to marry the miserable guinea-grabber for the rest of his days.

Rogan swore he'd never repeat his father's mistake. And he was not about to let his younger brother fall prey to some conniving commoner the way his father had.

No, he planned to keep a wary eye on Quinn's budding relationship with this . . . Hyde Park woman, just to be sure his battle-weary brother was not about to make the grandest mistake of his life.

"Brower rout tonight." Rogan turned around and looked to Quinn. "Might behoove you to look your best this eve. Who knows, your nameless lady might be in attendance."

Quinn's whole face seemed to brighten. "Do you think so?"

Rogan shrugged. "Don't know, but from what I've heard, half of London society shall be there. And since you claim she is highborn, which absolutely she is, because of the graceful curve of her back—"

Quinn laughed. "Then you must be sure to wear your blue coat, Rogan."

"And why is that?"

"So you will look your best as well—when I introduce you to my betrothed." Quinn grinned at him, then drained the last dark crimson droplets from his glass.

Rogan forced a chuckle, then tossed a wink at his brother and left the room. Instead of heading for his bedchamber, he turned straight down the passage and slipped into the library. There, he inked a short missive and sent it off with a footman.

He'd not leave his brother's choice in brides to chance. In the event Quinn's chit was indeed at the rout, Rogan intended to have a plan of contingency already in motion. And that plan included the beautiful young war widow, Lady Tidwell.

Lady Upperton stared across the carriage cabin and smiled at Mary with full approval. "That gown skims your contours so perfectly, dear, one might imagine that it is made from a wisp of spring sky, and overlaid with lace woven from airy clouds."

"I daresay I had the *very* same thought, Lady Upperton." Mary glanced down at the gown Lady Upperton had sent for her—a pale blue gossamer silk confection, iced with hair-thin threads of silver.

She sighed inwardly. The gown was beautiful, she had to admit. Still, she was not at all convinced that in light any stronger than that of the interior of the carriage, the mere whisper of a dress wouldn't be entirely transparent.

Though she had to admit that such a gown was bound to draw suitors. For modesty's sake she made a mental note to avoid all clusters of two or more candles, or two or more gentlemen this eve.

Elizabeth and Anne sat quietly beside her on

the leather bench, their backs straight and rigid. Practiced smiles were pasted firmly upon both their faces, but it was clear they were more tightly wound with nerves than she.

They were too aware of their finery to enjoy riding in such a splendid vehicle. Instead, they fretted over the possibility of the jostling carriage wrinkling their skirts before they reached the Browers' grand house.

But reach it they did. Carriages lined Grosvenor Square three deep. Shouting drivers jockeyed for position, each trying to deliver his passengers to the single prime spot before the Browers' imposing home.

Through the grand lower-floor windows and the open front door, Mary could see into the crowded, brightly-lit house, where elegantly dressed ladies and gentlemen moved shoulder to shoulder like dairy cows pushing through an open gate into a green meadow.

Within minutes, she, her sisters, and Lady Upperton were part of the lowing herd moving down the center hall toward the drawing room.

The movement of the crowd was so horribly slow and the sweaty press of bodies so great that Mary could hardly expand her ribs enough to breathe. It was only owing to her stature that she was able to draw a few gasps of air from above at all.

Elizabeth, however, did not share her misery. "Have a look, Mary." Her youngest sister was cinched between her and Anne, and held tight to their arms. "I can lift my slippers from the floor and still move forward. You should try it. Watch."

Mary felt a downward tug on her arm, and sure enough, Elizabeth was riding the *ton*. "Oh, good heavens. Stop that at once. We shall be inside the drawing room at any moment, and for certain there will be space enough for all."

When her lungs felt about to burst from lack of air, at last the crowd pushed through a set of double doors, and Mary and her sisters spilled out into the expansive, glittering room.

Dozens of candles burned brightly overhead, ensconced in no less than three sparkling crystal chandeliers. The walls were pleated with blue satin.

Mary's mouth parted in surprise. She could not look more than several feet in any direction without seeing a footman liveried in rich saffron silk serving wine from enormous silver trays.

Anne spun around, surveying their surroundings. Her nose wrinkled. "I do not see Lady Upperton. Where do you suppose she has gone?"

"Likely trapped in the mob near the door." Mary stood on the toes of her gleaming silk slippers, but she could not spy Lady Upperton either. "I am certain she will be about in a moment. Do not fret."

"I'm not." Elizabeth glanced around the room, and an excited flush rose into her cheeks. "How long may we stay?"

"Do you not mean how long *must* we stay?" Mary quipped.

"Well, dears, how many ticks of the minute hand we are here all depends on the three of you," came a small, high voice.

Mary looked down at her side, where the squeak had come from, and saw that Lady Upperton had suddenly appeared.

"And," the short round woman added, "how quickly you make the acquaintance of the Browers and their guests."

Mary's spirit seemed to drain from her body and into the toes of her slippers. She had not wanted to attend the rout this evening. Would have done almost anything to have simply remained at home. But by the time she'd sat down for her evening meal, she'd known that declining the Brower invitation had been quite out of the question.

True to Lord Lotharian's word, Lady Upperton had indeed dutifully seen to every possible detail.

When the sisters had returned from the Old Rakes of Marylebone Club late that afternoon, they had been stunned to find silken gowns with matching slippers, hair brilliants, strands of gleaming pearls, reticules, and shawls lying on each of their tester beds.

Even a lady's maid had been dispatched to help them dress and arrange their hair in classic curls atop their heads.

No, Mary could not have refused Lady Upperton's generosity without offending the kind old woman, and that she would not do.

"If you are ready, gels," their sponsor began, "allow me to launch you into London society."

Lady Upperton wasted no time beginning her introductions. Within a clutch of minutes, the Royle sisters were formally introduced to more than a dozen ladies of the *ton*. Lud, already Mary was more exhausted than she had been the month smallpox had stricken the parish.

Anne and Elizabeth did not seem likewise affected. Even now, they eagerly followed the short stub of a woman straight into the jaws of a rousing conversation. Mary, however, stepped backward and allowed the crowd to consume her whole. In an instant, she was whisked several feet away.

In truth, she had no other option but to slip away. Every fiber of her being told her she did not belong there mingling with London's crème de la crème.

She was an uneasy, jumbled nest of nerves, so when she spotted a petite chair beside a japanned folding screen in the corner of the room, she made for it.

Turning her head, she peered over her shoulder to be sure she would not be observed, then dragged the tiny chair behind the concealing screen and plopped down to weather the rout.

For several tedious minutes, she sat quite still,

eavesdropping on snippets of conversation or staring up at the ornate moldings edging the ceiling.

By degrees, Mary began to grow very, very bored.

She leaned back in the petite chair and yawned. Just then, she noticed a row of books sitting atop the mantel only an arm's length from the edge of the screen.

La, why hadn't she noticed them before?

She stood up and, keeping her body hidden behind the screen, reached out. Her fingertips barely brushed the cover of the book nearest to her.

Oh, perdition. Just . . . out . . . of . . . reach.

She strained; her shaking fingers scrabbled against the book leather, but they were unable to make purchase.

And then, suddenly, the book was floating before her eyes.

"Is this perhaps what you were reaching for, miss?" came an astonishingly low male voice.

The man's face peered around the edge of the screen.

Mary's eyes widened. "Y-you, you—"

She hadn't meant to say anything, but of all the people in this city to find her hiding away like a child—how horrid it was that it was *him*.

The viscount's despicable brother.

The man smiled. "I do not believe we have been properly introduced. I am Rogan Wetherly, Duke of Blackstone." He paused for a moment and his eyes seemed to rake her body, finally settling on her face. "Forgive me for staring. Am I incorrect, or have we met before?"

Heat suffused Mary's cheeks. *Oh yes, we've met. You are the ogre from the garden. And the beast who nearly ran us all down on Oxford Street only this afternoon.*

She opened her mouth but snapped it closed again.

There was no way she was going to admit anything to *him*. So, instead, she shook her head.

"No? Are you certain? You seem so familiar to my eye."

Mary shrugged her shoulders, then focused her gaze on the wedge of space between the giant of a man and the edge of the screen.

It was tight, but if she rushed through the gap she might make her escape.

"And you are?" He raised both dark, slashing eyebrows, waiting for her to offer her name.

Mary sucked in a lusty breath. "I am . . . I am *leaving*. Do excuse me, Your Grace."

Nerves propelled her forward, a bit faster than she intended. Pushing past him, she accidentally hit the screen with her left elbow and, with her right, knocked the duke a half stagger toward the wall.

She cringed and had just started for a cluster of gentlemen in dark coats when she heard a thud. And then, behind her, a chorus of gasps.

The sound she'd heard was no mystery, but she could not help herself from looking back over her shoulder at its source.

The screen had fallen to the floor, and Blackstone, still standing where he had been, appeared to everyone to have toppled it.

Even more ghastly was the fact that his blazing eyes were staring straight at her.

Nearly a dozen or so guests followed his potent gaze back to her, and chatter washed through the crowd in a wave of excitement.

A tremble raced over her limbs. Good heavens, she'd only been inside the house for a clutch of minutes and already she had made a goose of herself and an enemy of the brother of the man she would someday marry.

There was no other choice. She had to leave. *Now.*

Then she felt a small hand on her upper arm.

"There you are, Mary. Come with me, dear gel." Lady Upperton gestured across the drawing room. "This way, please. There is someone who wishes to make your acquaintance."

Mary exhaled in relief. Lud, she had no idea if Lady Upperton was the least bit aware that she had rescued her from a most awkward situation, but at that moment, she didn't really care. All she knew was that the tiny woman was leading her away from Blackstone.

Within moments, Lady Upperton had guided her to the farthest reaches of the drawing room, which suited Mary perfectly well. She would be glad to meet whomever Lady Upperton wished, for that introduction had saved her from unimaginable embarrassment before the *ton*.

"Here we are, dear." Lady Upperton smiled brightly at her.

Mary lifted her gaze forward and suddenly could not move.

Lord Wetherly, the handsome blond viscount, whom she was destined to marry, was standing directly before her.

She could hear that Lady Upperton was in the midst of an introduction, but the words were like buzzing in her ears. And she could not quite follow what was being said.

But here he was.

Lord above, what a night. Though they might have abandoned her earlier, all the angels in heaven were certainly smiling down upon her now.

Her eyes locked with his, and she bequeathed him a shy smile.

The edges of his mouth lifted, and he bowed before her. "Miss Royle." His tone was smooth and pleasing to her ear. Not at all like his brother's deep voice, which vibrated through her in the most annoying way when he spoke.

"Lord Wetherly." Mary bent and dropped a perfectly executed curtsy, having had the benefit of so much practice earlier that day at the Old Rakes of Marylebone Club. Of course, she would not mention that, and she trusted that Lady

Upperton would keep that secret to herself as well.

"I truly must thank you, Lady Upperton, for introducing me to your protégée. I own, Miss Royle and I have exchanged gazes from time to time in Hyde Park, but until this evening, we had never chanced to actually meet."

"I am honored you remembered me, Lord Wetherly."

Before he could reply, an even broader smile shaped the viscount's lips as he focused on a point somewhere behind her. "Ah, there you are, Rogan. Do come and meet Miss Royle. She is Lady Upperton's protégée."

The viscount leaned on his cane to reach past Mary and draw forth his brother, who had at one moment or another silently crept forth to stand right behind her.

Blackstone moved to his brother's left. He tilted his head to the side a bit, and a crooked grin took hold of his lips. "Miss Royle, is it?" He straightened his head above his shoulders and merely tipped his head to her.

Lady Upperton nudged Mary in her ribs. "Curtsy, dear," she whispered.

Mary smirked up at the duke and bent slightly at the knees. Even that was more than he was due.

Who did he think he was, giving her naught but a nod?

"Miss Royle and I have not met until this eve," the viscount said reprovingly as he shot his brother a loaded glance. "Though, coincidentally, we have crossed paths in Hyde Park on several occasions."

"Hyde Park?" The duke's eyebrows drifted toward his hairline. "Then she must be—" He looked straight into her eyes with his piercing gaze.

Mary felt a familiar hot flush sweep across her cheeks.

"Ah, there it is, Quinn," the duke said, gesturing to Mary's face. "A delicate rose hue."

"Yes, well . . ." Lord Wetherly shifted his feet in apparent unease, but it was nothing compared to the awkwardness Mary felt.

She turned her head, breaking free of the duke's gaze, and peered past Lady Upperton to locate her sisters.

"Damnation! I know where I've seen you."

Mary snapped her head back around just in time to see Lady Upperton wave her furled fan in the duke's direction.

"Ladies are present, sir," the old woman scolded. "And it doesn't matter to me if you are a duke or a prince. I demand respect and I will have it."

"I do beg your forgiveness, Lady Upperton, Miss Royle." He narrowed his eyes at Mary and seemed to study her.

Mary's breathing became faster. His words were apologetic, but the mischievous look in his eyes was anything but.

"I thought I recalled seeing you before, Miss Royle, and now I know where that was."

Mary swallowed deeply. *Oh no.*

His eyes seemed to widen to twice their earlier size. "Y-you are the statue from the garden!"

Chapter 5

"A statue?" Mary blinked and raised her eyebrows for effect. Despite the inconvenience of her insides swirling like dried leaves on a windy day, she at least had had a few moments to prepare for Blackstone's attack.

It had been fairly easy, in fact, to gauge the Black Duke's intent once she'd glimpsed the excited movement in his eyes.

All she'd had to do was imagine the absolute worst thing that could be said or done, which she oft did in any situation anyway, and that was precisely what the brute did.

"What ever could you mean by that, Your Grace?" Mary tossed a confused expression to Lord Wetherly, hoping to gain his support.

The duke seemed to realize her game. "Do you claim you do not understand me, Miss Royle? I am convinced you know precisely what I speak of."

Mary shrugged and remained silent.

"I was certain I had seen you—and I had—in the Underwoods' garden."

"I am sorry, Your Grace." Mary reached out and gave him a placating pat on the arm. "But I am not acquainted with the Underwoods."

"You were there . . . and in a toga." He narrowed his eyes at her. "For some reason or another you had powdered your hair and body and were posing as a piece of garden statuary."

"Posing as statuary? What nonsense is this?" Lady Upperton hooked Mary's hand and reeled her closer. "Do tell me. What is His Grace speaking of, dear?"

Mary forced a hard laugh. "Oh goodness. He is making a jest, Lady Upperton." She laughed, softly this time, and looked up timidly through her lashes at the viscount. "Lord Wetherly, you should have mentioned that your dear brother was so dryly diverting."

The duke's eyes flashed, and she knew her strategy of remaining one small chess move ahead of him was trying what modicum of patience he possessed. "Miss Royle, I know what I saw."

"Rogan, you are clearly mistaken." Lord Wetherly stared pleadingly at his brother.

"It *was* you." The duke's tone grew deeper as his ire increased. "Though you may wish our company to believe this eve marked our first exchange of glances, it was not, and I demand you admit it, Miss Royle."

What option had she now?

She could not lie.

Mary raised her eyes and peered up at Lord Wetherly.

Even he was waiting for a response that would put his brutish brother at ease again.

And then it suddenly occurred to her what to say. "How silly of me. You are absolutely correct, Your Grace."

The duke's chest seemed to puff out a bit at her admission. "Do you see, Quinn, even *she* admits it."

Lady Upperton pulled Mary closer to her again. "You were disguised as garden statuary, dear?"

Mary released a strained laugh again. "His Grace is correct about his assertion that we've exchanged glances before this night."

Several guests beyond their intimate circle hushed and gathered near to hear Mary's confession.

"It was this very day, in fact." Mary looked the duke straight in the eye and smiled confidently at him. "Do you not recall it, Your Grace? Why, you nearly ran me down in Oxford Street earlier." She glanced at Lord Wetherly and then Lady Upperton. "I own, 'twas only due to Lord Wetherly's quick thinking that my sisters and I were not trampled by His Grace's massive horse."

"Good heavens!" Lord Wetherly reached out and clasped a hand around Mary's upper arm. "That was you and your sisters? I do so apologize. Are you completely unharmed?"

"I am," she replied sweetly.

He was touching her. The heat of his fingers pressed through his gloves and warmed her skin. Though she didn't wish for him to release her, Mary could not resist looking down at where their skin met. She wanted to remember this moment. Remember the feel of him.

Lord Wetherly followed her gaze and immediately returned his hands to his sides. "Forgive me, Miss Royle."

"Think nothing of it, Lord Wetherly." Mary smiled coyly at him again. "I admit, I am greatly flattered by your kind concern."

Mary had the impression that the duke would have raised his head and howled at his defeat if it would have been socially acceptable.

A triumphant smile itched to show itself upon Mary's lips. But she knew the favorable footing she enjoyed now could be lost at any moment, so she began to plot her escape.

Just where were Anne and Elizabeth?

Lady Upperton pursed her tiny lips. "Dear, you and your sisters never mentioned your sweep with doom this day."

"There was no need. We were rescued from all harm by Lord Wetherly, here." Mary extended her hand to him. "At the time I am afraid I was too shaken to address you properly. So I shall do it now. Please accept my thanks, Lord Wetherly, for saving our lives."

"It was my duty, Miss Royle . . . and my pleasure." The viscount elbowed his brother. "Now my brother has something he wishes to say to you. Is that not correct, Rogan?"

"Miss Royle." The duke cleared his throat. "I beg your forgiveness for the near-accident this day. I am greatly relieved that you and your sisters were not harmed in any way." He leaned closer to her. "Might I suggest the use of a carriage in the future?"

"You might, Your Grace, but since we do not own a carriage, and hackneys are too dear to hire with any regularity, my sisters and I will likely continue to walk whenever possible. I am sure you understand."

He cocked his brow at her then, and his eyes brightened, as if he did suddenly understand, though, from the curious expression on his face, Mary was not at all sure what he might have gleaned from her innocent comment.

She leaned toward the great beast, although it made her heart thud hard in her chest to do so. She held the tone of her voice as low as possible. "Might I suggest keeping your mind focused in the future, so the lives of others are not imperiled?"

The duke grimaced at her, then exhaled loudly.

"I think I shall succumb to nausea if I do not locate a glass of wine. Perhaps the ladies might also enjoy a libation as well?"

"I would adore a sip or two of wine, Your Grace." Lady Upperton unfurled her fan and swished it across her powdered face.

"Very good, Lady Upperton." The duke looked to Mary. "And you, Miss Royle?"

"No, thank you, Your Grace."

The Black Duke started for the refreshment table, but before he had traveled a full step, he turned around. "Quinn, will you assist me?"

The sheen of disappointment was clear in the young viscount's eyes. "Do excuse me, ladies. I shall return promptly." He bowed politely—something the grand oaf had not troubled himself to do—then followed his brother through the heaving crowd.

The moment the two gentlemen were no longer discernable amongst the collection of dark dress coats, Lady Upperton's manner changed abruptly. "Mary, Lord Wetherly mightn't have realized you were lying, but I certainly did."

Mary frowned. "I didn't lie. In actuality, I was very careful to tell the truth."

Lady Upperton huffed a breath of air between her painted lips. "I was holding your hand, dear. I felt it twitch and saw your body tense whenever the duke made his ridiculous accusations about garden statuary."

"I didn't lie."

"You mightn't have, but you certainly danced a full quadrille around the truth." Lady Upperton leaned close and tilted her chin up. She studied Mary's face through squinted eyes. Then she gasped. "Oh, my word, Mary. He *wasn't* incorrect. You *were* the statue in the Underwoods' garden! What could you have been thinking?"

"I only wanted to show my sisters the gentleman I would one day marry." She paused, but Lady Upperton folded her arms across her chest and lifted her eyebrows, as though waiting for the rest of her story.

"You see, earlier, our cook asked for the evening off to earn a few extra shillings by helping to prepare the dinner for the Underwoods' garden party. We cannot afford to pay her much in the way of wages, so we agreed. Cook was very happy about this, as you might imagine. She began to tell us about the food that was to be served . . . and sometime during the conversation casually mentioned that Lord Wetherly, the young war hero, would be a guest."

"But you said you are not acquainted with the Underwoods."

"Well, we aren't. So we were not included on the guest list. But I did so want Anne and Elizabeth to see the man I have set my cap at, Lady Upperton. And la, he was going to be just next door. So close. I knew I daren't miss the opportunity, so we powdered ourselves and crept into the back garden—"

"Oh, dear me." Lady Upperton snatched a lace

handkerchief from her frothy sleeve of rose lace. "'Twas all *three* of you?"

"Please do not fret. No one saw my sisters. And no one saw me . . . well, except the duke. But it was dark, and I was completely marbleized with powder and a smear or two of paste."

"Heavens . . . is Lotharian aware of any of this?"

"Am I aware of what?" Lord Lotharian and his cohorts, Gallantine and Lilywhite, were suddenly standing in a tight ring around them.

Lady Upperton became instantly agitated. "Haven't got a tick of the minute hand to discuss this now, Lotharian. You must know, however, that our Mary has set her cap at Viscount Wetherly, and I would wager every jewel I own that he is *very* interested in such a match."

Lotharian scratched his chin. "Wetherly. Why do I know that name?"

Lilywhite raised a finger. "Perhaps because Wellington mentioned the lad in every dispatch from Toulouse. Or because the Prince Regent recently bestowed on him a viscountcy in recognition of his bravery and valor. Why, Wetherly led the Sixth Division in the heroic attack above Toulouse, you know. No small feat. He's a true hero."

"His father was the late Duke of Blackstone," Gallantine added. "His brother holds the title now. You certainly have heard of him—the Black Duke."

"Ah yes, the Black Duke. Have indeed." Lotharian chuckled, and the other two gentlemen joined him, as if the three were sharing a private joke of some sort. "Now *he* is a man to consider, Miss Royle."

"Blackstone?" Mary stared at Lord Lotharian in disbelief. "How can you suggest such a thing. W-why, he is . . . *horrid.*"

"No, no. You've got it jumbled." Lotharian waved her comment away like a foul odor. "Blackstone is naught but a spirited young fellow. I admit, he even reminds me of myself in my youth."

"Oh you do flatter yourself, Lotharian." Lady Upperton bent and peered around the towering lord. "But that is neither here nor there. The Black Duke holds some sort of a grudge against our Mary—"

"I slapped him," Mary said matter-of-factly. "Quite hard too."

Lady Upperton cringed. "I am almost afraid to ask, but I must. Did this occur in the Underwoods' garden?"

"It did. But I swear to you, he deserved it thoroughly. He was about to . . . to touch me," Mary bent at her knees and whispered into Lady Upperton's ear, "most inappropriately."

"Oh, dear." Lady Upperton dabbed her brow with her handkerchief, taking off a bit of her facial powder in the process. "Lotharian, Lord Wetherly is Miss Royle's choice, not his older brother. The viscount comes from an old family and has earned honor and distinction . . . despite his mother. Do you agree?"

"His mother?" Mary looked to each of the four for an answer, but it was as if her question fell on indifferent ears.

"Wetherly sounds like a perfectly suitable gentleman. I shall have my man investigate him further." Lotharian smiled down at Mary. "Miss Royle, I shall have your answer within the week."

"I fear we haven't that long." Lady Upperton hastened her next words. "My concern is that Blackstone will not support the match. Already this evening, he has taken great strides to shame our Mary. I fear he may do irreparable damage to the potential match unless he is persuaded to stop."

"I can certainly distract the duke this eve. Then we shall meet again in the morn to discuss a broader strategy for keeping our two young lovers together." Lotharian raised his quizzing glass to his eye.

"What do you mean to do?" Mary's head was beginning to throb.

She had already set off on the worst possible footing with the duke. The Old Rakes were only going to make things worse, of that she was sure.

"Ah, what have we here?" Lotharian, who stood a full head above most others in the grand drawing room, became suddenly alert. "That's him, the tall gentleman, with shoulders like a pugilist. Am I correct?"

Lilywhite lifted his glass as well and peered into the crowd. "You've got the right of it, Lotharian."

"Well, then." Lotharian glanced mischievously around the drawing room. "Leave Blackstone to me. Lady Upperton, you may see to the task of seeing that the viscount and Miss Royle connect again this eve."

Lady Upperton nodded, sending her double chins quivering.

Lotharian held his quizzing glass before his eye. "Hmm . . . best make haste though, dear. See there." He raised his chin, covertly gesturing to the center of the drawing room. "The duke seems to be introducing his brother to the lovely widow Lady Tidwell."

"Oh, dear me." Lady Upperton rose up on her toes to catch a glimpse of the young woman, who was indeed laughing with Lord Wetherly.

The duke, however, was no longer with them. With Lady Upperton's refreshment in his hand, he was heading straight back to their party.

Lady Upperton held her fan before her face and pulled Mary close. "Lady Tidwell is out of mourning. Oh, Mary, her connection with your young man is a poor turn of events, very poor—one we must reverse at once!"

"Do not worry overmuch, ladies," Lord Lotharian said with all confidence. "Miss Royle has innocence and superior breeding to recommend her.

Lord Wetherly will make the right decision. Now, if you will pardon me, ladies, I have my own task to complete." A wicked grin turned Lord Lotharian's lips, and the ancient rake set off on a course for certain collision with the Black Duke.

Rogan took one last glance at his brother before delivering Lady Upperton's glass of wine.

It was going well. Quinn was clearly taken with Lady Tidwell, which helped put his own mind at ease.

He just couldn't endure it if his brother formed a connection with Miss Royle. Why, the chit seemed to take great pleasure in irking him at every turn.

Certainly, he had never met a more irritating woman in all his life.

What else could he have expected from her, though? Everything he now knew of her served to bolster his belief that she was common, and penny-poor at that.

Still, she was dangerous, for she was pretty and knew how to use her wiles.

She belonged to the absolute worst class of woman. The sort that snared unsuspecting men by their heartstrings, then lured them to the altar solely for their money.

Miss Royle was a guinea-grabber. Worse yet, she had Quinn fixed firmly in her sights.

Not for long, though.

When he had mentioned to Portia, Lady Tidwell that Quinn meant to marry and begin a family before the year was through, she was more than a little intrigued.

Now, *she* would be his perfect match.

She was from a good family, possessed a sizeable portion, was well mannered, and maintained all the best society connections. Yes, she would do quite nicely.

He had just turned toward Lady Upperton when he felt a firm tap on his shoulder. He turned to see a well-muscled gentleman staring angrily up at him. "May I assist you, sir?" Rogan asked.

"I would speak with you in the garden, Your Grace." A web of red threads shot through the man's furious eyes. His cheeks burned crimson, and his foul breath was coming fast.

"Might I inquire what this is about, sir?"

The gentleman huffed at that. "You know exactly what this is in reference to. Several old gentlemen saw you do it. Pointed you out to me. I demand satisfaction—in the garden."

Rogan looked at the two elderly gentlemen watching the exchange with amused grins on their wrinkled faces. "I am afraid, sir, that there is some confusion. Might I know what I supposedly did that so incensed you?"

The man was practically snorting fire, but he was well enough trained to lower his voice to a near whisper. "You pinched my wife's backside."

"Did I? Are you sure?" Blackstone glanced around the room. "Which is your wife? Point her out to me, will you?"

A vein throbbed along the young man's wide forehead, and his red face almost seemed to pulse. "To the garden, *now*." He grabbed Rogan's sleeve and turned him toward the passage.

"You are making a dangerous mistake, sir," Rogan said, shaking the man's hand loose.

"The mistake was yours, Your Grace, the moment you touched my wife."

"But I didn't. I am sure I would remember."

"Outside."

Rogan lifted the edges of his lips and set Lady Upperton's glass of wine on the tray of a passing footman. "Then let us continue our discussion in the garden, as you suggested, sir. It is rather stifling in here, and I could use a bit of fresh air."

Rogan's full lips twisted into a smirk as he followed the irate fool down the passage and through the French windows into the garden.

He removed his gloves and shoved them between his waistcoat and lawn shirt for safekeeping.

Yes, perhaps a little air would cool his new friend's ire. But if not—Rogan flexed the fingers of his right hand, then curled them into a tight fist—he would take matters into his own hands.

The moment Blackstone left the drawing room, what Mary took to be the second part of the elderly quartet's scheme was put into place.

Lotharian eyed Lady Upperton and tugged upon his earlobe.

"Dear gel, the moment I distract Lady Tidwell—you will know the moment if you watch carefully—you must at once appear at your beau's side. Your opportunity shall not be available to you for long, so the sooner you can convince him to quit the room, so much the better."

Mary reached out and took Lady Upperton's chubby little hand. "Lady Upperton, I do appreciate your efforts, but truly—"

Her round face glowed. "I know you appreciate my help, which is why it so gladdens me to assist you in all ways. It has been so very long since I felt so needed."

Oh, that wasn't at all what she had been trying to say, but it was too late now. Mary winced. She had no choice but to play along.

Lady Upperton patted the top of Mary's hand, then slipped her own from her grasp. "Lotharian beckons again. It is my moment. Watch for your opportunity!" With that, the tiny woman barreled like a hogshead through the throng, paying no heed to the perturbed guests she left scattered in her wake.

Mary cupped her hands over her eyes momentarily. *When would this evening end?* Never before had she endured so many face-reddening moments in one night.

"Darling."

Mary lowered her hand and looked up to see Lord Lotharian standing before her, with Lord Wetherly beside him.

Lotharian grinned at her. "Miss Royle, I just made the acquaintance of Viscount Wetherly, the famous war hero. Of course, I wanted to introduce him to you, but I have just learned that you are already acquainted."

"Oh, yes, Lord Lotharian, we met only minutes ago." Mary turned to Lord Wetherly and felt her cheeks redden with the embarrassment from this insane scheme.

"Are you ill, Miss Royle?" True concern etched the corners of the viscount's vivid blue eyes.

She opened her mouth to assure him she was not, but it was Lotharian who responded.

"Miss Royle's cheeks do appear somewhat heated." Lotharian withdrew a handkerchief from inside his coat and dabbed his own high-set cheekbones. "I daresay, it is rather close in here. Perhaps a stroll in the fresh air would revive you, Miss Royle."

"I-I suppose it would." Mary looked from Lotharian to the viscount. "Shall we all go together?"

Lotharian flapped his handkerchief in the air. "Nothing would please me more, Miss Royle, though I promised Gallantine I would introduce him to Sir Corning." He looked to the viscount. "I wonder if you, Lord Wetherly, would do me the favor of seeing to Miss Royle?"

A most attractive smile appeared on Wetherly's lips. "I shall be honored, sir." He straightened his back and excitedly offered his arm to Mary. "Shall we, Miss Royle?"

She took Lord Wetherly's proffered arm and shyly looked up at him through her lashes. "Absolutely."

Good heavens. The scheme was actually working! Mary could not believe her luck.

Whyever had she doubted Lord Lotharian's plan to see her married off? Obviously, he had a fine mind when it came to matchmaking.

Mayhap tonight was not nearly as dreadful as she had first believed.

Chapter 6

～✦～

Mary shivered as she and Lord Wetherly stepped out upon the paving stones leading into the Brower garden.

The air in the courtyard was cool, especially when compared to the heat of the drawing room, but it was not the temperature of the night that sent Mary's body all aquiver.

Reading her shaking as a need for warmth, Lord Wetherly hurried back inside and collected her shawl from a footman.

When he returned but a moment later, she turned her head and smiled at him as he settled the wrap lightly about her shoulders.

She pulled the shawl close about her, wanting to

appear grateful, but the fine hairs on her arms and the back of her neck still prickled up from her skin.

It was not the chill that discomfited her.

Nor the excitement of walking with the man she would ultimately marry.

It was his wicked brother.

For though the sweeping garden ahead appeared deserted but for the two of them, Mary knew that Blackstone and his ready-fisted opponent lurked somewhere nearby.

"Would you like to walk down the pathway? Lady Brower mentioned a moon garden near the well. It is said that white flowers scent the night with sweet fragrance unmatched during the daylight hours." Lord Wetherly leveled his eyes with hers.

For several moments, without moving from where they stood in the golden light shining through the French windows, they stared dreamily into each other's eyes.

Or, at least she tried to match the sleepy look she saw in his eyes. But for some reason, she was having a devil of a time doing it.

"I-I" Mary broke her gaze and peered off into the moonlit garden.

She could not help thinking that at any minute the beastly duke could leap out from behind the boxwoods to wreak havoc.

"Forgive me, Miss Royle, I should not have asked

you to leave your sponsor and stray from the rout." Lord Wetherly leaned on his cane and lowered his gaze to the pavers.

"I beg your pardon, Lord Wetherly." Mary swung her head around to look at him again. "You have done naught wrong, I assure you."

"I should not have suggested a walk . . . alone."

Blast. She was going to lose him if she didn't focus her attention better.

"Lord Wetherly, I would greatly enjoy a walk in the garden with you. Nothing would please me more." Mary turned her head slightly to the side and gazed coyly up at him. "However, I neglected to inform my sisters where I was headed before you and I left the drawing room. I only thought to remain near the house . . . in the event they come to look for me. You understand, don't you?"

"I do, and I admit, I am greatly relieved." The viscount exhaled a sigh. "For an instant I was sure my invitation might have been misinterpreted and that you thought me a horrible rake intent on whisking you into the darkness for a wickedly passionate kiss."

"Lord Wetherly—"

"Please, do call me Quinn. I know we have only just properly met, but I feel . . . I know you so very well."

Though she had no experience in the stages of love, she was fairly certain he was smitten, and because of this, a proposal was likely in the weeks to come.

She could almost feel it.

Mary's head began to dance with thoughts of a future with . . . *Quinn.*

She could see their wedding clearly in her mind even now. They would live in a grand house in the country. They would have three beautiful children, all with Quinn's golden hair.

And . . . and . . . Suddenly she was being summoned back into the moment.

"Miss Royle?" There was that concerned look in his eyes again. "Miss Royle?"

W-what? Oh goodness. Focus your attention, Mary. Focus!

"*Mary*, please call me Mary." She laughed softly. "Do forgive my inattention, please. I confess, I was off gathering wool."

She looked into his eyes and he smiled.

God, he's so beautiful when he smiles.

"And what so consumed your thoughts, *Mary*?"

Well now, that was a good question. Just what *had* she been thinking? Or, rather, what might he like to hear?

She fluttered her eyelashes.

Lud, was that a bit much? She squinted her eyes and studied him.

No, no, he is smiling. Everything is well.

It is. Has to be.

And then, she suddenly knew just how to

answer his question. "I wondered if I would think you a horrible rake if . . ."—*go on, say it*—"if you kissed me *here,* right now." She widened her eyes in feigned innocence.

Quinn's eyes widened too, and he paused for several seconds before his look of surprise was replaced with one of eagerness. "I suppose there is only one way to know the answer to your question."

A tattoo thrummed in her chest and in her veins.

He was actually going to do it. At any moment, Lord Wetherly was going to press his lips to hers.

Zeus, should she close her eyes? Or wait until their mouths touched? Close them. Yes. That felt right.

Mary squeezed her eyes shut and tilted her lips upward and waited for Quinn, the man she would one day marry, to kiss her.

Any moment now. Any . . . moment.

Suddenly, she heard him shuffle his feet most peculiarly, and then the sound of his breath left his lungs.

A cool swoosh of air blew between them, and she knew for certain he had moved away from her.

Could she have read his ardor incorrectly?

She was about to lift her lids and blame her wanton behavior on the wine—well, she had no tolerance for the juice of grapes, so it made perfect sense, didn't it?

In the next instant, before she could say a word,

he swept her into his arms and crushed her against his hard, muscled chest.

She scarcely had a moment to gasp a small breath before his lips came down and claimed hers, hot and moist, moving so . . . so . . . passionately.

Oh my . . . oh God.

All at once, her legs softened to the consistency of marmalade, and heat surged through her entire body.

Heavens above, she never knew a kiss could be like this.

Or that Quinn, gentle Quinn, was the sort of man who could make her head spin so deliciously.

She had to be in love.

Of course, that was it. There was no other explanation for it. She and Quinn were meant to be together. She ought to tell him. Admit her feelings now.

He had to be feeling it too. Had to be. No one could kiss like *this* without being in love.

Do not think, Mary. Just tell him.

Tell him!

And so, the moment his mouth lifted from hers, she confessed her feelings. "I-I think I love you."

Then she heard his voice. "Stop!"

How odd. He sounded so far away.

"Stop at once!" he pleaded.

"W-what?" She held her eyes closed, not wishing to break the moment, and leaned into him for another kiss.

"Rogan, I *demand* it."

Rogan? Mary suddenly went stiff. She wrenched her head toward the garden. Her eyes flew open, expecting to see Quinn's beastly brother stepping from the bushes, just as she'd imagined. Just as she'd feared.

Instead, she saw Quinn standing beside her. *Quinn?*

Then w-who had been kissing her? She turned her head and blinked up. *Oh perdition.*

"Love me, do you, Miss Royle?" The Black Duke, still crushing her against his chest, chuckled wickedly. "And here I thought you despised me."

Tears pushed into Mary's eyes. "Let go of me, you—you vulgar beast."

"You heard her, Rogan. Do it now!" Quinn shouted. "I can't believe you did this. You are my brother. My *brother!*"

"Very well, I will release you, Miss Royle," the duke told her in an insulting whisper. "Anything for the woman who loves me." He straightened and settled her to her feet.

Mary glared at him. Her breath was coming so fast she spat out her words. "How dare you!" And for the second time, she drew back her hand and landed a stinging slap across his cheek.

She could not even bring herself to look back at Quinn as she flung open the French windows and ran, blinded by tears of humiliation, inside the house.

* * *

"Let her go, Quinn. For now." He rubbed his cheeks with the back of his hand. "I daresay she might need a few minutes to settle her head."

Quinn looked from the French windows to Rogan. "I ought to level you for what you've done."

"But you won't because I did it for your own good." When Quinn opened his mouth to protest, Rogan raised a hand to silence him. "I know an apology is not nearly enough, Quinn, but I vow someday you *will* thank me for this."

He reached a hand to his brother's shoulder, but Quinn swatted it away.

"Why? Tell me why you did this?" Quinn looked straight into Rogan's eyes. His own were glistening in the soft light from the house. "I was about to kiss Miss Royle—the gentlewoman I . . . I may marry someday . . . when you shoved me away and assaulted her!"

"I didn't hurt her. I only kissed her. And I am fair certain she liked it." He tried not to smile. Or mention that he might have rather enjoyed it as well. But he wasn't the beast the *ton* believed him to be. He hadn't kissed her to hurt his brother. No, when he'd kissed Miss Royle, it had been with the best of all intentions.

"Why, Rogan?" Quinn was overwrought, though he fought to hide it. "Why the hell did you do it?"

"Damn it all, Quinn. I did it to save you from the bloody parson's mousetrap."

Rogan walked to the marble bench and sank down upon it. He shoved his hand through his hair before looking up at Quinn again. "I was just returning from the back garden after a rather heated discussion with a gentleman who had been mistaken about my interest in his wife. That's when I heard her *luring* you into a kiss."

"She wasn't luring me. She was inviting me to do something I wanted very much to do!"

"Sometimes you can be so naïve. But I am not. It was a trap, one you were eagerly stepping into."

"It was no trap, Rogan."

"But I was certain it was. You would take her into your arms and kiss her, and at once Lady Upperton and a pack of censorious society matrons would rush into the garden from the house, accusing you of ruining Miss Royle. And, being the good man, the honorable man you are, you would protect her by asking her to become Viscountess Wetherly."

Odd, Quinn wasn't the least moved by his sacrifice. Instead, his brother's cheeks glowed red and his chest heaved. *Bloody hell.* He looked even more furious now, if that was possible.

He just didn't understand. And so, Rogan continued. "An honorable man would have no choice but to marry her. But society has dubbed me the Black Duke. I have a wicked reputation. No one could coerce me into a marriage by appealing to my honor—because as far as they are concerned, I have none. So you see, by kissing Miss Royle in your stead, I rescued you from a forced marriage."

He smiled at Quinn then, hoping to defuse his brother's anger. "You may thank me now if you like."

"You are mad, Rogan. You've spent so many years blindly distrusting all women that you see a villainous motive behind the most innocent of kisses."

Rogan exhaled hard. "You do not know women as I do. You place them upon a pedestal. But believe me, I know what they are truly capable of. I have seen her sort before. Many, many times before. Women who deceive, who use, who destroy—all to line their own purses with gold."

"Deuce it, Rogan. She isn't that sort of woman. Y-you do not know Miss Royle."

"Nor do you! Do you not understand, Quinn? That is my entire point. You haven't even known her name for more than an hour, and already you claim she may be a woman worthy of your heart."

"Had I kissed her, the whole of London could have poured through the French windows demanding I marry her that very instant—and Rogan, I would have been glad to do it. I want to marry, Rogan. And she is a good woman, a virtuous woman with a kind, gentle soul."

Rogan rubbed his cheek. "A gentle soul with one hell of a swing."

"You deserved nothing less. I can only hope that one day you will realize that everyone's heart is not as black as yours."

"And you will learn, Brother, that I can read a woman faster than she can tell me her name. Miss Royle is *not* Quality."

"She is. She possesses a grace that I have never witnessed before."

"True, she dressed well enough this eve, which might give anyone who met her the impression that she hails from a good family, but I saw her earlier today. Saw her country frock and absurd bonnet. I saw who she really is—an opportunist, concerned only with your title and your full pockets."

"You are wrong, Brother." Quinn turned and charged for the house.

Rogan rose from the bench and called after him. "You will see, Quinn. You will see."

When Rogan sat down to break his fast quite late the next morn, Quinn, dressed in a dark blue frock coat, had already filled his plate with bacon rashers, eggs, and bread, and was slowly sipping his coffee. He did not even seem to notice that Rogan had entered the room.

Quinn looked quite handsome, with his coat brushed, his neckcloth painstakingly tied, and his brass buttons sparkling as if they'd just been polished. This was not his brother's usual day garb. Not at all. And this worried Rogan.

"Look at you, Quinn. You're all the crack this morn, aren't you lad?" *Hmm.* He was hoping for an explanation for Quinn's fine garb, but his brother did not hurry to offer one.

In fact, Quinn said nothing at all.

Instead he munched on a thick slice of toasted bread smeared with a dollop of freshly churned butter.

"Come now, did I not apologize? If not, allow me to do it now. Dear brother, I vow I heartily regret kissing Miss Royle."

"You do not regret it. You seek only to prove your belief—your *incorrect* belief, I might add—that Miss Royle wants nothing more than my fortune."

Rogan filled his cup, then sipped his coffee noisily. "You must believe me when I tell you that I hope my assertion is a long stroll from the truth."

"Well, it matters naught, Rogan."

"No?" *Damn it all.* Quinn had set his thoughts on something, and Rogan had a good mind of what it might be.

"No, because I plan to call on Miss Royle early this afternoon to apologize for *your* barbaric actions at the Browers' rout." He fastened a smile to his mouth and looked pointedly at Rogan. "Then I shall make my way to Cavendish Square to discuss with Lady Upperton my intentions to court her protégée Miss Royle."

A jolt of worry blasted through Rogan, propelling his body up from the chair. "Quinn—"

He didn't have even a modicum of an idea what he would say to dissuade his brother from this preposterous notion.

It was for this reason that when the butler,

Clovis, entered with a letter atop a silver tray and headed straight for Quinn, Rogan closed his mouth and sat down again, grateful for a few more moments to craft his argument.

When Quinn noticed the butler, the fine skin at the outer corners of his eyes wrinkled and a look of confusion passed over his finely boned face. "Early for a letter, is it not?"

"Not so early, my lord." Clovis raised the tray a little higher before Quinn, urging him to take it.

It suddenly struck Rogan that something was not as it should be. "Take the card, Quinn."

Quinn peered at the cream-colored note on the tray. "I shall . . . finish my breakfast first, I think."

What was this? Rogan rose from his chair. Even from his position across the table from his brother, he could see that the direction on the outside of the letter was written in a woman's hand. Possibly Miss Royle's?

Could that be the reason Quinn was apprehensive about opening it? Did he fear the card might contain instructions to refrain from seeing her again? After all, to her it might have appeared that Quinn, a war hero and all, had done nothing to stop his roguish brother from attacking her. Or, more likely, she'd found another deep-pocketed target later on at the rout.

Yes, yes. Fanciful thoughts. But the prospect of hearing an end to Miss Royle's campaign to snare his brother's ring made Rogan nearly giddy.

Still Quinn made no move to open the letter.

Bloody hell, Rogan could endure no longer. He had to know what was inside that letter. "I have eaten all I can manage this morn," Rogan began, hoping Quinn would not notice his nearly full plate of food. "I shall read it aloud for you while you eat. After all, we have no secrets, do we, Brother?"

Before Quinn could reply, Rogan stole the card from the tray. He broke the gold wax wafer, unfolded the letter, glanced down the page and— *damn.*

Not from Miss Royle.

"'Tis from Lady Tidwell." Ah yes, his contingency scheme. But so soon? Now this was interesting. Rogan held the letter out to Quinn. "Surely you wish to read it."

"Oh, very well. Give it to me." Quinn brought the letter to his eyes and silently read for several seconds.

What was that he just saw? Rogan watched his brother intently for a reaction. *Could it be a hint of a smile? A glimmer of interest?*

"How does Lady Tidwell?" Rogan asked. "I scarcely had two words with her. And it was her first venture into society after her mourning period ended, too. You spoke with her, didn't you, Quinn?"

"I did." He seemed quite distracted at the moment, which Rogan took to be a good omen. "Her brother, Lieutenant Spinner, has accepted a commission with another regiment. Only in Town for a short while. Seems he's heading off to India in the morning. Good man, Spinner."

Quinn looked up at Rogan, his face no longer cinched with worry but instead suffused with brightness and cheer. "We, uh, served together in Toulouse, you know."

"Oh, did you? I hadn't been aware." But of course Rogan had been. In fact, it was Quinn's close association with Lady Tidwell's brother that made her the perfect choice as a distraction for Quinn.

"She has extended an invitation to me to dine with the two of them this afternoon . . . before he leaves." Quinn lowered the letter to his lap, his eyes suddenly astray in thought. "I do so wish to accept, but—"

"But nothing!" Rogan took a step closer and slapped his brother's back hard but good-naturedly, to snap him from his thoughts of calling upon Miss Royle instead. "I know where your mind is lingering. Look here. Accept Lady Tidwell's invitation. You, yourself, commented on how short life can be, especially for a soldier."

Quinn turned his gaze upward. Rogan's point had been taken. "But after last night . . . I should—"

"Bloody hell, Quinn. If you must, if you absolutely must call on Miss Royle and Lady Upperton, you can do so after dinner—or better yet, tomorrow, when Miss Royle has had a chance to calm herself properly after my . . . *indiscretion*."

"Yes, I suppose you could be right." Quinn happily popped an apple wedge into his mouth and began to chew.

"That's my man." Rogan patted Quinn's shoulder again, then quit the room and headed above stairs for his chamber.

He snapped his fingers at a nearby footman and asked him to summon his valet at once. He needed to look his best, for he had two very important calls to make right away.

First to Lady Upperton.

And then to the gel with the gleam of gold guineas in her eyes.

Miss Royle.

Mary lowered the spout of the chocolate pot over Elizabeth's chipped, but perfectly serviceable, cup and began to pour.

Last night had certainly been the worst of her life. Never before had she been so humiliated. The Duke of Blackstone was a blackguard and should be locked away for the good of all women.

"Mary!" Elizabeth grabbed Mary's hand and tilted the pot upright. "Where were your thoughts? For your mind was not on pouring. Look at the linen."

"W-what did you say?"

Elizabeth pointed her finger at her overflowing cup.

Criminy. There were the fat droplets of chocolate spotting the tablecloth too. "Oh dear. Let me fetch something to—"

"Never you mind, missy. I'll take care of the spillage," said Mrs. Polkshank, the cook and house-keeper whom Mary had engaged only two weeks before.

Mrs. Polkshank set down a plate of hot muffins on the table, and Elizabeth snatched one up. "Used to it, you know," she told them. "The later the hour at the tavern, you see, the more spills there were, so I learned to be always prepared."

Just as Anne entered the dining room, Mrs. Polkshank, who did not seem to concern herself with modesty, hoisted her pendulous right breast and snatched a homespun cloth from the waistband of her apron.

Anne stared in disgust as the cook dropped her breast back into place, wet the rag with the tip of her tongue, then began to dab away the chocolate stains.

"Oh, this ain't goin' to do it." The heavyset woman spun around and started for the door to the passage. "I'll be needin' some vinegar." She paused when she reached the threshold and looked back over her shoulder. "Shall I fetch some more chocolate? Maybe some tea for you, Miss Anne?"

Anne did not turn around to reply. Anger blazed in the golden bursts of her moss green eyes. She shook her head furiously.

"Well, then, I'll be back in a tick or two." Mary watched Mrs. Polkshank disappear into the passage.

Anne immediately addressed Elizabeth. "Sister, will you please tell Mary that Cook must go."

Mary frowned. "She is not going anywhere, Anne, and if you wish to discuss our staff, you may speak directly to me."

Two bright red dots appeared on Anne's cheeks. "Very well, I shall. Where did you find her, Mary, on a street corner in Drury Lane?"

Elizabeth took a large bite of her muffin and carefully lifted her cup to wash it down with a gulp of chocolate. "I do not agree with you, Anne. We never had meals in the country like Cook's. I think Mrs. Polkshank is quite talented. And she certainly keeps a cleaner house than Aunt Prudence's thief of a housekeeper did."

"She is quite gifted in the kitchen—and very economical," Mary added. "She always has at least a shilling or two spare after marketing. You must agree that with her creativity in piecing together meals and her skill in preparation, it almost slips my mind how limited our budget is."

"Our only shortages of funds are due to your frugality, Mary. We are not in want of coin. Why, with the portions we've been given, we could live like kings for several years at least."

"Or *princesses*, at the very least." Elizabeth hid her grin behind the lip of her cup.

Mary shook her head. "Anne, you are not angry because I engaged Mrs. Polkshank. You are not truly angry, at least not this morn, about my handling of our household accounts."

"Really, Mary, am I not?" Anne folded her arms over her chest.

"No, you are still fuming over last night."

Anne lowered her head, as if she'd been studying the cut-work edge on the serviette upon her lap. "Lady Upperton had just introduced me to a most diverting young man—an earl." The green rim of her eyes grew clear and sharp as she looked up again. "And then, you come rushing into the drawing room, hair all mussed, and within an instant we are all standing outside the Brower residence waiting for the carriage to scoop us up and transport us home."

"Blackstone kissed me." Mary felt her voice tremble. "That wicked rake did everything he could to make a mockery of me before his brother. He did it because somehow he knows I have set my cap at Lord Wetherly. That is the only explanation."

Elizabeth settled her hand on Mary's forearm, but her attention drifted to Anne. "We had to leave. Our sister was upset, and who is to say what Blackstone might have done had he found Mary inside."

Anne pushed back her chair and studied Mary. "What I do not understand is why a simple kiss, unwanted or not, rattled you so. *Our* Mary would have slapped him. Or worse."

"I did."

"But what he did brought you to tears. Now, were you some simpering miss just out, I might expect sobs. Might expect howls. But not from you."

Elizabeth turned and stared at Mary as well, as though she were suddenly seeing her in daylight for the first time. "I agree, Mary. Until Father died, you were so strong, confident, and, lud, so fiercely competitive. You would not have allowed anyone to get the better of you."

"Why now, Mary?" Anne said.

Mary settled her elbows atop her lap and rested her head in her hands. "I do not know. I really do not."

She looked up and was surprised to feel hot tears rolling down her cheeks. "Until Papa died, I knew who I was. I knew my place in this world. But now I feel so lost."

"Anne and I feel just as you do. This is a new world for us, Mary," Elizabeth told her. "We will find our way . . . with time."

"All I know is this money we have in our coffers is all that stands between us and the workhouse." Mary straightened her spine. "We must use it wisely to construct secure futures."

When Anne spoke, her voice was now soft and soothing. "And Blackstone is undermining your efforts to forge a future, a life, with Lord Wetherly. That is what frightens you so."

Mary peered down at the spot on the tablecloth and said nothing.

There was a knock at the door, but no one except MacTavish paid the interruption any heed.

Lady Upperton's mission to introduce the sisters into society had been a success last evening, and all that morning visiting cards and invitations to fetes, musicales, and routs had collected on the mantelpiece.

Mary swiped a tear from her cheek with the back of her hand. "The duke is stubbornly determined to keep me at arm's length from Quinn . . . Lord Wetherly. And I can do naught to prevent it."

"You *could*," Elizabeth said. "At least, the old Mary could."

Mary blinked back the last bit of moisture in her eyes. "You're right. Why should I stand by, awaiting his next ploy to humiliate me before his brother? I just need to be clever to keep him in check. To distract him so he does not have the time or opportunity to drive a wedge between Lord Wetherly and me."

"That's our Mary." Anne rose from her chair and circled around the table. She hugged her just as MacTavish stepped from the passage and into the dining room.

Mary stood and raised her fist in the air most dramatically. "Blackstone, you have met your equal."

"Have I now?" came a deep, all-too-familiar voice from the passage.

Mary thought her eyes would pop from their sockets the moment she realized who was standing just behind the butler.

She gulped down the huge lump that suddenly seemed to be lodged in her throat.

"Oh my Lord. *Blackstone,*" she gasped.

The duke lifted his eyebrows significantly. "My dear Miss Royle, I understand that you are fresh from the wilds of Cornwall, so I choose to believe you did not intend to insult me. My title is not 'My Lord Blackstone.' I am a duke. Therefore, the polite way to address me is *Your Grace.*"

"Oh, I do apologize—I . . . I didn't say 'My Lord Blackstone. I did pause after 'Oh my Lord,' " Mary stammered.

"Miss Royle, I know what I heard," he insisted.

"No, no. You've got it all wrong." She looked pleadingly at her sister. "Anne, fetch a sheet of paper and a pen. I will show you, Your Grace."

"Just . . . say it again."

Mary looked back at him to oblige. Even started to open her mouth. But then she saw the mischievous glint in the duke's eyes and his wide, crooked grin.

Blast. She had allowed him to do it again. Allowed him to humiliate her.

Well then, she'd give him this one. He was quick, and she hadn't been prepared.

But this would be the very last time.

The very last.

Chapter 7

"**P**lease do forgive me, Your Grace," Mary said most politely to the duke, though in her head, her tone was anything but civil. "I assure you my grasp of forms of address is quite adequate. Though I confess, I had not expected to find you in our dining room at this hour—or any other."

Mary edged past her sisters to reach Blackstone and extended her hand. "Let us begin again. Welcome to our home, *Your Grace*." Mary dipped into an overemphasized curtsy deep enough to honor the Prince Regent himself.

When she rose, she glanced at her sisters, who, though appearing obviously shaken that the infamous Black Duke was actually standing inside their home, honored him in like manner. When they straightened, Mary tapped her outer thigh, beckoning them, like one might a puppy, to her side.

"Will you not join us in the parlor, Your Grace? I vow we shall all be much more comfortable there." As any good hostess would, Mary smiled brightly at her guest and stepped into the passage, gesturing for him to follow.

Outwardly, she was calm and serene. Inwardly, she was a tangle of raw nerves.

When they entered the parlor, Mary, as was her habit, snatched the drained cordial glass from her sleeping great-aunt's bony hands.

She turned and saw that Blackstone was staring at the old woman.

"Should we perhaps retire to another room so that"—the duke gestured to Aunt Prudence—"she is not disturbed?"

"No need." Mary shook her head and rested her hand on the old woman's shoulder. She did not move or awaken. "This is Mrs. Winks, our great-aunt."

Blackstone bowed to their dozing aunt. The edge of Mary's mouth twitched with amusement. "She is a dear, but well into her dotage. We shan't bother her, you needn't worry. It has always been my belief that she enjoys the company of young folk, even if she mightn't be fully aware." She extended her hand toward the chair opposite Aunt Prudence. "Please, be seated, Your Grace."

As they sat down in the parlor, Mary thanked

the heavens above that her full skirts concealed her ridiculously knocking knees. It wouldn't do for the wretch to see how clearly unprepared she was for such a surprise attack.

And this *was* an attack. It was the only explanation she could muster. For why else would he have come?

Certainly not to apologize for kissing her. That would be the gentlemanly thing to do, and Blackstone was *no* gentleman.

"Your Grace, I am sure it is abundantly clear that we had not expected you this day," Mary began. Her voice was steady and even, which surprised her. "Might I inquire the purpose of your visit?"

Anne and Elizabeth sat silently, practically huddled together, as they stared at the duke like two field mice cornered by a hungry barn cat.

Blackstone fixed his eyes on Mary then, and suddenly she felt as though she could not draw a breath.

"I have come, my dear lady, to apologize for my actions last night." He swallowed deeply, and his glance flicked across at Anne and Elizabeth for the briefest moment, eliciting a tiny gasp from each of them. "I should not ask it, but . . . might I speak with you privately for a moment or two?"

The duke's words had only just left his mouth when Anne and Elizabeth stood from the settee and, as if they were stitched together, scurried from the parlor.

Cowards. Mary's pulse thrummed in her wrists. Now she was left all alone with him. Well, except for Aunt Prudence, who was now snoring loudly as if to remind Mary of her presence.

Still, she was as good as alone, and Lord knew, she wasn't prepared in the least for that. Why, she could not sit here with a man who had taken improper advantage of her only yesterday.

Mary stood and opened her mouth to make her own excuses.

"Please, Miss Royle. Do not go. You have naught to fear from me, I swear it." He came to his feet and in a single stride was standing before her. "Please."

With a gentleness that surprised her, he laid his hand on her shoulder and guided her back to sit upon the settee once more. He knelt down before her and took her hand into his.

Saints be blessed, what was he going to do now?

Blackstone covered her hand with his fingers and held tight. "I do hope you can bring yourself to forgive me, Miss Royle. What I did was despicable, and I have no excuse for it . . . other than I did it for Quinn."

Mary tried to unobtrusively slip her hand from his grasp, but his own were so large that it was quite impossible. "Yes, what you did was horrid, and you must excuse me, Your Grace, for not understanding your reasoning, but your brother did not seem appreciative of what you did *for him.*"

Without meaning to, Mary glanced past their clasped hands to his chest. Even beneath his waist-coat and coat she could see the curve of his firm muscles. Suddenly all the sensations of being pressed against that hard chest came crashing into her mind.

Tiny beads of perspiration moistened the cleft between her breasts. My, it was getting rather warm in the parlor.

She turned her gaze away from his form and fixed it instead on the bell on the table near the hearth. If only he would return to his chair, she could summon MacTavish and have the windows opened to the breeze.

Mary tugged a little, but his grip on her hand only tightened.

He lowered his head, and his eyes seemed to search the rug's pattern for a prompt as to what to say next. When he looked up again, he looked al-most unsure of himself.

No, this cannot be. It is just a ruse, that's all.

"Allow me to be brutally honest with you, Miss Royle," he finally said.

"I would wish it no other way, Your Grace."

"When I heard you coax Quinn into kissing you, I had the notion that the sharp teeth of a marriage trap were about to snap closed around my brother."

He leaned his handsome face close toward hers then, requiring Mary to press her back against the settee to avoid rubbing noses.

"I was certain that the moment his lips touched yours, your sponsor would emerge from the house, claim that he had ruined you, and demand marriage."

A single burst of laughter slipped through Mary's closed lips. "Your Grace, you must think me far cleverer than I truly am, if you are under the impression that I am capable of carrying off such a devious strategy."

"I do not believe I underestimated your cleverness, Miss Royle. Though I fear I completely misread your intent."

"If you thought I was about to entrap your brother," Mary said as she cocked her head, "why did you not call Quinn away? Why did you step in and claim the kiss for yourself?"

Blackstone released her hand and came to his feet then. He turned away and walked toward the hearth.

The moment his back was turned, Mary slapped her hands to her chest and gasped in a draught of air.

"Because I had to know." He settled his elbow on the mantel and swiveled his head to look at her. "I had to know if I was right—that you had a plan. That you were the sort looking to marry for money."

Mary was quite taken aback by his words.

Did he think she truly found his brother attractive because of his fortune?

How preposterous!

"Your Grace, I have no need for coin, I assure you. I have an adequate portion and quite a substantial dowry."

Blackstone looked around the room, taking particular note of the threadbare settee and frayed carpet. "If that is true, I beg your forgiveness, Miss Royle."

"It *is* true." Mary glanced down at her worn cambric frock and suddenly wished she had dressed in anything else. "Appearances, perhaps, notwithstanding. This is our great-aunt's house. When we came to live with her, her staff were already well into stripping the house of all valuables. Thankfully, we arrived when we did."

Blackstone nodded his head thoughtfully.

Lud! Why did she care what he thought of the furnishings? Or her dress?

He was a beast. What did his good opinion of her matter? Mary swallowed and returned to the core of their conversation. "So, Your Grace, you tested me? How did I fare?"

"Do you think that I would condescend to come here and beg your forgiveness if I still doubted your motives regarding my brother?"

Mary paused in her reply. She would be mad to blindly believe his words, but at the moment, she could not summon any reason to disbelieve him. "No, I suppose you would not."

"So . . . you will accept my apology?"

"Your Grace, I do thank you for explaining your actions to me. I gladly accept your apology." She summoned a smile to her lips. The sort of obligatory expression meant to communicate to a guest that his visit was over but it had been ever so pleasant to see him.

Still grimacing, Mary leapt up, turned, and passed him as she started for the door. "Thank you for coming, Your Grace. Allow me to show you the way out."

Suddenly she felt him behind her, his warm hands gently squeezing her shoulders and turning her around to face him. She raised her eyes and peered into his. At once her breath seemed torn from her lungs. "Is . . . is there something else, Your Grace?"

"Just one more request. Let me try to make amends for my indiscretion last evening." His eyes seemed to search hers for an answer. "*Please.*"

"What is your request?" Her own voice sounded thick and breathy to her ears, but it was all she could manage with Blackstone so impossibly close.

"Just this, Miss Royle. Consent to share a ride in my phaeton. My brother has mentioned how you do so enjoy taking the air in Hyde Park. Allow me this, and if you never wish to see me again, I shall abide by your wishes." He seemed to hold his breath in his lungs. "Please, say you will."

Mary did not speak for some moments. Instead, she peered into his eyes, wondering if he was sincere—for indeed he seemed earnest—or was this, too, some trick of his?

Still, he did offer the choice of never being in his presence again. For this alone it was worth risking an hour in the park with the rogue.

"Very well, Your Grace." Mary pressed on her hostess smile again. "Shall I expect you around three this afternoon?"

"You may, Miss Royle." He released her shoulders then but reached down, lifted her right hand to his lips, and kissed it ever so softly. "Thank you."

Without another word, he cut a half-circle past her and disappeared through the parlor doorway.

Mary stared at her hand where his lips had been.

Oh my word.

To what, pray, had she just agreed?

Somehow, Mary had had the impression that Blackstone would not arrive in Berkeley Square at the appointed time.

She had been wrong.

Not only did he cast the brass door knock to its base at the precise moment the tall case clock in the library pinged the correct hour but he also arrived with a gathering of damask roses bound with a silken blush-hued ribbon.

Mary found this exasperating. How horribly considerate of him. For certain, there was some insulting message hidden amongst the velvety red petals and glossy green leaves.

But Mary had never been very good at puzzles.

So, since she could not decipher the cryptic message conveyed by the flowers, she simply passed the flowers to MacTavish and bade him see the stems to a vase.

Then she thanked the duke for his thoughtfulness.

What else could she have done?

He was behaving like a gentleman, and though she suspected his polite manners were more feigned than an ingredient of his innate character, she could find no fault with his demeanor.

He even invited Anne and Elizabeth to join them for an outing in the park.

Likely not wishing to remain in the presence of the Black Duke beyond the few minutes it took to greet their guest, they declined, of course.

This was just as well, since the vehicle halted before their Berkeley Square town home was a high-perch phaeton—capable of transporting only two people.

Within a quarter hour of Blackstone's having knocked upon the Royle sisters' door, Mary found herself swaying inside the phaeton, her right thigh pressing against his left, racing down Oxford Street for Hyde Park.

At first, she thought his leg touching hers was a most rakish thing to do, but as she looked at the sheer size of his body she gave him the benefit of the doubt.

He was extraordinarily large, and, well, the phaeton had been built to accommodate an ordinary person. And he was nowhere near an ordinary man.

The duke cracked his whip in the air, and the horses broke from a fast trot to a canter. Mary tightened her grip on the metal edge of the cushioned seat. Not that the clamp of four fingers would prevent her from being hurled from the phaeton if the duke took the next corner at such speed.

"Your Grace, *please*." She saw him glance at her. "I believe your invitation was for a ride in Hyde Park."

"It was." His voice was barely audible over the roar of the wheels on the road.

"Then please rein in the horses," she shouted frantically. "Else we shall never reach the park . . . *alive*."

Blackstone laughed and pulled back on the reins. The horses, their sides already glistening and heaving from the exertion, slowed to a far saner trot.

Mary's own breathing, however, was still at a canter. She laid her hand to her chest and did her best to steady her senses.

The duke pulled the left rein and angled his team to the side of the road. "If I frightened you, Miss Royle, I do apologize. I have only just acquired the conveyance and the matched pair. I was wondering how the phaeton would perform at a good clip, and I suppose I let my musings leap from my mind and into Oxford Street."

"You are obviously far more accustomed to

riding than driving." Mary felt one eyebrow rise. "Mayhap I should take the ribbons. I likely have far more experience than you, Your Grace. Why, I drove a gig to church on Sundays. I began ten years ago." She gave her head a confident nod.

Yes, it was a jab to his ribs. A necessary jab, however, if she wanted to survive this jaunt to Hyde Park.

"Splendid idea, Miss Royle."

"W-what?"

Blackstone handed the reins over to Mary, then leapt from the phaeton to the road. He strode around the back of the vehicle, pausing beside Mary. "Just slide across the seat to the other side. I find it more natural to drive from there. You might as well." He shooed her across the seat. "You offered, I accepted. You shall take the reins, and I shall relax and enjoy the view from this side."

"But—"

He knocked his knuckles against the upper edge of the phaeton, then he flashed her a bright smile. "Come now. Do not tarry."

Mary knew she had no choice.

There was only one small hitch to the situation.

She had actually only taken the gig's reins twice. Once on a Sunday ten years ago, and then again when she had had to transport the reverend to give her father his last rites.

Blast.

* * *

With a slight snap of the leather reins, Mary urged the horses slowly, *very* slowly, down Oxford Street toward Hyde Park.

From time to time she heard a frustrated shout, or a string of lively oaths, and a moment later a red-faced hackney driver, an angry coachman, or a scowling drayman would roar past the phaeton waving a wild fist or whip in the air.

At first she attributed the rude rebukes to a pitiful lack of patience. Nothing she had done.

After the second or third hackney driver jeered at her as his vehicle overtook the phaeton, however, it finally occurred to her that perhaps she could free up the reins a little bit.

Still, she did not entertain this thought overlong. To her way of thinking, it truly did not matter how hard she drove the duke's team, but rather how straight a course she could maintain, given her limited experience with a pair of ribbons in her grip.

Besides, if she walked the horses any faster, she knew the chances of losing control and toppling the phaeton were probably as high as if the duke had still been driving. Therefore, it seemed logical to her to handle the team conservatively.

At one point, from the corner of her eye, she observed Blackstone tipping his hat to a pair of ladies walking on the flagway beside the phaeton. Several minutes later, Mary caught a glimpse of the pair walking beside the phaeton again. Or rather . . . *still*.

No, this cannot be.

"Are those the same women we passed a few minutes ago? Surely not."

"The women we *passed*?" He chuckled. "We *never* passed them. They have been strolling alongside the phaeton for some time now. You do maintain quite the leisurely pace."

Mary felt her cheeks heat. "The street is busy this day. And, well, taking the reins of a gig is one thing, driving a high-perch phaeton clearly another, Your Grace."

"Your Grace." The duke groaned. "My dear Miss Royle, I realize that 'twas only this morn that I worried you over the proper way to address me, but every time I hear you refer to me as 'Your Grace,' I find myself looking over my shoulder for my father. Do me the honor, please, of calling me by my Christian name—Rogan."

Mary blinked. "I do not believe I can manage that, Your Grace. After all, we hardly know each other. Blackstone, perhaps?"

"No, I think not. I hear Blackstone too often from the mouths of gentlemen at the track, or the clubs." He reached across, gently took the reins from her hands, and clucked to the team. "Only Quinn calls me Rogan, and I own it has been far too long since I heard my given name roll softly from a woman's lips. I rather miss that." He snapped the reins, and the horses hastened to a trot.

A tremor raced through Mary's body, and she stiffened.

Pressed against her as he was, the duke noticed her reaction. "I think you misunderstood my comment, Miss Royle." He turned his face toward hers. He wasn't even looking at the road.

"Have I?" Mary swung her head around and stared at the street before them. "There's a hackney just ahead. Do take heed."

But still he looked at her as he drove. "I only meant, Miss Royle, that my grandmother was the last woman to speak my name with kindness. And that was many years ago."

Mary held her eyes wide and stared ever forward. She curled her fingers around the lip of the seat cushion again. "Surely there have been others . . . lady friends, for instance. *The hackney*. Oh, God. Look out for the hackney!"

"You are aware of my black reputation, Miss Royle. Some of what you have heard is naught but exaggeration and hearsay, but I would venture to say that other parts are true enough. And, I must admit, the story that I never favor a woman long enough for my beard to darken my face, well, that claim is not too many steps from the truth."

The duke turned his eyes forward just long enough to swerve the team to the right and avoid plowing into the very-solid looking hackney. Then he leveled his gaze upon her once more. "Only those closest to me call me Rogan."

His voice, so low and rich, hummed through

her as deeply as the rumble of the wheels on the road. "I beg your pardon, but it hardly could be said that I have earned such a distinction."

"But you will. I can feel it." He smiled at her.

"I fear you must explain yourself, else I shall believe that you suppose too much." A town carriage was crossing the road only twenty strides before the phaeton. "Please, Your Grace, do humor me by looking ahead. The street is teeming with vehicles."

"My dear Miss Royle, my brother believes he may have found a kindred spirit in you. My every instinct tells me that you will forge some sort of connection with our family. We should be friends, at the very least. Do you not agree?"

Could this really be true? He wished to be friends? "Yes, Your Grace, I see your point. It is only logical to assume we will be in each other's company quite often, so I agree, we should be friends."

"So please, call me Rogan, even if only when no others will hear. Do it as a favor to me—your friend."

"Very well, if you will do me the favor of watching the road before us." Mary collected a deep breath in her lungs to prepare for the moment the phaeton would careen into the carriage.

"Very well, *who*?" A teasing grin sat upon his lips as the moment of sure impact grew more imminent.

"Very well—*Rogan*!" Mary closed her eyes. "Yes, I shall call you Rogan. And you may refer to me as Mary, but please, please, stop!"

The phaeton bounced. Mary opened her eyes in time to see the duke brace his right leg on the phaeton's footboard and yank back the reins hard.

The horses slowed immediately, then reared slightly. Their hooves seemed almost to dance as they came to a full halt just as the carriage screamed by.

"Thank you . . . Rogan." Mary's heart pounded so hard that she could scarce hear her own words.

"Darling Mary, you never had anything to fear. Believe me. I had at least five more seconds for you to agree to call me Rogan. And I would have used every one. It was all worth it, for now we are friends."

Mary drew a handkerchief from her reticule and dabbed her forehead before looking up at Rogan, beside her. "Yes, we are friends. But I would have agreed far more quickly had I not feared for my very existence."

"Really?" He slanted a single dark eyebrow and grinned at her. "I shall try to remember that in the future."

"Please do." Then, for no clear reason she could name, Mary realized, quite unexpectedly, that she felt quite at ease with the Black Duke.

With Rogan.

She looked across at him and did not resist when the corners of her mouth lifted.

* * *

It was clearly a day for unexpected visits. Except this time, when the door knocker sounded, the sun had long since set.

Mary was just finishing a late supper with her sisters when MacTavish entered the dining room and informed her that a gentleman caller was awaiting her in the parlor.

It was long past the sort of visiting hours propriety recommended, which told Mary that the caller could be none other than her new friend who did not always abide by society's rules—Rogan, the Duke of Blackstone.

And, for some reason as yet unknown to her, Mary wasn't the least bit bothered that he'd come so late in the eve. Her hair was a bit mussed, and she was wearing the same threadbare cambric frock she'd had on earlier in the day.

It is only Rogan, she told herself, so she did not even bother to glance into the gilt-framed looking glass hanging in the passage. Instead, she walked straight into the parlor without a care.

Only it wasn't Rogan she saw pointing his cane into the carpet and pacing.

It was Quinn.

A jolt of dread raced down her spine.

Lud, this changed everything. Her appearance *was* of consequence. Lord Wetherly was her intended, after all. She had decided that almost a month ago.

Quinn lifted his clear blue eyes the moment her

first slipper crossed the threshold, leaving her absolutely no chance for retreat to see to her toilette.

Mary hurriedly tucked a loose coil of hair behind her ear and bit her lips to draw a bit of color into them, but she knew she still looked rather like a rag girl. It could not be helped now, however.

"Oh, Miss Royle." He started for her at once. "I do so apologize for the late hour, but I simply could not wait until tomorrow to call upon you."

Mary bobbed a quick curtsy. "Think nothing of the time, Lord Wetherly . . . Quinn. You are always welcome in our home."

He rested his cane against his thigh and took both of her hands in his. "As I said, I could not wait, though I realize it is entirely ill-mannered of me to arrive unannounced."

His expression was nerve-bound, and he seemed to be having difficulty holding her gaze. His cane slid from his leg to the floor, and he glanced longingly at the settee.

"Come." Mary stepped over the cane, then hurriedly led him to the cushioned seat, settling the both of them into it. "Do tell me what troubles you so. I can see worry in the lines of your face."

Quinn withdrew his hands from hers and lowered his head. "I have something to confess, yet I do not know how to go about it, for, more than anything, I do not wish to hurt you."

"And why would you think yourself capable of that?" When Quinn did not immediately reply,

Mary reached out to his hand resting on the cushion between them and laid her hand comfortingly on his.

"My dear Lord Wetherly, please tell me what it is that so distresses you. I cannot bear to see you in such a fretful state."

Quinn raised his eyes to hers once more. "You are very good, Miss Royle. So very good." He lifted his free hand and placed it over hers, enclosing her hand between both of his. "I had thought to call early this afternoon, but I received a note from Lady Tidwell."

Lady Tidwell? Lady Upperton had warned her that the widow might give cause for worry.

He gazed deep into her eyes, and at once Mary knew he was looking for a response.

And though she did feel a painful punch of surprise in her middle, she did not permit herself any reaction to his words. There would be a suitable explanation, she was sure of it. And so, she waited.

"Her brother, Lieutenant Spinner, a man . . . no, he is more than that—*a friend*—I served with him on the Peninsula . . . in Toulouse. He stopped to visit his sister before he shipped off to India in the morning. He wished to speak with me of a matter of some importance. And so, given his limited availability, I went to see him and Lady Tidwell."

"How very kind of you." God, it was getting difficult to remain restrained. The drawn-out overture was making her imagine all manner of horrid news he might deliver. "But please, go on. You've not told me what vexes you so."

"Dear Mary, please believe me when I tell you I hold you in the highest esteem."

Another prelude. And a complimentary one too.

Whatever he would tell her next would not be good. Mary held her breath, waiting for the "but" clause to be added.

And then it came.

"But Spinner asks a great favor of me—one I cannot refuse. Please understand, he practically saved my life in Toulouse. I owe him much."

Mary's throat began to work, and she swallowed deeply. "Tell me then, what did you promise?"

Moisture must have risen into Quinn's blue eyes, for now they glistened in the candlelight like morning sun on the Serpentine. "Lady Tidwell has just emerged from mourning and wishes to reclaim her place within society."

"Yes, I saw her speaking with you at the Browers' rout. She is . . . quite lovely."

"Yes, that was she." Quinn squeezed Mary's hand between his own. "But she is not as well as she appears. Her brother claims she often thinks too much of her husband, who died at Salamanca, and when she does, she sometimes falls into a state of melancholy."

The skin between Mary's brow furrowed. "I am confused, sir. How does her state affect you?"

"Spinner believes that if she were kept busy,

socially, she might emerge from her downhearted-ness. He asked me to escort her for the rest of the season."

Mary shot to her feet. "What?" *What about me . . . about us?*

"Oh, Mary, know that I am greatly fond of you. A few weeks of consideration is all I ask of you. Please. I owe Spinner my life. I must help him."

Mary felt a little dizzy. She took a few steps and sat down in a wing chair near the hearth.

"Do not fret. You shan't be alone whilst I carry out my duty. My brother will escort you in my stead."

His words struck Mary like a bucket of icy water.

"The duke? The man who shoved you out of the way and kissed me?"

"He told me he apologized to you earlier this day—and that you accepted. Is this not true?" Quinn stood.

Mary paused to steady herself. "He did apologize and yes, I accepted." Mary cupped her hand over her eyes.

"Then there should be no problem with the ar-rangement."

"Forgive me, Quinn, but you needn't worry about my loneliness. I do not require the company of your brother. I have my sisters, after all."

"Please, Mary, he would be doing this for me as well. You are a beautiful woman. Very beautiful. Oh, I know it is wrong of me to feel this way, but I could not bear if I saw you dancing and conversing with another gentleman."

"Oh, dear sir, you have naught to fret about. I have no interest in any other."

"Please, Mary." Quinn went to her. He bent at the waist and pried her hand from her eyes. "Please, endure my brother for a few weeks—for me."

Mary looked at Quinn squarely.

This was no rakish game he played. Quinn was the most honorable man she had ever known, aside from her father. She could not ask him to refuse the lieutenant's request.

And so, she must do the honorable thing as well.

"Very well," she belatedly said. "I shall *endure* your brother's company—but only until the end of the season." Mary smiled playfully at Quinn, trying, as best she could, to make light of the situation.

"Brilliant!" Quinn retrieved his cane from the floor. "Now, I will leave you to your evening. Again, I apologize for coming so late. I knew I would not be able to live with myself if I did not discuss this with you immediately."

Before Mary could stand herself, Quinn started for the parlor door, twirling his cane twice. He spun around at the mouth of the passage and bowed. A moment later, Mary heard the front door close with a click.

Lovely. Just lovely.

Mary rose and wearily started for the library

to search for the book of medical maladies that Elizabeth had found in their father's document box a few days earlier.

She would need it for certain. It would be ridiculous to think that she could feign a headache every night during the season.

Yes, she would need a full selection of ailments to present to excuse her from society events.

For there was no possible way she could survive a season on the arm of Rogan, the Black Duke.

Absolutely none at all.

Chapter 8

❧

Bond Street
The next morning

"Look there, Anne." Elizabeth gestured to Mary, who stood in the middle of Madame Devy's elegant dressmaking shop, arms curled upward as if she'd been balancing a Roman water urn on each shoulder. "Blackstone's garden statue has followed us here."

Anne brought her hand to her lips, but Mary heard the muffled giggle anyway. She was not the least amused.

She craned her neck to see past the petite modiste and brocade privacy screen to glimpse the table clock.

Two hours. They'd been here for two mind-numbing hours.

First they'd spent an hour poring over countless fashion plates from *La Belle Assemblée*. Then, once a design had finally been selected, the modiste had begun draping her with fabrics, ribbons, and lace.

Two horrid hours had passed—and her sisters had not yet taken their turns standing beneath the modiste's assessing gaze.

Mary could endure no more.

"Are we nearly finished, Lady Upperton? My arms feel leaden and my back is beginning to ache. And, truth to tell, I do like this silk quite a lot. So why don't we choose it and be done with it all, hmm?"

Lady Upperton clucked her tongue as the modiste finished draping a swathe of rose silk over Mary's shoulder. She took the sight in for several moments, considering, before shaking her head. "No, Madame Devy, the color does not suit her. The hue is too bold and mutes the natural rosiness of Miss Royle's cheeks and lips. No, no, it will not do. Have you a softer shade in the same palette?"

The round old woman, immersed in her duties as fashion counselor, did not seem to hear Mary.

Mary crinkled her nose. "Lady Upperton?"

"A more demure shade? *Oui*, my lady, I do." The modiste whisked the silk from Mary's body, then ordered her assistant, a quiet young girl with mousy-brown hair and a pointed nose, to fetch yet another bolt of silk from the shelves.

Silently, the girl eased the roll of silk into the French modiste's arms, then assisted her in unfurling several lengths and wrapping it around Mary three times.

"That's it!" Elizabeth's eyes went bright. "Oh, yes, that's the one. You will see, Mary. The gown in *this* fabric will become your favorite."

"Mademoiselle has a sharp eye. I think she is correct. What say you to this, Lady Upperton? *Parfait!*"

"Oh, yes, madame. I think this will do very well for the Heroes' Fete next week." Lady Upperton's plump face suddenly looked very concerned. "You can hurry the gown along and deliver it in plenty of time? You promised me if we came to the shop and selected everything at once you could rush completion of the gowns."

The modiste looked at the hand-colored fashion plate on the table nearby, then at the lengths of silk wound around Mary. She looked a bit concerned. "One gown, *oui*, but three?"

"Whatever it takes, I shall pay it. We must have three new gowns for the event." Lady Upperton whisked her reticule from the table and shook it so that the coins inside jingled. "Can you finish in time?"

The modiste nodded. "*Oui.* I shall engage every seamstress in Town if I must to deliver the misses' gowns before the ball. Is it true, my lady, that Wellington himself might attend?"

"I do not know. Though his attendance would make the affair most exciting, would it not?" She slanted an eyebrow at the modiste. "Even more reason to turn out these gels in the most stunning gowns possible, eh?"

Mary tensed. "Lady Upperton. Please do not do this. Do not spend your money on me. I can pay Madame Devy myself . . . or better yet, wear the blue silk I wore to the Brower rout."

Lady Upperton clucked her tongue again. "Nonsense, dear. He has seen you in that gown. Mustn't let him think you have but one proper gown for evening."

"Why not? 'Tis true."

Lady Upperton looked up at her. "Yes, dear, I am aware of that—which is why we are here today. If you are to receive an offer by the end of the summer, you will need a proper wardrobe right away. Today's selections will be the first of many, of that you can be sure."

"But—"

"Do not even bother to try to dissuade her, Mary." Anne fingered a pale lavender ribbon. "Lady Upperton knows her mind. I intend to comply. So should you."

"Besides, Mary. Lady Upperton is quite correct. You must admit, even our best Sunday frocks that we wore in the country are not at all suitable for London's drawing rooms."

By now, Lady Upperton was circling around Mary like a bird of prey. Her face was pinched with concentration, her little fingers steepled, and the ridiculously high heels of her Turkish slippers were clicking maddeningly on the wooden floor as she moved about.

"The silk perfectly complements your complexion, dear. The gown will turn the head of every lady and gentleman in the Argyle Rooms." Lady Upperton rested her hands on her wide hips and smiled brightly. "Why, I daresay, the duke shan't be able to remove his gaze from you." Then she tossed Mary a sly wink.

No, surely, she could not have heard the old lady correctly.

"I-I am rather confused, Lady Upperton," Mary said. "You mentioned the duke. But . . . in truth, you meant Viscount Wetherly, did you not?"

Anne and Elizabeth set the lace sample cards they held in their hands on the counter and leaned closer to listen.

Lady Upperton did not immediately reply. Instead, she handed a sash of ivory satin to Madame Devy, who wrapped it around Mary's ribs. "No, not enough dash. Let us try the claret satin."

"*Oui*, my lady."

Then the tiny, plump woman turned her eyes up to Mary. "No, dear. I meant the *duke*." She smiled at Mary and gave her a little nudge. "He called upon me yesterday for permission to squire you about in his brother's stead. Very gentlemanly of him, don't you agree?"

"He called upon you yesterday—during the day, not that evening?" Mary was stunned. "What hour was this, might I ask?"

Lady Upperton's eyes wedged to one side and she tapped her index finger on her lower lip as she thought. "I suppose it must have been around one o'clock in the afternoon." She glanced back up at Mary. "Why do you ask, dear?"

"Because he came to Berkeley Square in the morning to apologize for kissing me—then he called again at three o'clock for a phaeton ride in Hyde Park. But Lord Wetherly did not call until . . ." Mary narrowed her eyes.

"Oh, dear." Elizabeth's gaze locked with Anne's. "Do you know what this means?"

"I do." Anne cringed.

"Well, I do not!" Lady Upperton scuttled over to Anne. "What consequence does the time of the duke's visit with me hold?"

"Lord Wetherly did not call upon Mary to inform her of his promise to escort Lady Tidwell to the season's events"—Anne's gaze flitted over Mary with every third word—"*and* the duke's promise to watch over Mary . . . *until late last evening.*"

Mary could not believe what she was hearing. "It means, Lady Upperton, that the duke is no gentleman. He has not changed at all. He knew Lord Wetherly would be asked to escort Lady Tidwell to events—well *before* his brother was asked for the favor."

She grabbed a small tufted cushion from the modiste's hand and started plucking out the pins that held the silk in place, jabbing them into the cushion. "He very nearly had me fooled into believing he was actually a considerate, well-mannered gentleman. But I was wrong. Oh! I was *so* wrong."

Mary ground her teeth while she struggled to withdraw a pin just behind her shoulder. "Why, I believe this whole Lady Tidwell scheme was crafted by Blackstone's hand as a means to keep Lord Wetherly and me apart!"

Finally, Mary pulled the last pin free and unwound herself from the silken cocoon. "The *ton* got the right of it when they dubbed him the Black Duke, for there is no one with a more wicked soul. But this time he has gone too far."

Mary disappeared behind the screen and quickly dressed. Then, without a word of explanation to anyone, she snatched up her shawl and charged out the door, angrily muttering to herself.

"Go ahead and play your horrid little games, Blackstone, you . . . you brimstone beast. I can outlast you. I can. Two months is not so very long."

"Yes, Miss Royle, I'm certain." Mrs. Polkshank bobbed her double chin as she topped off Mary's teacup. "The duke won't be pinchin' anyone's bottom at the musicale this evenin'—oh, me language. I beg your pardon, Miss Royle, I did overhear that bit when you and your sisters were talking last night."

"Are you sure he will not be there?" Mary asked.

"Oh, I am sure of it. He ain't on the guest list at all." She widened her mouth in a proud smile. "Only cost me a wee kiss to get one of the Harringtons' footmen to slip above stairs and snatch that bit of news for you."

"A kiss?" Mary narrowed her eyes. "What happened to the two shillings I gave you?"

Sheepishly, Mrs. Polkshank revealed the two shillings and slid them onto the parlor tea table. "I was thinkin' that since I got the information you needed, that I might be able to . . . keep the coins?"

Mary sighed. A shilling here, a tuppence there.

Avoiding the Black Duke was going to get very expensive before the summer was through.

Still, she'd gladly pay a half crown every night if it could keep her from running into the all-too-clever duke.

"Very well, Mrs. Polkshank, the money is yours to keep. Thank you for your report." She took a sip of her steaming tea.

Lady Upperton would be very pleased to see her at the musicale, especially after she missed Lady Holland's dinner party the previous night owing to the sick pain in her head. "What have you heard about the Heroes' Fete? Anything yet?"

"Far as I know, all of London society will be

there, miss. And, seein' as how Lord Wetherly is one of the heroes bein' celebrated . . ."

"I must attend," Mary said to herself, "for Lord Wetherly."

"Well, yes. But what I was about to say was that his brother will no doubt be there too. Don't you think so? I would certainly attend if everyone was makin' a royal fuss about my brother—if I had one. Which I don't."

"What?" Mary looked up at the cook. "Oh, I believe you are correct, Mrs. Polkshank. By the way, I left several more invitations for you on the table in the kitchen."

"Oh, thank you, miss."

"You need not dread the task. I hid a few more shillings in the water bucket by the meat spit. Use them, or keep them for yourself—as long as you let me know whether or not the Duke of Blackstone will be attending the events."

Mrs. Polkshank grinned, revealing the gap where one of her front teeth used to be. "As long as the household's got footmen," she puckered her lips saucily, "I can find *some* way of learnin' if the duke is attendin' or not." The entire right half of Mrs. Polkshank's face contorted as she winked. "If you get my meanin'.'"

When Mary looked up, Anne was standing directly behind the cook.

Oh no. Mary rested her head in her hand. Redirect the conversation. Quick. "Yes, Cook, a roast would be perfect for our Sunday meal. Good day."

"What? A roast? Beggin' your pardon, Miss Royle, but this is short notice, Miss Royle." Mrs. Polkshank picked up the near empty teapot. "I'll have to see what the butcher has. Maybe give him a little sugar too." She laughed heartily, then turned around to see Anne glaring at her. Her expression sobered at once.

"That will be all, Cook," Mary managed. "Thank you."

"Yes, miss." Mrs. Polkshank slinked out of the parlor and headed below stairs.

"Well?" Anne folded her arms over her chest.

"How long have you been standing there?"

"Long enough to hear that you, our frugal sister who will not even allow us to hail a hackney in the rain, is paying our cook . . . and housekeeper . . . to steal peeks at society's guest lists!"

"Do you know of another way I can survive the next two months? I cannot abide the duke."

Anne unfolded her arms and slapped a hand to the table.

"Yes. Act like a mature woman. Lady Upperton has provided us with unmatched entrée into society. You might be a little grateful."

"I am grateful for what she is doing for you and Elizabeth, but I have already met the gentleman I intend to marry. What good can come of my attending events?"

"To help us, Mary."

"To help you and Elizabeth scout for mates? How could I be of assistance with that? I know almost no one in Town. And the Old Rakes, who are fully ensconced in society, have already committed themselves to seeing each of you matched."

"Oh, you are wearing blinders." Anne sat down beside her. "You are clever, Mary. You are curious. We need your help to investigate the story we've been told. All we have is a document box filled with scribbles and letters, none seeming to relate to another."

Mary laid her hand on the book sitting beside her on the table. "We also have Papa's medical reference."

"And two empty laudanum bottles," came their sister's voice.

Mary and Anne looked up to see Elizabeth standing in the doorway with two small, dark amber labeled bottles in her hand.

Anne stood and crossed to her sister. She took the two bottles and held them up to the bright sunlight streaming through the window.

"Where did you find these? I don't recall seeing them in either box." Anne handed one of the bottles to Mary.

"Nor do I." Mary turned the bottle over in her hand, then looked at Elizabeth.

"This morning, I accidentally knocked Papa's document box off the table. When it hit the floor, I heard a clinking sound," Elizabeth began. "Documents and letters do not clink, so I emptied the contents onto the carpet. It was just as before, a ledger, some papers. Nothing that could have made the noise I heard. I knew something else was in that box. I just couldn't see it. So I shook it, and heard it again, that faint tinkling sound."

"I don't understand. Where did you find the bottles?" Anne asked.

Elizabeth's gaze brightened. "There was something I wasn't seeing, so I ran my fingers all around the inside. Then I felt it—a tiny metal depression."

She tugged at the ribbon she wore around her neck and revealed the key to the document box. She twisted the oval finger grip and removed it, revealing a hexagonal-shaped driver. "Do you remember what Lotharian told us, that Papa told him that the key opened a trapdoor?"

Mary came to her feet. "In our home in Cornwall."

"Yes, that is what we all assumed. But we were wrong." Elizabeth held the small driver out before them all.

Mary and Anne craned their necks to view the hidden portion of the key more closely.

"When I inserted this into the hole and turned it, the base suddenly sprang open. That's when I realized that the box had a false bottom—a trapdoor. When I opened it, I found the bottles, wrapped up in a filthy cloth."

"To mute the noise." Anne gripped the back of

Mary's chair and steadied herself. "You do not think those bottles contained the laudanum used to . . ."

Elizabeth nodded her head slowly. "Drug our mother—*Mrs. Fitzherbert.*"

Slowly Mary returned her gaze to the bottle in her hand. She lifted the stopper and sniffed. "Nooo, this is not possible."

Chapter 9

The Harringtons' home, though located just diagonally from Lady Upperton's residence and the Old Rakes of Marylebone Club, was small in comparison to the other grand homes packed cheek by jowl on Cavendish Square.

Still, when Mary was ushered into the gallery room for the musicale with her sisters, her mouth fell open in awe.

Every wall was filled with paintings—landscapes, still-life compositions, and portraits with allegorical, religious, or mythological themes. Clearly, the stunning paintings were the work of a single artist of unmatched talent.

What so intrigued Mary, however, was the fact that beautiful, aristocratic-looking women—she recognized some from biting caricatures she'd seen on display at Hatchard's—were prominently featured in almost every single one.

As she and her sisters moved past at least ten rows of chattering guests, Mary's ears suddenly filled with a collection of random notes. She had just turned her gaze to the musicians, tuning their instruments at the front of the gallery, when she noticed Lord Lotharian in the distance.

Lotharian managed to rise from his chair situated in the first row of gallery seating. He beckoned forth the footman, who quickly guided the Royle sisters to several chairs near Lady Upperton and himself, Sir Lilywhite, and Lord Gallantine.

Lady Upperton hugged Anne and Elizabeth, then allowed them to take their seats toward the far end of the row beside the Old Rakes.

When she greeted Mary, however, she snatched up her hand and held it firm. "You may sit beside me, my dear," she told Mary, with a mischievous twinkle in her eye. She gestured to a chair beside her near the center aisle.

"Why, thank you, Lady Upperton." When Mary sat down, she realized that the chair beside her was still unoccupied.

Ordinarily, this would not have concerned her in the least, but when Lady Upperton, on two separate occasions just moments apart, shooed guests from sitting in the single empty chair, Mary knew that a plan was afoot. She studied the round old woman and the lanky lord beside her. They merely peered innocently back at her.

But Mary knew better. She only hoped the scheme did not include the wretched Duke of Blackstone.

Suddenly, from somewhere behind her, a wave of enthusiastic applause rolled forward toward the small dais where the musicians had assembled for their performance.

She twisted around in her seat just in time to see that the crowd was applauding Quinn, the famous war hero, who was just starting up the aisle. On his arm, to Mary's dismay, was the lovely widow Lady Tidwell.

Mary felt a twinge in her middle.

Blast. She should have also asked Mrs. Polkshank if Lord Wetherly was to attend. Why hadn't she thought to do that? She mightn't have attended the musicale at all, or at the very least could have better prepared herself to see Quinn . . . with *her.*

As Quinn escorted Lady Tidwell closer, his eyes sought out Mary's, and once found, he smiled brightly at her.

The click of his cane grew louder, and abruptly she realized that he was perhaps coming to speak with her. She bit her lower lip, then sucked the top one into her mouth for a moment, hoping to send a little color into them. She glanced down at her gown.

Yes, she was ready to face him now.

As gracefully as she could manage, Mary rose

from her seat, beaming at Quinn. She lifted a welcoming hand to him. He reached out his hand as he moved toward her, when suddenly the musicians struck the first chord.

Quinn stilled his step, and both he and Lady Tidwell quickly began to scan the rows nearby for open chairs.

Perdition! Mary wrenched her head around and glared at the conductor. He was ruining everything. She only required a moment more to speak with Quinn.

Just time to exchange a few words, to reassure him that she would wait as long as it took for them to be together.

When she turned back to look at Quinn, she saw that he was no longer moving toward her. Instead, he and Lady Tidwell were moving back down the aisle to two unoccupied seats in the middle of the gallery.

When they were about to seat themselves, Quinn paused and did something very odd. He smiled at Mary once more, then raised his eyebrows and angled his head and eyes toward the center aisle.

Mary followed the direction of his gaze.

Oh no . . . there he was—Rogan.

He was wearing that cocky lopsided grin of his and, worse yet, was moving straight for the empty chair beside her.

No, no, no, this can't be happening.

Mrs. Polkshank had told her that the duke

would not be in attendance this evening! It was the only reason she'd agreed to come.

Thinking quickly, Mary tossed her reticule and lace fan on the chair, hoping he might believe the seat was already taken.

But he didn't.

He was not the least concerned that he was distracting the musicians when he nudged past the conductor and headed straight for the chair beside her.

"Thank you, my dear Miss Royle." Quite casually, he lifted her reticule and fan and handed them to her. "How good of you to hold a chair for me."

Mary thought to imply that the reticule and fan belonged to someone else and that he was taking some unknown lady's seat, but that would be lying. She looked down at the articles now sitting in her lap. No, such a lie would not have been successful anyway. After all, the fan had been created from the exact same lace as her dress. Even a man was sure to notice that.

For more than two hours the musicians played and played.

Mary had decided right away that she wasn't going to look at Rogan, though her eyes were straining to do just that.

She would not allow herself to look.

He would just smile back at her in a condescending way, thinking to himself how he'd fooled her so completely. That she actually had believed that he had been doing Quinn a grand favor by watching over her—when in fact she was almost certain that he had devised their separation to begin with.

The *beast*.

To occupy herself, Mary watched the minute hand on the tall case clock in the corner start its full-circle journey around the dial.

Hardly amusing. And after just one minute her eyes were inching toward Rogan. Couldn't allow that.

So Mary played a little game whereby she would close her eyes and count to sixty, then open them again just as the minute hand moved on.

She grew bored with that activity after just two minutes.

How would she last the evening with the duke sitting right beside her and Quinn just a few rows behind with the lovely widow? She would go mad if she had to endure it much longer.

As the moments passed, she began to wonder if Quinn was enjoying his evening with Lady Tidwell.

A quick look at the couple would not be so very improper, would it? Not if it was a small glance, and nothing more.

Mary set her fan atop her knee, and over the next seconds, removed her hand. The lace fan tumbled to the floor between her seat and Rogan's.

She bent to retrieve it, but immediately the duke's hand shot down between the seats and wrapped his fingers around the fan.

Luck was not with her. Of course the wretched man chose that very moment to act in a gentlemanly manner.

Brilliant, just brilliant.

Still, Mary bent at her waist and plunged her hand between the chairs as well. She fished her hand around the feet of chairs, pretending she was not aware Rogan had already picked up the fan. As her hand scrabbled around the floor, she turned her head as much as she dared and wedged her eyes as far to the left as she could manage, hoping to catch a glimpse of Quinn.

And catch it, she did. Only the appalling sight she glimpsed made her turn around completely in her chair to be sure of what she had seen.

Quinn was holding Lady Tidwell's hand between both of his own. Oh God. He held her hand the very same way he had held hers in the parlor, not so many evenings ago.

The backs of Mary's eyes pricked as she caught Quinn staring, most adoringly, into the widow's eyes. He squeezed her hand in his.

A tear breached Mary's lower lashes and splashed onto her cheek.

"Turn around, gel. People are taking notice." Lady Upperton grasped Mary's arm and turned her around in her chair.

"Your fan, Miss Royle." Rogan glanced down at her, no doubt seeing her tears, as he closed her fan and placed it into her gloved hand, along with his handkerchief.

Deuce it. Mary tried hard to blink back the tears welling in her eyes without needing Rogan's linen.

She took a deep breath, then raised her chin, trying to keep the tears poised in her eyes.

It was then that she noticed she was peering up at a very large painting positioned behind the musicians.

Focus on the painting. Not on what Quinn might be doing.

It was a full-length oil portrait of a beautiful woman. Clearly, she was highborn. She had an aristocratic look about her.

Her expression was demure, yet in her eyes Mary could almost believe she saw sparks. The painted sky behind the woman was dark and dramatic, which made her white gown vivid and fresh. Her hair was piled high upon her head, with coils of ringlets spilling down the sides of her throat. Around her shoulders, in stark contrast with her almost virginal appearance, was a crimson-and-gold Kashmir shawl.

Mary looked at the shawl, so bold and vivid, and then once more she focused on the woman's eyes. They seemed to flicker with a sly vitality.

With feminine power.

A knowing smile lifted Mary's lips.

She felt almost as though she knew this woman. Could see her soul through her eyes.

"Mary?" Lady Upperton nudged her shoulder.

She turned to look across at the old woman, but the moment she did, the tears she'd fought slipped down her cheeks. She scrubbed them away with Rogan's handkerchief, then folded the linen in a square and squeezed it in her palm.

"Mary?"

Belatedly, Mary realized that the musicians had finally stopped playing at last, and that Lady Upperton was peering pointedly at her. "Oh, dear, I do apologize, Lady Upperton. I found myself quite taken by the woman in that painting."

"You would not be the first." Then it almost sounded as if Lady Upperton huffed. "Sir Joseph possesses many paintings by the artist George Romney, but this one is his prize."

"Why is that?"

"Because 'tis rumored that the Prince Regent himself commissioned the painting . . . when the lady was his mistress." Lady Upperton caught Mary's arm and pulled her near. "But when she lost his favor to another, he never paid the commission or claimed the painting. So there it sat in Romney's studio until his death, when the house and its contents were sold by his heir."

Mary leaned back in her chair and gazed up at the painting.

From the corner of her eye, she could see that Rogan was looking up at it as well.

"She was a classic beauty," he admitted, punctuating his words with a greatly affected sigh.

Mary did not look at him. Instead she directed her next question to Lady Upperton. "Who was she?"

"Are you serious? You really do not know?" Rogan rudely broke into the conversation. "My, you *are* a country miss, aren't you?"

"Yes, I am." Mary glowered at him. "But I was not addressing you, Your Grace."

Rogan chuckled. "My, my, Miss Royle. Either you have taken a sudden dislike to me . . . or you are working very hard to play *unattainable*. Which is it?" He lifted one eyebrow, which only served to infuriate her further.

"I think you know, Your Grace." Mary glared at him, holding her angry gaze as long as she could manage.

Those ladies and gentleman of society who sat nearby suddenly quieted and watched them, as if eagerly awaiting a sparring match between the country miss and the highborn duke.

Lady Upperton noticed the other guests' focused attention and was quick about stopping the heated exchange.

She snorted an overdone laugh. "Goodness now, the war is over, let us not begin another." She tapped Mary's arm with her fan, forcing her to break her daggered gaze, then tamped down her tone. "The woman is Frances, Countess of Jersey."

A cold finger seemed to run down Mary's spine. "You do not mean *the* Lady Jersey."

The woman who wrapped up the cold, blue babies in her shawl and handed them off to Papa?

She shook the idea from her head.

Impossible. Impossible!

"Yes, I do." Lady Upperton sighed. "As you can see, she was quite beautiful in her day. And she took full advantage of that beauty."

"So, she is no longer living."

"No, Miss Royle, she is alive. I saw her only last year," Rogan mentioned nonchalantly. "She . . . was an acquaintance of my father's."

"You actually have been introduced to Lady Jersey?" She asked, with badly feigned indifference. As much as she wished she was not interested, she was.

"I was, only in passing though." Then, his tone grew richer, as smooth and sweet as port and chocolate. The sort of voice a man draws forth to lure, to woo. His tone dropped as well, and he began speaking so quietly that Mary was compelled to lean nearer to hear what he was saying at all.

"She no longer resembles the siren in these paintings, however," he told her. "She is handsome enough, but no longer beautiful, *unlike you*, my dear." He paused for several moments and merely stared into Mary's eyes, making her heart pound ridiculously.

He reached out his hand then and for the briefest moment slid two fingers down the length of a dark curl dangling at her throat. "Her hair color is not silky and rich, as yours is. Instead, it is gray."

Mary swallowed hard.

Rogan's gaze slid slowly down her form, riding every curve like a lover's caress. "She no longer possesses the slim yet supple body a man dreams of pressing against his own."

Mary flipped open her fan. The gallery had grown very warm now that the audience had started to move about. How she wished he would just go away. Go speak with his brother . . . *and his lady friend.*

She turned away from Rogan, hoping that perhaps Lady Upperton had heard something of the duke's lascivious words and would cease creating opportunities for their meeting. But the old woman was deep in conversation with Lord Lotharian, too preoccupied to have noticed that anything was amiss.

Rogan evidently noticed this too. For he brought his mouth to Mary's ear and whispered hotly into it. "Shall I tell you more, Miss Royle? Or would you like to step into the courtyard for some cool air? I seem to recall you enjoy night walks in the garden."

She stared at him. "I cannot believe your gall. No, no, that is not right. I *do* believe it. I just should have expected it."

"You wound me, Miss Royle." He took her free hand in his and pressed it to his heart. "I only sought to make you feel better . . . after your up-set."

She raised her open fan beside her mouth. "And you expect me to believe that? You are quite wicked, Your Grace," she told him in a hushed tone.

She had wished her words to carry power, but instead they'd come out weak and missish.

It was all she could manage, for suddenly she found herself quite breathless.

Oh, botheration. Snapping her fan to her side, she tore her gaze from Rogan's and rudely interrupted the conversation in progress beside her. "Lady Upperton, does Lady Jersey still reside in London?"

It was a valid question, not just a means to avoid Rogan and his annoyingly heated whispers. Perhaps Anne and Elizabeth could speak with Lady Jersey and put their fanciful notions of being blood royals to rest.

Lady Upperton shrugged. "I vow, I have not seen her in society in many months. I had heard she was in Cheltenham recently."

Rogan suddenly stood from his chair, star-tling Mary with his overwhelming presence. She couldn't help but stare up at him. Once again she was taken with how enormous he really was.

His height was nothing less than extraordinary, and his form, well, it was muscled and solid—so different from Quinn's lean, elegant body.

She tried to act calm and collected as she gazed up at his strong, square jaw, glittering dark brown eyes, and . . . those lips. Oh, she remembered that mouth all too well. Mary swished her fan before her face.

It was sweltering in the gallery. Was she the only guest who noticed?

Rogan smiled down at her, making her flush.

She could not deny that some women might find him incredibly handsome, if they favored that dark, rugged look of his. Which, of course, she did not.

Still, there was something very appealing about him. Though that was reasonable. He was Quinn's brother after all, and they did share blood.

Still, nothing about them was similar. While Rogan's wavy hair was dark as ebony, so black that it glinted blue in the candlelight, his brother's hair was fair and brought to Mary's mind the color of wheat just before harvest.

She raised her eyes from his lips and, to her embarrassment, met his gaze directly. Lud, he'd been all too aware of her study, and the grin on his lips told her he was quite amused by it as well.

Unexpectedly, he extended a hand to her. "Despite what you *think* you saw happen a moment ago, I know Quinn would be most pleased to see you, Miss Royle. He mentioned his hope that you would be in attendance this evening."

"Really? He did?"

"He did, indeed." Rogan's voice had instantly returned to a more civil, less rakish tone. "I was about to go and convince him and his guest to drink a glass of wine with me. Would you care to join us?"

Was it possible she had misinterpreted Quinn's affection for Lady Tidwell?

She supposed it could have been compassion in his eyes for a widow lost in her melancholy.

She turned a smile up at Rogan. "Yes, Your Grace. I should very much like to . . . if Lady Upperton will permit it." Mary looked at the plump elderly woman, who exchanged a quick glance with Lotharian beside her.

"Very well, Mary," Lady Upperton said, "but we'll away within the hour. Take care that you have returned to us before then." Her painted red lips slanted with amusement. "I trust you remember where the clock is?"

Mary flushed at the comment. "Yes, I do." She looked up at Rogan again, then, lifting her hand, placed it gently in his gloved palm.

His fingers curled around hers, and at once she felt the heat of him, even through her silk gloves.

The warmth rose into her cheeks again, much to her humiliation, as he drew her up from the chair. He offered her his arm, and together they walked past the conductor arranging his music and down the crowded center aisle toward Quinn.

And Lady Tidwell.

Mary rose up on her toes as they squeezed through the crush of guests, hoping to snare a glimpse of Quinn, her viscount. Her intended.

Rogan, whose height in this instance was a clear

advantage, did not share her problem of impeded view.

"Damn me," Rogan hissed. "He's gone."

"What?" Mary heard the desperation in her own voice and cringed at the sound of it.

She had no desire for Rogan to detect her lack of confidence. Though what else should she feel, when her future husband was obligated to take the arm of a beautiful, lonely widow every night?

And so Mary added, "The musicale was longer than most, don't you agree? Your brother has likely gone to the refreshment table." She looked up at Rogan and smiled prettily at him. "Shall we do the same?"

Rogan locked her arm tightly against his side while they walked, as if he thought she might flee. He looked down at her then with a gaze so smoldering that Mary trembled, suddenly realizing the danger of her feigned flirtation.

But he wanted her to feel that way, didn't he? Nerve-shot and unsure of herself?

This was how rakes maintained the advantage, was it not?

And at that moment, as she and Rogan walked down the aisle together, it occurred to her that there was no avoiding the duke, no escaping him, no matter how diligently she plotted to do just that.

As much as she hated to believe it, she knew that she must accept the fact that Rogan had taken control of her relationship with his brother.

If she neared Quinn, Rogan would simply taunt her with his wickedness, and in an instant she'd be knocked from her footing.

He knows just how to shake my confidence. I should slap him. She gazed fiercely at the duke. *Again.*

Yes, he was a master at wielding his sensuality like a weapon against her. He had had years of practice playing the rake, after all.

From what she'd heard, he'd had years of experience too, thrusting and parrying with the most skilled and beautiful of society women.

She, however, was naught but an inexperienced country miss. *Clearly, I am no match for him.*

Mary stilled her step suddenly as a thought occurred to her. She peered into his eyes as he gazed down at her.

Or am I?

How adept is he in warding off the advances of an innocent? A little smile pulled upward at her lips.

Well, she decided, perhaps it was time to find out.

Rogan, feeling her delay, paused too. "Are you well?" he asked.

"Perfectly." Mary smiled up at him.

For now I have the perfect plan.

One that you, given your nature, cannot possibly be prepared for.

One that would send the Black Duke running for his country house.

Yes, the seducer was about to become . . . the seduced.

Chapter 10

C ourage. That was all she needed to regain control of her future with Quinn.

Sadly, though, as Rogan led her into the dining room toward the refreshment table, Mary knew she sorely lacked that important commodity.

"Odd." Rogan was scanning the bustling room in earnest. "I do not see Quinn in here, either. I was sure he'd be fetching Lady Tidwell a libation."

A glass of wine. Yes.

What did it matter if her constitution had little tolerance for spirits of any sort? The smallest amount had the power to make her all muddle-headed. But tonight, it might be just the thing to boost her bravery.

While Rogan was distracted with the task of

peering through the crowd to locate his brother, Mary took the opportunity to extricate her arm from the duke's steel-banded grasp.

"The night is mild and the house is very close this evening," she told him. "Do you think it likely that he and Lady Tidwell stepped outside for air . . . as you, yourself, had earlier suggested we do?"

"Yes, perhaps so," he murmured distractedly as his gaze flitted this way and that about the room.

"Shall we each collect a glass of wine and venture into the courtyard to join them?" She raised her brows, as if her suggestion had been innocently conceived.

Rogan turned and pinned her with his gaze. "Wine? Oh, quite right." He started for a footman, who was circling the dining room balancing a silver tray filled with goblets of claret, but he stopped suddenly and turned around to look back at her.

"Your Grace? Would you like me to assist you?" She served him a gentle smile.

"Y-you will wait here for me, will you not?" The expression on his face seemed altogether too serious for the words he had spoken. "I shall return in but a moment."

Mary tilted her head to the side and considered his peculiar reaction.

Did he really think that the moment he had turned his back to her she would dart off into the courtyard to woo Quinn? "I'll not step from this spot, Your Grace. I promise you. I shall not leave."

"Very good, Miss Royle." His expression brightened.

Mary watched as he hurried through the throng to reach the footman, who was now on the farthest edge of the dining room.

What an odd gentleman.

Just then, her sisters appeared beside her.

"Such a dull gathering, is it not?" Elizabeth raised her own goblet of wine to her lips and took a sip. "When Lady Upperton mentioned quitting the musicale, I encouraged her to do so as soon as possible."

"So, are you ready?" Anne quizzed. "Lady Upperton's carriage already waits at the door."

"Leave, *now*?" Mary glaced at Rogan just as he lifted two goblets from the footman's silver tray. "Oh, no. I am not yet prepared to leave. I have yet to speak with Lord Wetherly."

Anne leveled an annoyed look at her. "Well, do go and bid him farewell now, please—if you must."

"Do, Mary." Elizabeth raised her wineglass and gestured about the room. "There are no bachelors here. Look about. Only dreary married ladies and gentlemen."

"See here, I can walk back to Berkeley Square. The night air is soft and warm this evening." Mary flicked her fingers at each of her sisters. "So go ahead without me. Quit the musicale. I shall return home soon enough."

"But we can't leave without you," Elizabeth said.

"Nonsense." Mary reached out and snatched

Elizabeth's goblet from her, nearly spilling the half glass of wine that remained. "Go on."

"You can't walk all the way home at night—especially not in that gown. You, and it, will be ruined if you attempt it." Anne was completely serious, for she folded her arms over her chest the way she always did when Mary proposed some indecorous course of action.

Mary looked up and her stomach muscles tensed. Rogan had paused momentarily to speak with their host, but he was only a few strides away now. He would return in an instant. "Do not fret, Anne. I shall ask Lord Wetherly, Lady Tidwell, and the duke to see me home. Off with you now. I shall be along soon enough."

"Very well, then," Anne amended. "I suppose your plan is reasonable enough."

"*Finally.* Let us away." Elizabeth took Anne's hand and, without a look back, drew her toward the passage. Good eve, Mary."

"Good eve," she called back softly.

My plan is reasonable enough.

She grinned to herself. *If they only knew.*

Mary looked down at Elizabeth's wineglass in her hand. *Courage,* she told herself, as she swallowed the claret in a single draught and slipped the empty goblet onto the tray of an unsuspecting footman passing by.

She knew, or thought she knew, exactly how to seduce the duke.

All she needed to do was pretend to be receptive

to his roguish passes. Act as if she had suddenly set her cap at him.

Yes, all she needed was a little courage, and she'd have Rogan running for his rakish life.

She'd changed.

Rogan realized it the very moment he returned to Miss Royle's side, having balanced two goblets of wine through a revolving gauntlet of the Harringtons' horde of guests.

"Here you are, Miss Royle." When he pressed the glass of wine into her hand, she lifted it quickly to her mouth. Her hand quivered fiercely.

She raised her gaze to his and thanked him for the wine. Though she smiled pleasantly and her countenance was the portrait of serenity, she seemed quite unable to stop her fingers from trembling.

For some reason, she was conspicuously anxious and tense, far more so than before.

He didn't enjoy seeing her this way. Bloody hell, it was his fault. Her shaking made him almost regret toying with her earlier. Almost.

It was not as if he'd had a choice in the matter. He had a duty to protect his brother. His seductive words had been necessary to distract her and keep her thoughts solidly with him, rather than with his deuced marriage-minded brother.

Clearly, she was aware of his study of her. Had there been a japanned folding screen anywhere nearby, he was certain she would have ducked behind it for refuge.

Positioning her lace fan between them like a tempered shield, she flicked it hard, and it snapped open with a click.

Damn it all. Am I that menacing?

Evidently to her I am.

Her amber eyes were wide and round, and she nervously raised the wine-filled goblet to her mouth again and again, until the claret was drained completely.

Rogan raised his eyebrows. "You seemed to have enjoyed your wine. Shall I fetch you another, Miss Royle?"

"No, this one will do." But then she held her trembling hand before her and looked into the hollow of her glass. "*Oh.*" She angled her eyes back up at him, her cheeks flushing red with embarrassment.

She inhaled deeply, and when she released her pent breath, a calmness of sorts descended over her. "On second thought, yes, I should like another. But do allow me to walk with you this time, if you will."

Her lids looked heavy, and her eyes glinted in the candlelight. "The footman serving the wine is just there," she said as she tipped her head, gesturing toward the doors that led to the rear of the center hall. "We can step into the courtyard afterward and breathe some cool air. What say

you"—she lowered her voice and leaned close—
"*Rogan?*"

And there it was again. Another change in her
demeanor.

One moment she was quaking like a frightened
child, the next plying her feminine wiles like the
most practiced of French courtesans.

This made no sense to Rogan.

What is the chit's game?

Ah, well, the hour was not so very late. He had
time to indulge her long enough to determine
what she was truly about.

She smiled and, without a prompt, reached
out and looped her arm tightly around his.
"Shall we?"

She was shaking again. Now that was disheart-
ening.

Deuce it. She was so damned transparent in her
effort to appear brave and resistant to his taunts.

But he knew better. He had played this game
many times before and with far more skilled op-
ponents.

"Mayhap we shall stumble across your brother."
Her lips pulled back, revealing the falsest of
smiles.

"Do you think so, Miss Royle?"

Ah, now he understood.

True, it was stifling inside the house, but he knew
it was not the evening breeze she truly sought.

It was his cursed brother.

She feared, and perhaps rightly so, that Quinn

was developing affections for another. And Mary was not about to step back and let Lady Tidwell claim her golden prize.

"It's only l-logical, Your Grace." She shook her head lazily. "Do you not agree?" The wine seemed to be affecting her very quickly, thickening her tongue and weighting her eyelids.

"I am not so convinced, but if you would like to be sure, Miss Royle, let us go and see. If nothing else, we shall enjoy the air. Right this way, if you please."

As Rogan led her toward a tray of filled goblets, the heaving crowd pressed them tightly together, and she leaned against him for support. He felt the softness of her breast against his side.

At once he felt a tightening in his groin.

Bloody hell. Not now.

He could not feel such things for *her.* Anyone but her.

The cool air would help. Had to.

Because Rogan knew that Quinn and Lady Tidwell would not be found in the courtyard.

Nor the garden.

For Sir Joseph had told him only moments before that Lady Tidwell was not feeling herself and had been escorted home by his brother half an hour earlier.

And in all likelihood, he and Miss Royle would be in the courtyard . . . alone.

* * *

The crescent moon seemed unnaturally bright on this particular evening, bringing to Mary's mind the night when Rogan had slipped between her and Quinn and kissed her, sending her body all to jelly.

Tonight, however, such a rakish act was not a concern. She and the Black Duke would not be alone. Another female, even if Lady Tidwell was that woman, would be present, and Rogan would not dare to repeat such an offense in her presence.

Nor would the blackheart chance piercing his brother's heart again, not when it had wounded him so keenly before.

No, she would be completely protected from any more roguish exploits this evening, for even a rake must hold some boundaries sacred.

Mary surveyed the moonlit courtyard. "I do not see Lord Wetherly and Lady Tidwell. Do you, Your Grace—" She turned her head to look up at him, and at once her head began to spin. "I mean, *Rogan?*"

My, she was beginning to feel so . . . very sleepy.

Her legs were a little wobbly too, now that she thought about it, and she felt unsteady on her feet. She braced herself against Rogan for support and focused her blurry gaze upon him.

Goodness, but he looked rather dashing.

Her gaze drifted to his lips, and she started thinking about their kiss. It had certainly been good, though admittedly, she hadn't much experience kissing. She wondered if she'd enjoy it if he kissed her right then.

Rogan looked down at her with a most curious expression on his face. "My brother and Lady Tidwell? Oh, they are not here. I did not truly expect them to be."

"You never mentioned that to *me*."

Or did he? Bah, she couldn't remember.

Mary felt her body swoon fully against Rogan, and his hands suddenly upon her. "I might not have come outside had I known your brother and Lady Tidwell would not be taking the air as well."

"Well, they aren't here, so we may step back inside if you wish." He had that cocky glint in his eyes again. "I had heard that my brother and Lady Tidwell left the musicale early. But I thought a breath of cool air would be most invigorating."

Mary's head was spinning when she tilted her face back to look up at Rogan. "So we are all *alone*."

"It would seem so, Miss Royle."

"Mary. I granted you leave to call me Mary." She squinted her eyes up at him. Lord, her head felt so heavy. "Why don't you call me Mary? Don't you like me?"

I like you, Rogan.

No, no. I hate you. That's right.

Rogan tried to take a step backward. But Mary held firm, lest she lose her own balance. When she pressed up against him for support again, she felt a hardness between them.

Good heavens.

It seemed he did like her. Quite a bit actually.

A grin seized Mary's lips just then. She was feeling quite courageous just now. Maybe a mite off-kilter, but infinitely brave.

And oh-so-ready to shift the balance of power between them. First, she would caress his cheek with her bare hand.

She flashed him what she hoped was a seductive glance as she peeled one glove down to her wrist. But then, she couldn't pull her fingers out, so she left it bunched where it was.

Did she just hear him chuckle? She looked up at him. "Rogan." Though she did not intend it, her voice was husky and low. "Have you thought about it?"

His eyes quizzed her. "Have I thought about what, Mary?"

She stood on her toes and slanted her mouth toward his. "Kissing me . . . *again.*"

Her fingers slipped around Rogan's neck and pulled his head down to her. She closed her eyelids and opened her mouth slightly for him.

"Mary," he whispered, "I vow you are not used to the effects of the wine. You should stop now, before you do something you will regret in the morning."

"Haven't you thought about it? You must have." She lifted her lids and peered up at him earnestly.

"Rogan, I have tried to forget the feeling of your body pressed against mine. Fought to wipe away the memory of your mouth, so hot and wet, moving over my lips. But God save me, I can't do it."

"Mary, please, do not say another word." He caught her wrist and made to pull her hand from the back of his neck.

She doesn't know what she is doing. Make her stop. Stop now.

"No, please don't. You don't understand. I took the wine this night for courage. So I would not retreat." She placed her hand softly upon his cheek for a moment, then slipped her fingers to his temple and through his hair.

Rogan closed his eyes and drew a deep breath through his nose.

It had been so long since he'd been touched so tenderly. And though he wanted nothing more than for her to continue, he knew he could not allow it.

He caught her hand and removed it from his hair. "Mary, stop—"

Instead she laid her finger vertically across his lips. "Shh. Listen to me. What I felt when you kissed me was like . . . nothing I have ever known."

Rogan grabbed her wrist and pulled her finger from his mouth. "You are an innocent."

"Not so innocent as you might believe."

"Somehow, my dear, I doubt that."

"Then you would be wrong, sir." She lowered

her eyes to the pavers for an instant, before meeting his gaze again with an impish grin on her lips. "Believe me, I know how a kiss feels. Yours was not my first."

"Wasn't it?"

She shook her head and colored most becomingly. "But I do not lie when I admit that when you touched your mouth to mine, every part of me felt so . . . so alive—like never before."

Rogan let his gaze flutter over her flushed cheeks and delve deep into her eyes. "What do you want of me, Mary?"

"I want you to kiss me again—now. I have to know."

"What?"

"If it's you, Rogan, who awakened me—or if it was my belief that I was in Quinn's arms."

Quinn's arms? Damn you.

He caught her waist with both hands and held her at arm's length. "What game is this, Miss Royle?"

Her eyes suddenly took on a sheen in the moonlight. " 'Tis no game, Rogan. I want to know. I *need* to know. *Please.*"

Rogan's breath came faster. *Walk away. Just turn and walk away from her. Now.*

Why, despite his attempts to separate this woman from Quinn, by the end of summer she could become Viscountess Wetherly—his brother's wife.

"Please, Rogan," she said breathily. "One kiss."

Damn it. He couldn't seem to help himself.

His grip tightened around her and he pulled her to him, closer and closer still, until they stood only a breath apart.

"Kiss me," she whispered again.

And in the cool light of the moon, Rogan swept her into his arms and leaned toward her.

He rested his hand in the small of her back, making her arch against him as he moved his lips along the tender skin of her throat.

Mary moaned and softened against him.

His mouth moved upward along her neck, pausing for just a moment to murmur in her ear. "Is it the same?"

"I do not know yet." Mary settled her hand on his chest, the tips of her fingers digging into his muscles. "Kiss me, Rogan. *Please.*"

Gently, he brushed his fingers along her jaw, then firmly took her chin and turned her face upward to his, before catching her mouth with his own.

Excitement surged through his body, and he knew, for certain, what she had meant about being awakened.

She angled her lips against his, opening her mouth to deepen the kiss, giving herself to him, and desire like he'd never felt exploded through his veins.

He could smell the scent of roses on her skin, taste the wine on her tongue, feel the warmth of her breath mingling with his own.

He was drowning in her and never wanted to surface.

The courtyard dissolved into nothingness around them. Thought evaporated.

All he knew was Mary, and his need for her.

Rogan pulled her hard to him, felt her full breasts crush against him. She wrapped her hands tightly around his neck and clung to him.

He pulled back for the briefest moment and gazed into her eyes. "Is it the same, Mary?"

She peered sleepily into his eyes, and her lips curved upward. *"Yesss."*

He drove his tongue deep into her mouth, wanting, needing urgently to possess her. As he kissed her so deeply, one hand slid over her hip and ground her against the hardness between his legs.

She broke their kiss then and peered up at him queerly.

"Mary, I don't know what made me—"

"What did you say?" Her eyes seemed to roll back, and her lids closed.

"Mary? Oh, God." He shook her, and he saw she tried to open her eyes. "Can you hear me? Are you well?"

But then her eyes closed again and she crumpled against him. Rogan stared down at the woman, limp in his arms.

"Mary!"

Chapter 11

Her eyes were so heavy, her limbs so weighted, that Mary was in no hurry to rouse herself from her slumber . . . and this wicked, but oh-so-delicious dream.

She was rocking ever so gently, her back resting upon his chest, with his hands securely wrapped around her waist, holding her against him.

Even through the layers of petticoat and skirts, she could feel his hardness branding her. She wriggled against him, reveling in the proof of his desire for her.

Around them was a roaring sound, grating annoyingly in her head. Making her awaken.

She slowly opened her eyes and turned to face

Rogan. It was completely dark inside the carriage that carried them through the night.

She blinked. This dream was different.

As she moved, he slipped his hands under her arms and drew her closer, holding her securely against him on the seat.

She couldn't resist smiling. Since the night she and Rogan had first met, she'd had many similar dreams, wanton and willful, but never in a carriage.

Never one so visceral as this.

In the small finger of moonlight breaking through the cloaked window, she could just discern Rogan's face. She smiled and pressed up on the seat high enough that she could nuzzle the exposed skin between the top of his starched neckcloth and the lobe of his ear.

"Mary," he whispered, halfheartedly nudging her away. "I am bringing you home."

"No, not yet, please." Mary tried to sit up straight, but her head began to whirl. She reached out for Rogan, who sat straight and rigid on the carriage seat. Using his lapels as leverage, she slid her knee over his legs, straddling him. "I want you to kiss me again."

His hands came around her waist. He seemed more than a little stunned at her boldness. He tried to lift her from him. "Mary, we can't do this."

Throwing her arms around his neck, Mary clung to him. "Yes we can. No one will know. Besides, it will not be the first time."

It was true. In her dreams, they'd been together dozens of times, like this. Just like this.

She skimmed her fingers through his thick hair and kissed him deeply. He groaned against her mouth, low and deep, making her tingle all over.

His hips seemed to move of their own accord, and she felt his erection press against the crushed skirts between her legs.

Her own body heated from within, and instinctively, she arched her back and pushed down against him.

He drew back his head, just enough to see her eyes, without breaking her kiss. Even in the dimness the question in his gaze was clear.

"Rogan," she whispered rather hoarsely as her fingers worked to unwind and remove his neckcloth.

He trailed his mouth from hers, running the tip of his tongue along the curve of her upper lip before plunging it inside her mouth.

Mary moaned and allowed him to deepen his kiss as she fumbled to open his waistcoat and wrenched his shirttails from his breeches.

She slid her hands over the ripples of his stomach muscles, then higher until she touched the hard swells of his chest. *Yes, just as she'd imagined.*

He lifted his mouth from hers and whispered her name, so queerly, as if her own name were a question.

And so she answered him. "Yes, Rogan. Yes."

In a sudden move, he roughly scooped her up, turned, and settled her back against the length of the leather seat cushion.

Then he knelt beside the seat, gazing at her through those dark, smoldering eyes.

Without a word, he skimmed her face with his fingertips, down and along the line of her jaw, then rode swiftly down the center of her throat to the base of her gown's lacy neckline.

His thumb slid to the left, over the upper mound of her breast. She arched against his hand, shivering with pleasure at the searing heat of his touch.

Now *this* was the rake she had dreamed about.

His hands caught her gown and her silk chemise at her shoulders, then dragged them down her arms, baring her breasts to him.

She was panting now, but he did nothing more; instead, he only watched her. She felt so wanton. So wicked. But still she wanted to feel more.

"I want you to touch me," she murmured. "I want . . . to touch you."

His gaze trailed slowly down her body, then returned to her face.

"Are you sure of this?" He bent and took her nipple inside his mouth for just an instant, making her gasp.

She tried to speak but managed only to nod.

When he lifted his mouth from her, she could feel the heat of his breath upon her skin. "*This* is what you want?"

"And more." Why shouldn't she? This was her dream, her fantasy.

Grasping his coat, she yanked the side closest to her from his shoulder.

Rogan came to his feet. He bent to avoid hitting his head on the ceiling as he shrugged his coat to the floor and tore off his waistcoat as well.

Her heart pounded as she watched his silhouette move purposefully to the end of the seat. He turned to face her, then slipped his hands beneath her knees and roughly pushed them apart.

He kissed the top of her knee, then knelt between her spread legs and eased his body over her, bracing himself on his hands on either side of her head.

The look in his eyes was primitive and all male, and it sent color rushing up past her bare breasts and into her cheeks.

Just a dream. Just a dream.

Please, don't let me wake up this time.

"Don't stop," she whispered.

He glanced up at her as she spoke, then he turned his eyes to gaze at her breasts. He moved his head, and she knew what he was about to do, or at least, what she hoped he would. At once, her nipples became hard and erect.

He looked back into her eyes and smiled wickedly at her. Then he lowered his mouth and dragged his wet tongue over her nipple, swirling it in hot, agonizingly slow circles, before taking it hard into his mouth.

He leaned against the backrest and cupped her other breast, squeezing it gently as he sucked harder.

Her head swirled with the sensation, and she writhed against his hard body as he sucked, nipped, and touched her, arousing her as she had never been before.

His erection grew harder and began to throb against her.

Raising one knee, she flung one leg over his hip and pressed her body against his groin.

He raised his dark head from the paleness of her breast and pinned her with his gaze. "Are you sure?" He lifted himself up from her, and as he knelt between her thighs, he shoved the layers of skirts to her hips.

"Yes, *yes.*"

It was about to happen. He was about to claim her body.

But she always woke up the instant before he possessed her, and she knew she would again at any moment if she didn't hurry this dream along.

"Rogan, don't wait," she begged. "Please."

Over the crumpled mounds of skirts at her hips, she could see that he fumbled at his front fall.

"Hurry."

He came up on his knees and moved close to her.

He grinned most wickedly as he positioned his thumb against her most private of parts and began to rub a slow circle that made her whimper and thrash about.

Please do not wake. Please.

So close.

Then she felt a hardness touching her, just there. *Yes.* Intimately sliding between her moist folds, separating them. *Yes.*

Her head was spinning, and her body throbbed.

She wanted nothing more than to push down upon him. To feel him inside of her before—

"Now, Rogan, *please.*"

Rogan lowered his body over hers and positioned his hands on either side of her head once more.

God, he wanted her.

Somewhere in the back of his mind, something told him to stop. Stop now.

But hadn't she told him herself she was not the innocent? That she had done this before?

She was young, but hardly in the first blush of her youth.

And so he looked down into her wide, needful eyes, then closed his lids and thrust into her heat.

There was a scream.

His eyelids snapped open only to see her staring at him in pain and horror.

Suddenly the carriage came to an abrupt halt, bouncing slightly on its springs, sending Mary's naked breasts quivering beneath him.

"Berkeley Square, Your Grace."

* * *

"Bloody hell. She's a virgin—*was* a virgin."

Rogan's hand shook as he shoved it through his hair. He paced before the large mullioned windows in his parlor.

He was such a fool.

He'd been so convinced that Quinn was the guinea-eyed wench's target that he had not seen her greedy scheme to snare *him* coming.

Damn it all, but she was good.

So comely and innocent, yet so skilled in seduction that he had not been able to refuse her.

Hadn't wanted to.

The way she'd made him feel, by God, he'd never wanted any woman so badly.

As he passed the settee, he stopped and dropped back into it.

Where the hell was Quinn? He had to tell him what happened. Had to confess.

Rogan set his elbows on his knees and rested his head in his hands. But then, he could not tell his brother, could he?

For all he knew, Quinn might really love the chit—even if the clever country gel wasn't even close to deserving his affections.

Rogan lifted his head from his hands and slammed his fist on the walnut tea table before him.

How could he have been so blind, so stupid?

He came to his feet and hastened to the open

windows and peered out into the dark and deserted square so late at night.

It was nearly two o'clock in the morn. Quinn and Lady Tidwell had left the musicale hours ago. Just where the hell was he?

Rogan leaned back against the narrow portion of the plaster wall near the left window and banged the back of his head against it.

He'd spent the past two hours mulling over what had happened and his options.

But as far as he could reckon, he had but one course of action.

One that mightn't break his brother's heart.

One that might slip the notice of the *on-dit* columnists' weekly smudges of ink.

One choice.

Rogan's body slid down the wall, folding like an accordion fan. He closed his eyes, resigned to the truth of his predicament.

He had to marry Miss Royle.

Damn her.

He opened his eyes again when the clock in the passage tinged the sixth hour and he heard the click of the front door closing.

"Quinn? Is that you?"

He heard footsteps in the passage, then his brother peered into the parlor. "Rogan? What the deuce are you doing awake? Just came home yourself, did you?"

"No." Rogan struggled to his feet. "I've been waiting here for you—for some time now."

A dark red suffused the pale skin of Quinn's cheeks. "Got me."

Rogan was not in the mind to play fools' games. "Where were you?"

"You're a gentleman. Ought not ask such a question."

"Where were you?"

"Damn it, Rogan. I am sure you know the answer." Quinn moved his cane forward and walked stiffly into the parlor. "I was with *her.*"

"Lady Tidwell."

"Yes. I am not proud of my behavior." He clicked his way to the settee and sat down.

"Why not?" Rogan's tone was harsher than he intended, but somehow it served him better if Quinn was already riled when he admitted his rakish deed.

"She is fragile. My God, she's a widow."

"Obviously, that didn't deter you, Quinn."

Quinn narrowed his eyes at Rogan. "Why so dark this morning? I would think, given your own proclivities, you mightn't be so judgmental." He exhaled slowly. "I have no doubt that you are already aware that Lady Tidwell and I left the festivities early."

"I am. But that does not explain why you are slipping into my house like a thief before dawn."

"She was feeling sad. The orchestra played a concerto that her husband had especially enjoyed."

Rogan said nothing. He folded his arms over his chest and waited for Quinn to continue, lest he be set into the uncomfortable task of explaining his own base behavior this night.

"I took her to her home and tried to comfort her. She was inconsolable at first, but then she softened and warmed to my presence."

"Oh, good Lord."

"Deuce it, Rogan, I did not intend for my relationship with Lady Tidwell to progress. I am quite fond of Miss Royle. But . . ." His gaze shifted to the cold hearth and remained there.

Rogan sighed, feeling some modicum of relief.

Oh, he knew he should admit all to his brother now, while Quinn swam about in his own guilt. But he was who he was, after all. And what good would hurting his brother do anyone?

Met with silence, Quinn raised his eyes to Rogan's. "I . . . I think I have feelings for her."

Rogan straightened. "For Miss Royle?"

Quinn shook his head. "No, no. I thought I might have, that is, until I came to *know* Lady Tidwell this evening."

"You can't tell Miss Royle."

"What? Why not? I must. It is the honorable road to take."

"It might be the proper course, but it might also break her heart." Rogan came to stand before the settee. "Have you not considered that she may be in love with you?"

"I have. I have considered it." Quinn's chest

seemed to puff out heroically. "Which is why I must confess."

"Confession will only ease your own conscience. It will not help her."

"Then what, pray, do you suggest, Rogan?"

"Let me do what I promised. Let me stand for you. Let me court Miss Royle in your stead."

Quinn shook his head in apparent disbelief. "What possible good could that do her, or anyone?"

"Why, I might win her heart."

"Win her—what?" Quinn sputtered. "Why would you do this?"

For a moment, Rogan actually considered telling Quinn the truth. But only a breath later, he thought better of it. Confession would only ease his own conscience. "Because perhaps it is time I set aside my bachelor's ways and find a wife myself."

Quinn's mouth fell wide open. "God's teeth. I never thought I'd hear you speak those words!"

"Well, now you have."

And soon, Mary will hear those words as well.

When the rising sun broke through Mary's window and fell across her face, she awoke with a start.

"Glad to see you are finally awake." Anne was seated in the spindle chair beside Mary's tester bed, and Elizabeth was standing before the window, sweeping her finger across a roundel of condensation.

"What is the hour?" Mary rubbed her eyes.

"Almost seven," Elizabeth replied, then opened her mouth and blew a burst of hot breath on the window.

"So early?" Mary pulled herself into a sitting position and pulled out a pin that dangled from her hair before her eyes. "I am aware that the two of you returned home early last night, but I did not, and I could have used more sleep."

"Oh, we know you returned late." Anne's lips were pursed bitterly.

"We carried you to your room." Elizabeth pressed her finger to the window and drew a heart. "Well, the Duke of Blackstone carried you here, and Cherie set you into your nightdress and put you to bed."

Anne skewered Mary with the sharpest of gazes. "We could not believe what was happening, and so we stood back and watched. My word, Mary. The Black Duke laid you into bed. There simply must be a logical explanation for what happened."

"Logical . . ." Mary held herself very still. Her head was throbbing, and her mouth felt packed with cotton.

The wine.

Oh my word.

No.

A frenzy of images filled her mind's eye.

No, it wasn't real.

"Carried you in his arms from his town carriage." Anne stood and came to sit on the edge of the bed. "Do you want to tell us what happened?"

The carriage. Oh, no. What had she done?

"H-he did not explain?" Mary swallowed hard and stared hopefully at her sisters.

"No, he did not." Elizabeth chuckled into her hand. "But I have my own suspicions. I think Anne and I are of like minds on that point."

Mary fashioned a glower and shot it at each of her sisters in turn. "I should think it quite evident. I simply indulged in the Harringtons' excellent wine. You know I have no tolerance for spirits of any sort."

"That much is obvious." Anne leaned close, too close for Mary's comfort. "Did you make a spectacle of yourself? Or don't you know, and must we read about it in the *on-dit* columns on the morrow?"

Mary thought a moment on that question.

In truth, she did not know. "How silly you are being, the both of you. There is quite a simple explanation for everything. Lady Tidwell wasn't feeling well, so Lord Wetherly escorted her to her home. I had no other means of transportation, so Blackstone offered his carriage."

Anne smirked. "And when will you provide us with the 'simple explanation'?"

"The rock of the carriage, the wine and warmth

of the night air lulled me to sleep. That's all." Mary started to draw back the coverlet, then thought better of it. "Now, if you both will excuse me, I should like to see to my toilette."

"Very well." Anne narrowed her eyes but rose from the bed and led Elizabeth toward the door. "We shall speak more of this when we break our fast, for I know there is more to the story than you are sharing, Mary."

The moment the door closed, Mary whisked back the coverlet and lifted the hem of her night-dress.

No . . . no. She was sure it had just been a dream.

But there was no denying the evidence before her.

There, between the jointure of her thighs, were twin smudges of blood.

Mary threw the coverlet back over her legs and slapped her palms to her eyes.

God help her.

She was ruined.

Chapter 12

After dressing, Mary did not go below stairs to join Anne and Elizabeth for breakfast. She turned the key in her bedchamber door, thus ensuring her privacy for at least a short while.

She had to consider the situation in which she now found herself, as well as the options—what few she still had—available to her.

With a nicked sterling spoon, she stirred the willow bark powder into a small amount of water and drank the mixture down. At least she assumed it was willow bark powder the young, mute maid had given her.

Mary had not even asked for the powder, but somehow the new maid had known—she always knew what the Royle sisters needed before they themselves thought of it—and had brought it right away.

How she did it, they did not know, so they decided that this was simply the way of her.

She had been engaged as a maid-of-all-things only two weeks past, after responding, Mary assumed, to the notice she had placed in *Bell's Weekly Messenger* advertising the position.

During the short interview, which had consisted of a series of nods and head shakes in response to Mary's questions, it had become apparent that the girl did not, or possibly could not, speak, nor did she exhibit the ability to write or cipher. Still, she had seemed to understand every word said to her.

And, after Anne's constant quibbles with both the outspoken butler and brash cook, the fact that the would-be maid did not speak had actually been a tick in her favor.

Like MacTavish and Mrs. Polkshank, she had appeared upon Aunt Prudence's doorstep without references, but, amazingly, she had seemed experienced in all manner of maid's work, from scullery to intricate coiffures.

Her abilities, joined with the fact that she would accept the meager wage Mary could offer, had made her instantly welcome in the household.

Her name remained a mystery, however. Not even Mrs. Polkshank could pry it from her, therefore becoming quickly convinced that the brown-eyed beauty was, in truth, a French spy.

Mary and her sisters were not so convinced, but

they humored Mrs. Polkshank by using the name the cook had given her—*Cherie.*

Mary rubbed her fingertips to her temples. What had she been thinking to have taken so much wine?

There was a soft knock at her door. Mary's head snapped around, amplifying the noise all the more. "Who is there?"

When there was no reply, Mary removed the key from her dressing table and crossed the chamber to insert it, warily, into the lock. She opened the door but a crack and saw that it was the maid, Cherie.

Cherie's huge brown eyes looked down at the portmanteau sitting beside her. She lifted it, which hardly seemed possible given her petite frame, but when Mary opened the door fully, she carried it into the bedchamber and hoisted it upon the tester bed.

Mary stared at the large leather bag, and moisture began to well in her eyes.

The maid waited silently for several moments, but when Mary made no move to remove it or open it, Cherie grabbed the handle.

"No! No, you are correct, Cherie." Mary scrubbed a heavy tear that had caught in the edge of her eyelashes. "It is my only choice. I must return to Cornwall. It is only a matter of days, perhaps only hours, before all of London hears of my indiscretion."

Cherie gave Mary a sad smile, and all at once,

Mary broke down and gave in to the tears she'd been holding back.

"What a fool I was, Cherie. Such a fool. I was no match for his rakish ways, and still I thought to send him for the hills by playing the innocent who wanted him."

Cherie took a handkerchief from the chest of drawers and wiped the tear from Mary's cheek.

"But the wine, the wine ruined it all. And now I must leave. I cannot stay here and risk ruining my sisters' good names as well."

The maid touched Mary's arm. Once she had her full attention, she pointed to herself with a pleading look in her eyes.

It took several seconds before Mary realized what the maid's gesture meant, but then she knew. "No, I must go alone." She managed a weak smile. "Besides, Anne could never part with you. You are the only member of our staff she truly likes." Mary gripped both of the maid's bony upper arms. "You will stay, won't you, Cherie? *Please.*"

The girl nodded her head slowly, then turned and opened the portmanteau for Mary.

"Thank you, but I can manage the packing myself. If you have gone missing too long, Anne will come to seek you out, and I do not wish her to know that I am leaving before I am prepared."

The maid nodded again before suddenly throwing her arms around Mary and hugging her tight.

Then, she spun around and scurried from the room.

Mary followed the maid to the door and closed and locked it behind her.

She opened her wardrobe, removed a few articles of clothing, and settled them inside the portmanteau.

Her mind was filled with tasks to complete. She'd have to see to the household accounts before she left. Anne and Elizabeth certainly had no mind for ciphering, and Aunt Prudence, well, the dear was simply too old to manage.

She turned and gazed out the window onto Berkeley Square. Her sisters would have to be told, of course, but not until Mary called upon Lady Upperton and the Old Rakes to explain everything.

Laying her hand atop the lip of the faded leather, she closed the portmanteau and heaved it beneath her bed to conceal it from her curious sisters' notice.

Lud, she should make her way to Cavendish Square right away. She couldn't bear it if her sponsor learned of her disgrace from another.

Especially if that person was the absolute worst of debauchers, the Duke of Blackstone.

It was early yet when Rogan arrived in Cavendish Square.

He had arrived at Doctor's Commons at first

light and had waited for the archbishop's office to open. Now, his business there completed, he held in his coat pocket the special license inscribed with both his title and Miss Royle's name. They could be married this very day if she so desired, which he expected she would, since a wedding was obviously the purpose behind her clever plan.

He was not looking forward to this, but his own lust had cast him into this position, and there was naught he could do to change that.

He threw his leg across the saddle and dismounted, then wrapped the reins around the post ring outside of Number Two, Cavendish Square.

It was time to face Mary's sponsor, Lady Upperton.

Within minutes of knocking at the door, Rogan was led down to the passage to the library where Lady Upperton was seated.

As his eyes fixed on the tiny woman, his ears picked up a distinctive metallic click, and from the corner of his eye he almost thought he saw a case of books move.

"Come, come in Your Grace." Lady Upperton's smile was as bright as the sun in the sky, and she beckoned to him to join her for tea. "We have—*I* have been expecting you."

"Have you?"

"Indeed, I have."

Rogan dropped his chin to his chest. This was going to be more difficult to stomach than he'd imagined.

He lifted his head. "Then you have already spoken to Miss Royle."

"I was at the musicale last evening. Do you not recall speaking with me?" Lady Upperton chuckled merrily.

"I d-do." *What in blazes did she mean?*

"Your Grace, do you forget that I was witness to your conversations with Miss Royle?"

Rogan stared blankly at the old woman.

"Oh, goodness me. Neither of you could say a civil word to the other. One might think the two of you dislike one another." She leaned close and patted his knee. "And yet your eyes told a completely different tale."

"I do apologize, Lady Upperton, but I do not understand."

"Dear sir, everyone but the two of you could see how enamored you were with each other. Why, you and Miss Royle are the talk of the *ton* this day."

"Are we?" Rogan did not like what he was hearing. Just how much did London society know of what had passed between him and Mary?

"I have heard rumors that White's book is filled with wagers for a wedding before Michaelmas."

Rogan cleared his throat and, without thinking, slipped his hand inside his coat pocket and touched the special license. "My good lady, you have seen my heart."

Or rather, my conscience.

"If Miss Royle would accept me and you gave me your blessing, I would wed her this very day."

The color ran from Lady Upperton's face, and her lips began to tremble.

"Good heavens," she stammered. "I must say, the depth of your feelings for each other are far more advanced than I had been aware. Why, this is wonderful!"

Rogan raised his hand. "I am wealthy and titled. I feel quite certain she will accept my offer."

Lady Upperton narrowed her eyes suspiciously. "Then why are you not more jubilant? If Miss Royle wishes to marry you, I will certainly offer my blessing, as will Lotharian."

Rogan thrummed his fingers on his knee. "There is no question, she must marry me. My concern is only that she may still possess some fondness for my brother, Lord Wetherly."

"Oh, dear." She brought her fingers to her lips. "Are you certain?"

"No, I am not. I do not know her heart. However, I do know my brother's . . . and his is held by Lady Tidwell."

Suddenly there was a loud noise behind the bookcases. Rogan leapt to his feet, though Lady Upperton was quite unworried and remained in her seat.

He peered down at her for an explanation.

"Rats." She shrugged her shoulders. "Just a few rats between the walls."

"They must be rather *large* . . . rats."

"Hmm, indeed." She turned her round little face to the row of bookcases near the hearth and narrowed her eyes. "Do you, perhaps, know a good rat catcher?"

Mary swung her blue Bourbon mantle over her shoulders as she hurried down the stairs.

She hoped to slip out the front door unobserved and to walk unaccompanied by her sisters to see Lady Upperton and the Old Rakes of Marylebone.

Her hand had just skimmed the newel post when Mrs. Polkshank called out from the far end of the passage. "Heard you had nothin' to eat this morn, Miss Royle."

Mary stopped and remained standing on the bottom step. She listened, hoping her sisters would not have heard Mrs. Polkshank and realized she had emerged from her bedchamber.

"I can prepare somethin' for you, if you like. Just set the water to boil. I can make some tea in no time at all. Baked some fresh biscuits, too."

"No, thank you, Mrs. Polkshank, I was heading—" Then Mary caught sight of a rich red swath of fabric wrapped around Cook's waist.

Slowly, she came down from the last step and walked over to view the material closer. "Your sash, may I see it, Mrs. Polkshank?"

The cook dutifully untied the swath and handed

it to Mary, who shook out its folds and ran her fingers over it.

It was soft, and though it was quite badly stained in the center, there was no mistaking the gold-shot crimson fabric.

It was Kashmir.

A Kashmir shawl.

Anxiously, Mary carried Mrs. Polkshank's shawl into the parlor and held it up to the sunlight washing through the windows.

"Where did you get this?" Mary turned and pinned Mrs. Polkshank with her gaze. "Did you know this is a Kashmir shawl? A very expensive shawl—when this was new it probably cost as much as a house. But it's ruined now, isn't it?"

Mrs. Polkshank blanched. "I didn't steal it or nothin', Miss Royle. Found it in the dustbin, I did. I figured nobody would mind the least bit if I cut it up for rags."

Mary couldn't believe what she was hearing. "You were going to cut up *this* for rags?"

"Well, it didn't look like that then, did it now? It was all dark and mussed with soot and such, like it'd been stuffed up the chimney to keep the drafts out."

Mary studied the shawl again. "It certainly doesn't look that way now."

"Cherie washed it up real nice for me. She's a good girl, even if she's French and all. But you can't choose where you come from, now, can you?"

"No, you can't." She lowered the shawl and held

it tightly to her middle. "Mrs. Polkshank, I believe this shawl is the rag Elizabeth found inside Papa's document box. I should like to keep it."

The cook stared hard at the shawl, and her fingers twitched as if they wanted to grab the Kashmir away. "You said it yourself though, it's ruined. Ain't worth nothin' anymore."

"It mightn't be worth much money anymore, but it may be worth quite a lot to Anne and Elizabeth."

Mrs. Polkshank grunted.

Mary bit her lip, not really believing what she, frugal Mary, was about to say. "Would you take . . . a guinea for it?"

Mrs. Polkshank's wide face began to glow, and a sly smile tilted her lips. "Well, it is Kashmir, like you said. The edges might be worth something. Did you see the gold threads?"

"Mrs. Polkshank, the shawl was found in this household. Rightfully, it already belongs to me."

"Very well. Thank you, Miss Royle. A guinea is fair compensation for my savin' the shawl."

"You are welcome, Mrs. Polkshank." Mary stepped past the cook and into the passage and peered up at the tall case-clock for the hour. "Where are my sisters? Have you seen them of late?"

"Oh, they're in the library lookin' over some papers. Shall I tell them that you are inquirin' about them?"

Mary started for the library. "No, thank you. I am headed there myself."

When she reached the library, she stopped just outside and spread the ornate crimson shawl carefully over her arm.

This is madness.

Utter madness.

But even she had to admit that with each day that passed, the tale of Mrs. Fitzherbert's babies was getting harder and harder to deny.

Mary arrived at Lady Upperton's Cavendish Square home two hours later.

She was not alone, for both Anne and Elizabeth were with her.

Nor did she arrive empty-handed. Carefully folded and concealed inside the basket swinging from the crook of her arm rested the Kashmir shawl.

Quite possibly, the shawl Lady Jersey had whisked from her own shoulders and used to swaddle the secret babies.

But they would need Lady Upperton and Lord Lotharian's assistance to be sure.

When the Royle sisters were ushered into the library, Lady Upperton was, as she was oft found, sitting on the settee serving tea.

"Do not move your cup, Lotharian. Leave it still on the tabletop."

"I heard you the first time, dear lady." Lord Lotharian glanced up. Noting the presence of the footman waiting to announce the sisters, he brought a finger to his lips to silence the girls.

"All I need to do is touch this cord and..." She reached out and gently pulled a piece of corded silk.

She wrung her hands and held her breath as a metal contraption of some sort wheeled forward until it bumped the tea dish.

Elizabeth, unable to restrain her curiosity, crept forward and stood behind the settee where Lady Upperton sat.

"Watch now." The old woman began to giggle with excitement. "The tea server has not spilled even one drop since I made the adjustment to the handle tension. Not one drop, I tell you."

Though Mary was near bursting with the news about the Kashmir shawl, she knew that at this moment, nothing was more important to Lady Upperton than her tea-pouring mechanism.

Lady Upperton's invention stood at least two feet high, quite large for such a small tea table. At least a dozen or more metal wheels spun and connected and resembled, more than anything else, the moving workings of a grand clock.

The server lowered a thin wire a finger's width into the cup. A tiny bell began to ring, and a silver teapot tipped forward and poured steaming tea into the dish until the liquid met the wire tip.

Abruptly, the teapot was righted, and four small wheels transported the server to its starting position on the far end of the table.

"Brilliant!" Lotharian cried out. "Why, ladies all

over England shall be clamoring for a mechanized tea server."

"Well." Lady Upperton angled her head, making her appear very proud indeed. "They can clamor all they like. No one shall have a server such as this but me." She giggled again. "Honestly, I have begun working with the power of steam. I have finished with tea servers for now."

"My lady, if I may." The footman cleared his throat. "My lady, Lord Lotharian, the Misses Royles have arrived."

The elderly inventor raised her brows. "Yes, I see that. Do be seated, gels."

She looked at the young women and reached out her hand to greet each one, before returning her gaze to the footman once more. "Mayhap I should begin designing a mechanized announcement system." She lifted a white eyebrow at her inperturbable footman.

Mary hurried to sit down on the settee. "Lady Upperton, I must speak with you on a matter of great importance."

The lady and Lord Lotharian shared a private, knowing glance.

"No doubt you do." She settled her hand atop Mary's and squeezed it. "I have already had one young visitor this day. Would you care to guess who that might have been, Miss Royle?"

Confusion was plain on Anne's and Elizabeth's faces.

Mary had not yet decided how to admit to her sisters what had happened between her and the Duke of Blackstone. But she did know that doing so now, and in the presence of Lord Lotharian, one of the most famed rakes of all, was not the best way.

"Lady Upperton," she began. "I will venture to guess that the Duke of Blackstone called upon you. But please, let us not speak of him now. *Please*." Mary hoped her pleading gaze imparted the meaning she hoped.

Elizabeth rose and snatched Mary's basket from her. "We have stumbled upon a clue . . . no, more than that—we may have evidence of our noble birth!"

"Evidence?" Lotharian leaned forward, his interest highly piqued. "What have you got there in the basket?"

Elizabeth plunged her fingers into the basket, but before she could withdraw the shawl, Mary stilled her sister's hand.

"First, we need to know if you can get us into the Harrington gallery without raising suspicion." Mary looked pointedly at the elderly pair.

"Why, certainly." It was clear that Lady Upperton could not wait to have the contents of the basket revealed to her. Her words came forth in a torrent. "I can appeal to Sir Joseph's pride in his paintings. And Lord Lotharian, here, is a master of distraction. But why, dear, do you need to enter the gallery?"

"Because we found something hidden inside one of Papa's document boxes," Anne announced.

"Last night, during the musicale," Mary explained, "I might have seen something in Lady Jersey's portrait that quite closely resembles—*this*."

Mary gave Elizabeth a nod, and her sister slowly lifted out the fragile Kashmir shawl and laid it across Anne's awaiting arms.

Lord Lotharian lifted his stunned gaze from the ornately patterned crimson shawl and looked straight into Lady Upperton's widened eyes.

"Good Lord. Could it be?" he asked.

"I daren't allow myself to believe it." Mary swallowed deeply. "But, yes, this may be Lady Jersey's shawl."

"Do you know what this may mean, gel?" Lotharian asked.

"I do," Mary replied solemnly.

Chapter 13

Mary would never have guessed that Lady Upperton's clever way of gaining entry into the Harrington's gallery that evening would have involved Rogan, the Duke of Blackstone.

But it did.

Nor would she have believed that she herself would have been dangled as bait to lure the duke into unwittingly participating in their scheme.

But she was.

She had no recourse in this matter, for she had not admitted the twining of her bared body with Rogan's to anyone. Well, except the maid, Cherie, but since Cherie could not speak, Mary knew she could be trusted to keep her silence.

So Mary just did her best to avert her eyes from the duke as Sir Joseph and Lady Harrington led their party into the gallery that evening.

"Blackstone," Sir Joseph began, "Lady Harrington and I are honored that you remembered our hospitality and were able to extend to us invitations for the Heroes' Fete this night."

"The pleasure is all mine, Sir Joseph."

Sir Joseph bowed over his round belly. "Lady Harrington was beside herself with excitement when Lady Upperton called this afternoon. The newspapers reported that Wellington himself might return to London in time to attend."

Rogan rocked slightly on his feet and clasped his hands behind his back. "I am pleased you and your lady will be able to join us." He slid an annoyed glance at Lady Upperton. "Shall we be going? My brother is being honored at the fete, and I do not wish to miss a single moment."

To her horror, Mary saw that Elizabeth and Anne had walked away from the group and were standing below the portrait of Lady Jersey.

"Er . . . yes, I agree, we should be going very soon," said Mary, "only I wonder, Lady Harrington, if you and your husband might allow us to view the paintings in the dining room. I fear Lady Upperton and I, due to the popularity of your musicale, were unable to make our way in to see them . . . though we heard that there is a landscape that is particularly stunning."

Lady Harrington was beaming. "Why, certainly. Do come this way. I know just the painting you mean."

Lotharian noticed the Royle sisters beneath the portrait of Lady Jersey.

"Oh, Miss Royle," he said to Mary. "I wonder if you could fetch your sisters and join us in the dining room momentarily? I see they are quite taken with the paintings here, but do not be too long. The Heroes' Fete awaits."

Then he swung his arm around Rogan's shoulder and brought him in line behind Lady Upperton and Sir Joseph and Lady Harrington. "I daresay, Blackstone, from what I hear, you will not wish to miss it."

The minute the others had left the gallery, Mary rushed over to her sisters.

"Now, Mary, let us see and compare."

Mary glanced about to be sure no servant had wandered into the room. Then, she whisked from her shoulders her Platoff cape of pale pink satin and handed it to Anne, revealing the folded, gold-threaded, crimson Kashmir shawl beneath it.

Elizabeth lifted it gently from Mary's shoulders and held it up before the painting. "Oh my word." Her lips trembled, and her eyes welled with unshed tears. "Do you see—do you see?"

Mary did see. Anne saw too.

The hand-woven pattern, which would have taken the weaver months to complete, was identical.

The crimson background was exactly the same.

The spare use of hair-thin gold-hued threads . . . why, there was no question.

The Kashmir in Elizabeth's hands, though stained and aged, was in fact the same shawl as the one in the portrait of Lady Jersey.

The fine hairs at the back of Mary's neck rose up, and though the air in the room was thick with heat, a chill raced up her body and over her scalp, as if she'd been touched by a specter. She wriggled, trying to shake off the uneasy feeling.

Anne's face went white, and she suddenly pitched forward. Elizabeth dropped the shawl and lunged to catch her sister just before her head met the floor.

Mary crouched beside Anne, while Elizabeth tried to pat the color back into her sister's cheeks. "Anne, Anne?"

Anne smiled and shook her head. "No need to fret, Mary. I am well. 'Twas just the excitement."

"The excitement of what?" came Rogan's familiar deep voice from the far side of the gallery.

Elizabeth's eyes were wild as she met Mary's startled gaze.

Mary did not turn around but remained crouched before Anne. Her fingers scrabbled for the shawl, finally catching the edge and dragging it toward her.

Mary could hear his approaching footsteps.

Quickly, she lifted the Mechlin lace hem of her underdress and shoved the shawl as high up between her skirts and chemise as she could manage.

As she rose, she clenched her fingers around the flowing China crape overdress and the layers beneath, and held the shawl in place as best she could as she stood.

She forced a pleasant smile and looked straight into Rogan's eyes. "What excitement? How amusing you are." She manufactured a laugh. "Why, Your Grace, tonight's fete is only the most grand social event of the season." A smirk pulled at her mouth then. "And we are just country gels, as you so often remind me."

"The carriages are at the door. We are leaving." He peered down at Anne, still on the floor resting against Elizabeth. "Is everything all right? Shall I call for assistance?"

Mary glanced over her shoulder at the portrait of Lady Jersey, then back at the duke once more. "Everything is splendid, Your Grace. Quite splendid, indeed."

Lending her sisters a hand, Rogan helped them to their feet. "Very well, then. Shall we go?" he asked.

"Absolutely," Anne replied as she snatched up the pink satin cape and positioned it around Mary's shoulders for her.

The sisters' gazes leapt from one to the other before Anne and Elizabeth started for the passage, glancing nervously back at Mary every few seconds as she followed along behind them with Rogan.

She gripped the shawl through her skirts and walked very slowly, praying that the shawl—the evidence, perhaps, of their lineage—would not fall to the floor as she moved.

Rogan offered her his arm, and she knew she ought to take it, if only to avoid unwanted scrutiny, but there simply was no way to accept it without dropping Lady Jersey's shawl.

So instead she spurned him, earning herself an almost inaudible growl of disappointment from the duke.

Couldn't be helped. She was not about to let go of the shawl.

And so she looked straight ahead, chin upright, and walked through the gallery, then the passage, and to the front door, where Lady Upperton and Lord Lotharian were waiting with the Harringtons.

Three gleaming carriages made their way from the Harrington house on Cavendish Square to the opulent Argyle Rooms, where the Heroes' Fete was to commence.

Mary stared out the window as the Duke of Blackstone's carriage rumbled down the road.

She could not believe she was sitting upon the same seat where just the night before the man now opposite her had taken her maidenhead.

She could feel Rogan's heated gaze upon her, no doubt feeling the irony of the situation, just as she was.

Tonight they each sat on opposite sides of the carriage, gloved hands folded in their laps.

How ironic. Less than twenty hours past, they'd been panting, and kissing . . . and, well, tonight was completely different, that was all.

My, it was warm in the carriage.

She glanced over at Elizabeth, who seemed not at all bothered by the heat.

Moisture had begun to bead at Mary's own brow, and the lace trim of her underdress was beginning to stick to her skin.

The only part of her that wasn't steeping in the closed carriage was her hand holding the shawl in place beneath her skirts. Her hand was ice cold from gripping the Kashmir so tightly, and deuce it if it wasn't beginning to cramp.

"How did Lady Upperton convince you to extend an invitation for the fete to the Harringtons?" Elizabeth suddenly asked the duke. "Did you break a valuable at their musicale and feel you owed them something in return?"

"*Elizabeth,*" Mary hissed. Involuntarily her gaze lifted to Rogan's face, and she saw that he was watching her.

"No, nothing like that." Rogan's gaze was quite serious. "She simply asked me to do it as a personal favor to her. And in exchange, she would give me something I require."

Elizabeth braced her hands on her knees and leaned forward. "And what would that be? Will you tell us?"

"Sister, you are being most rude. Sit back please and stop questioning the gentleman."

That wicked grin of his suddenly appeared on his lips. "I will tell you, since Lady Upperton has already given me what I needed."

Mary could not breathe. She had no idea what he might say next, only that it would not be good given the way he was now looking upon her.

"I asked her to ask Lotharian, your guardian, for his blessing."

"His blessing? Whatever for?" Elizabeth asked.

"As a gentleman, without it I could not ask your sister here to marry me." He did not smile, did not move. "But you will be pleased to know he gave it without hesitation."

Good heavens. He was not serious. He could not be.

Rakes did not marry. Lud, there was a whole club full of aging rakes on Cavendish Square that proved that unequivocally.

And then she saw it. A tiny smile twitching on his mouth. Ah, it was just another of his depraved games.

"So, Miss Royle, what say you? Will you marry me?"

Mary sat up straight in her seat and met his steely gaze with one of her own.

She could see it in his eyes. He was not serious. No, this new game of his was called "retribution" for stopping him from slaking his lust with her last night.

She was certain his proposal was not sincere. He didn't drop to one knee, or confess his undying love.

This was just a game. A competition.

Who would back off first?

Well, she could play along. Make him cringe with her next words.

"Yes, I will." Mary smiled confidently, though already this game of nerves was exhausting her. "How soon?"

Rogan leaned forward too, until their noses almost met in the middle. "Tonight, if you like."

Mary shook her head. "We'd need a special license."

Rogan nodded thoughtfully, then, as if he'd just remembered something, he reached into his pocket and withdrew a special license. "Oh. Fancy that. I happen to have one. So tonight, is it?"

God, he was good!

"Your brother is being honored tonight. It would be horrid of us to steal his moment."

"You're right." He paused for a moment and peered out the window.

Ha, he was backing down.

Then he snapped his head back around. "How about just after the fete? We'd have plenty of witnesses—no doubt there will be several ecclesiastical authorities present at the Heroes' Fete."

"Several, you say?" Mary gulped. "Well then, we shall have our choice."

Rogan gave her a flat smile. "So, we are agreed then."

"Absolutely." Mary's hand began to spasm. So distracted was she by the discussion that she inadvertently flexed her hand, and the shawl slipped to the floor.

Oh, perdition! Mary frantically lifted her foot and dragged the edge of the Kashmir shawl beneath the cover of her flowing skirts and into the narrow gap at the base of the carriage seat.

When she looked up again, Elizabeth was staring at both her and Rogan in turn, her mouth opening and closing like a landed fish.

"No . . . this is pure folly." A small nervous laugh escaped Elizabeth. "You will not truly marry this evening."

Rogan folded his arms at his chest. "I assure you, I am most serious in this matter. I fully intend to marry your sister before the sun rises."

Mary's heart played a riotous tattoo in her chest. She sniffed in three short breaths, trying to calm herself.

No matter what he said, she told herself, this was just a grand game of nerves.

A *game*—one she intended to win.

"What say you, Miss Royle?" he asked, just waiting for her to back down. But she wasn't going to do that.

Mary could not meet Elizabeth's gaze. She had to sound confident, and she knew that if she looked into her sister's eyes, her voice would quaver. "Oh, yes. Definitely before the sun rises."

Elizabeth squealed and clapped her gloved hands enthusiastically. "I cannot believe it. Anne will be so disappointed that she had to ride with Lady Upperton and Lord Lotharian! She is missing everything! What wonderful news, Mary!"

"Yes, wonderful," Mary murmured.

Leaning across, Elizabeth hugged Mary, then stared up at Rogan and began chattering away in her excitement. "Our sister Anne will be beside herself. She was certain she'd be the first wed. But no—'tis our Mary!"

Mary swallowed deeply. What was she doing? She was actually lying to her sister to beat Rogan at his own horrid game.

But she'd set everything to rights at the fete. She'd pull both her sisters aside at the celebration and explain everything. They would understand. They would.

It wasn't as if she was really going to marry the Duke of Blackstone.

By the time the Blackstone carriage wheeled before the entrance to the Argyle Rooms, Mary was numb.

During the course of her brief journey from the Harringtons' home to the fete, she had not only kicked beneath the seat the only shred of evidence they possessed of their births but she had also agreed to marry the man she despised most in this entire world.

She should have never risen from bed this morning, for the day could not have unfolded more wrongly.

Unaware that the shawl was wedged beneath the seat, Elizabeth practically leapt from the carriage, so eager was she to share the news of Mary's surprise nuptials. "Are you coming, Mary? Do hurry!" Without waiting for a reply, she started for the doors.

Rogan rose and offered a hand to Mary, but she pretended not to notice and sat very still. There was no possible way she could retrieve the shawl without him taking notice and asking questions.

Then, given his nature, he would use the shawl as leverage or as a flag to wave over his head to humiliate her. She wanted neither, so she decided it was best to leave the shawl inside the carriage for now and retrieve it later.

As she rose to climb from the carriage, she surreptitiously slipped her fan into the narrow gap between the carriage wall and the seat.

Then, she took the footman's hand and descended the steps to the pavers, where she waited several heart-pounding moments before Rogan emerged from the cabin. She worried for naught, however, for his hands were empty, and his slim-fitted coat did not reveal any shawl-like lumps or bumps.

Mary smiled inwardly. More likely Rogan had needed a few spare seconds to collect himself before facing all of society—and Quinn—if indeed he had the nerve to announce his plans to marry an unsophisticated country miss.

"Mary, please." Elizabeth stood just outside the door, waiting—something that she had never excelled at.

"Your Grace." As a taunt, Mary lifted her arm for him to take and to lead her inside.

"My darling," he replied.

Then, while Mary still reeled from his words, he caught up her hand and raised it slowly to his mouth. Before she could snatch her hand away, he pressed a hot kiss that seemed to sear the tops of her fingers right through her glove.

A tingle raced upward from her hand and spread like fire across the whole of her body. She blinked slowly and moistened her lips.

A chaste kiss to her hand and she was all atwitter.

Oh, God.

I can't do this. I can't.

When Rogan straightened and looked her in the eyes, it was the wryest of smiles that greeted her. "Allow me to be the first to tell you, my dear, how very lovely you look on your wedding day."

And then he gave her a furtive wink.

Mary stiffened, her resolve instantly renewed.

"Shall we go inside, Your Grace?" she replied

excitedly. "I know Elizabeth is eager to tell everyone our joyous news."

Rogan's jaw tightened, and the corded muscles that ran the length of his neck tensed.

That was all she needed to see.

For now she knew with all certainty that she was ready for his game.

Ready to win it.

Chapter 14

Despite Mary's best efforts to hurry along her *betrothed* so that she might catch up with Elizabeth to speak with her before reaching the Argyle Rooms, her sister's excitement to share the glad tidings seemed to have imbued her with an unmatched lightness of step.

As they passed through a set of crimson folding doors, Mary finally slipped her arm from Rogan's. "Forgive me, Your Grace, but I would like to ask my sister to refrain from announcing our nuptials . . . until after your brother and the other heroes have been honored."

Mary glanced up to see Elizabeth midway up the grand staircase ahead of them.

Lifting the hem of her gown from the floor, she

started forward, belatedly pausing to toss a co-quettish glance over her shoulder. "Please excuse me—*my love.*"

At first, both of his eyebrows shot toward his hairline, but then he returned an amused grin.

Mary hastened up the treads, finally catching Elizabeth at the top of the staircase. She grabbed her sister's hand and pulled her into a lounge at the head of the staircase.

At first, Mary was completely distracted by her surroundings. The lounge resembled a Grecian temple of old, complete with classical statues and Ionic columns for support.

Elizabeth tried to remove her hand from her grasp. Mary wrenched her gaze back to her sister. "You mustn't say a word to anyone about what you heard. Promise me. *Promise.*"

"But why? Were I marrying a handsome, rich duke, I would stand in the middle of the Argyle Rooms and shout it to the *ton.*" She freed her hand. "And so should you. But if you won't, I shall."

"You can't, Elizabeth."

"Why not?"

"Because he has no wish to marry me, nor I him."

Three vertical lines appeared between Elizabeth's eyes. "I do not understand. I saw the special license. I know he means to marry you." Elizabeth's cheeks colored. "I *saw* it."

"What do you mean, *saw it?*" Mary stared at her

sister for several seconds. "Oh, no. *No.* I thought we were beyond all of this."

"I still have the dreams, Mary. Only I no longer tell you and Anne about them. I know the two of you do not believe me, but I tell you, I can see the future unfold—and I saw you marry the Duke of Blackstone. You will become his wife, *tonight.*"

A high-pitched screech rode inside Mary's laughter. Yes, it was true that sometimes Elizabeth did forecast events before they happened. But then, just as often, she was completely wrong about her so-called predictions. Why, one could just as easily flip a coin into the air and have the same degree of accuracy as her sister.

And this time, she had it all wrong.

Elizabeth pointed her index finger at Mary. "I *saw* that gown. When you married him, you were wearing that exact gown."

"But you encouraged me to choose it. Do you not remember?"

"I do not deny influencing your choice of silk, or lace, or design. I did it because I had already dreamed of the gown. I already knew how special the gown would be. I had already dreamed of *your* wedding."

Mary expelled a long sigh. "Elizabeth, I admit that there is a physical bond between me and Rog—the Duke of Blackstone. But it was a mistake."

"No it wasn't. It was meant to be. It was all meant to be."

Mary grabbed her sister's wrists and shook her. "I know you believe as much, but I do not, and I am asking you, as my sister, please do not speak of what you heard in the carriage. It is a game of nerves between me and the duke. Nothing more." She pulled Elizabeth to her and hugged her tightly. "*Please.* I am begging you."

When the two separated, Elizabeth nodded her head. "I will not tell anyone. Until the sun rises. But you will see, Mary, by then you will be the Duchess of Blackstone."

Elizabeth's confidence that Mary would soon wed Rogan did concern her, though she refused to admit it.

Elizabeth's skill in influencing and persuading was quite developed and powerful. Because of her childlike enthusiasm and her sincerity, rarely did anyone realize her manipulation, however unintentional it might have been.

"Ah, there you are, my dear," exclaimed Lady Upperton. "How was your drive?"

The tiny, old woman stood in stark contrast next to tall, lean Lord Lotharian.

Lotharian bent as if bowing, but as he did so, he turned his head and whispered in her ear. "What of the shawl? Was it a match?"

"It was," Mary whispered, then she raised her

voice to a normal level for the benefit of those surrounding them. "Yes, Lady Upperton, the drive was quite uneventful. Such a lovely evening for the fete, don't you agree?"

She leaned close to the old woman and dropped her voice to a hushed tone. "It seems I am to marry the Duke of Blackstone this eve, and you are to thank for securing Lotharian's blessing." Mary shot a glare to her guardian.

Lady Upperton exchanged concerned glances with Lotharian. "Yes, the air is quite soft for such an auspicious event as this." She rose up on her toes and put her mouth to Mary's ear. "Married this eve? Goodness me."

"It is not but a lark," Mary insisted. "Some wicked game Blackstone is playing with me to shatter my nerves. Lud, the man is despicable."

Lotharian suddenly waved to someone in the distance. "Do forgive me. There is someone who owes me a rather large gambling debt, and I do not intend to allow him to slip away this time." Like a hawk, Lotharian watched the gentleman move across the room. "Excuse me, please. He's seen me. Mustn't tarry now."

Mary exhaled through her nose. Lotharian was leaving in the middle of their conversation? *Unbelievable.*

Lady Upperton took Mary's arm and turned her away from Lotharian's departing figure. "Despicable, say you? Bah, Mary, you are being far too harsh.

Blackstone is much more suited to you than his brother, Lord Wetherly."

"How can you say that?" Mary wrinkled her nose. "Wetherly is just the sort of man every woman dreams of marrying."

"Yes, he is. Wetherly is a good man, a compassionate man, but a soft man, too. You are too impulsive for him, and he too malleable for you. Do you not prefer a man who can set your blood to boiling? I think you do. No, I *know* you do. I did, too."

The old woman dropped back to the heels of her Turkish slippers and looked up at Mary.

Mary narrowed her eyes.

There was that curious look in Lady Upperton's faded blue eyes again. Why, it was almost as if she really did know. Knew what passionate urges for Rogan lived in Mary's body.

And in her heart.

"Lady Upperton, wherever do you get such notions?"

Suddenly Mary felt a hand at her waist and another at her elbow. "Miss Royle, the master of ceremonies has announced the first dance. May I have the pleasure?" Rogan asked.

"Well, I—"

Now he leaned close and whispered in her ear. "I am to be your husband in but a few short hours, after all."

Heat surged within her. How that man could make her blush.

Around them, a flurry of society matrons gathered, listening and watching.

"I am honored, Your Grace." She raised her head high, and looking up through her lashes at the handsome duke, she allowed him to lead her through the crowd to the dance floor.

The Saloon Theatre, where the fete was in progress, was the largest chamber Mary had ever seen.

Impressions of columns rose high into what appeared to be the sky itself.

Six glittering, balloon-cut crystal chandeliers, each holding a dozen wax tapers, hung from the ceiling, casting an almost magical glow over the entirety of the dance floor.

The golden flicker above seemed only to accentuate the glistening blue highlights scattered about in Rogan's hair. Lady Upperton was right. Rogan was extraordinarily handsome.

As the orchestra's lively tones took to the air and Mary settled into Rogan's arms to dance, a warmth, a comfort coursed through her. It was a feeling she'd never truly known before. But she felt it, and, much to her surprise, she realized that she never wanted this moment to end.

She gazed up into Rogan's eyes and saw that he was watching her, his eyes filled with wonderment. His hands tightened around her body, and suddenly Mary grew uneasy in her bliss.

This was not possible. She could not feel anything for *him*, the infamous Black Duke.

It was all an illusion. One that would come

crashing down around her the moment she let herself love him.

Love?

Good heavens. Where had that thought hailed from?

This was wrong, all wrong.

So, rather than wait for Rogan to set some beastly ploy into motion, which he certainly would eventually, Mary set about causing the collapse of this moment of happiness.

She spun a circle around the gentleman to Rogan's left, and then because the dance steps required it, returned to the duke's arms once more. She lifted her eyebrows high.

"Your Grace, have you selected a church official from amongst the eligible?" They joined hands and she felt his body jerk. She could not help but smile triumphantly as they stepped into the archway of dancers.

He gazed down at her, and heat surged into her middle.

This is all folly, she reminded herself. *Not real.*

She manufactured a cold smile, but beneath, to her horror, her body still simmered uncontrollably from the nearness of his form.

Rogan's touch changed from comforting and warm to hard and mechanical. "Do not fret, Miss Royle. I asked you to marry me, and I intend to do just that."

"Your Grace, do you not think this farce has continued long enough? Look around you. The cream of society are circling about like vultures, waiting for you to cast me aside. Miss Royle, the mushroom who cannot tell when she is being played the fool."

Rogan lifted her hand over her head and spun her around. He did not say a word.

And so Mary verbally prodded him again. "Everyone is expecting it. You must know this. Do it, and no one will think ill of you."

"I will marry you."

"Why do you play this game? It is nonsensical to me."

A dark glint appeared in his eyes then. "Do you forget what happened between us last night?"

"I am not completely certain anything did. I haven't a head for wine, and as you know, I was drowning in my cups."

An ache began deep within her heart. She did not know why. But it was there. Hurting.

"You agreed to marry me this very night."

"I-I did."

"While all of London may believe me to be an unrepentant rake of the highest order, I do believe in honoring one's promises."

"As do I," she replied. A sickness began to swirl in her belly. She saw now where this uncomfortable conversation was headed.

The game was still in play.

"And yet you do not intend to honor your promise made to me this very eve," he responded.

Mary glared up at him. "You are wrong, Your

Grace. I will. The very minute this set has concluded, if you desire it."

"Actually, I prefer to marry this very moment." He twirled her around. "How else can I be sure you will not beg off?"

Mary pursed her lips. "How else can I be certain that *you* will not walk off?"

Abruptly, Rogan ceased dancing. He laced his fingers through Mary's and whisked her from the dance floor. When they reached the perimeter, he planted her between Lady Upperton and her sisters.

"Lord Lotharian introduced me, a few minutes ago, to someone I must speak with." Rogan stretched his neck and glanced around the Saloon Theater. "Ah, there is Lotharian, and there is my man." He turned back to Mary. "Do not fret, Miss Royle, I am not abandoning you. I shall return promptly, and when I do, a duchess you shall become."

Mary folded her arms at her chest. "I shan't move from this spot, Your Grace."

Anne appeared quite shaken. "A duchess? Mary, what did he mean?"

Mary glanced at Elizabeth. To her great relief, her sister did not burst with the news of the sudden betrothal but rather kept her promise and dramatically sucked the seam of her lips into her mouth.

"Anne, I haven't time to explain." She pulled her sisters near. "Before Blackstone returns, I need for you to go out to the street, find his carriage, and have it opened for you. If the driver questions you, tell him that I may have left my fan on the seat. You'll find it wedged between the wall and left door."

Anne huffed out a breath. "I am not going to miss the honoring of the heroes simply to collect your fan for you." She shoved her own fan toward Mary. "Here, take mine if you are over-warm."

Mary ground her teeth. "Do not speak. Just listen to me. You are not truly looking for the fan. I dropped the shawl inside the carriage cabin and kicked it beneath the seat."

"The Kashmir shawl?" Anne snapped open her painted fan and waved it before her face. "Mary, it's our only proof of who we are. Who we were born to be."

Lord Lotharian approached the trio just then.

"Oh, dear, Lotharian." Lady Upperton actually looked as though she might faint. "Mary left the Kashmir shawl in Blackstone's carriage."

"Not wise. Not wise at all, gel." Lotharian shook his head at Mary as if she had done it intentionally.

"Please, take Anne and Elizabeth to retrieve the shawl. They have received instructions, you only need to find it before Blackstone's tiger or coachman finds it."

"Very well. You can depend on me." Lotharian snapped the heels of his pumps together and ushered Anne and Elizabeth quickly through the theater and down the grand staircase.

Mary rested her hand on her chest and steadied her breathing. "Thank you, Lady Upperton." When she turned to the old woman, she saw that she had raised a lorgnette and was peering across the dance floor.

"Look there, gel." Lady Upperton twisted and offered Mary her lorgnette. "What is Blackstone doing?"

Mary waved away the lorgnette and focused her eyes. Then she squinted. Rogan slapped a gentleman on the back. Then he slyly looked in both directions and covertly pressed a small leather sack into the man's hand. "I believe he just slipped that gentleman a bag of coins."

"I knew he was up to something. It was in his eyes, you know. Kept looking about." Lady Upperton retrained her lorgnette on the duke. "Most suspicious, if you ask me."

After witnessing that very interesting exchange, Mary could not refrain from watching him as he next approached Quinn and drew him away from Lady Tidwell and an elderly matron.

As she and Lady Upperton watched for some minutes, it occurred to Mary that her attention was pinned exclusively on Rogan.

Quinn could have been any other gentleman for as little as she noticed him. It was the tall, ebony-haired, handsome duke who held her focus. He made her remember things she ought not. Made her wonder what the muscled chest she'd felt under her fingertips would look like, stripped of his coat and shirt and bared in the candlelight.

Suddenly Lady Upperton whirled around. "Oh! He's coming back. Turn away, turn away, Mary!"

A moment later, Rogan turned from the orchestra stand and strode toward the ladies.

Mary turned her head and saw the man Rogan had paid only a quarter of an hour before was now standing near the conductor, with a parcel under his arm.

"Lady Upperton, Miss Royle." Rogan stood erect. As he spoke, his eyes did not leave Mary's for an instant. "Will the two of you do me the honor of joining me in the Turkish room for a few minutes?" He gestured toward the doors near the grand staircase. *"Please."*

Lady Upperton looked confused. "Why, yes, Your Grace." She looked to Mary, who offered no explanation.

"Miss Royle?" Rogan offered her his arm. "Shall we?"

Mary nodded dumbly. Lady Upperton might not know what was about to occur, but Mary certainly did.

It was time to play her final trump.

Chapter 15

The Turkish room was awash in blue, from the luxurious carpets to the drapery panels lining the walls.

Rogan gestured to the nearest of the Ottoman sofas lining the perimeter of the room. Both Mary and Lady Upperton, obviously ill at ease, sat down obediently.

"The others should be here presently. Shouldn't be long." Rogan began to pace the open doorway.

"What is going to happen, dear?" Lady Upperton's white brows fluttered nervously.

Honestly, Mary didn't know . . . not for certain, anyway. She had an idea, though, and that idea sent her teetering to the edge of her nerves.

To pass the creeping time, she glanced up at the

massive, glittering crystal chandelier suspended above. There was something painted on the ceiling, and she drew a shading hand to her eyes and peered up at the painting of a soaring eagle grasping a thunderbolt.

Low voices from just outside lured Mary's gaze to the open doors. She leaned forward on the sofa, just far enough to see Rogan reaching, and the hands of two different men stretched outward.

Then he turned and gestured inside. Mary sat back upright and stared straight ahead.

"Lady Upperton, Miss Royle, my I present Mr. Archer? Lord Lotharian introduced us just this night. Such good fortune too, our meeting. Mr. Archer is a vicar and has agreed to preside over our wedding ceremony."

Mary bobbed a small curtsy, but before she rose completely, Lady Upperton nudged her arm and nodded to the gentleman.

It was *him*. The gentleman whose outstretched hand had taken the bag of coins Rogan had covertly offered him.

Ah, so this was his plan. Pay a gentleman to pose as a minister, then watch her squirm.

Well, thanks to Lady Upperton's keen attention and well-aimed lorgnette, she wasn't going to fall for Rogan's grand ruse.

Ha! Now that she'd viewed his hand, she could actually enjoy bluffing the duke.

"Mr. Archer, how good of you to officiate, especially at such late notice." She smiled brightly, then turned and watched Rogan's own smug grin dissolve from his lips.

"And you are both well acquainted with my brother." Rogan moved his large frame aside, and Quinn stepped forward.

"Lady Upperton." He bowed, then turned and looked sheepishly at Mary. "Miss Royle, how pleased I am to welcome you into our family." He stepped forward, clasped her right hand with both of his, and squeezed it gently. It felt like an apology.

Mentally bracing herself, Mary gazed deep into Quinn's eyes. She was ready for the blow that seeing him would inflict, knowing that he was willingly handing her off to his wicked brother.

But surprisingly, she felt no pain.

No disappointment at all.

How could that be? She had set her cap at him. Believed him to be her future. And yet . . . at this moment, she felt absolutely nothing.

Rogan stepped forward and broke the lock of their hands. Possessively, he took her hand and set it in place around his own arm. He looked down at her. "Quinn will be a witness."

The Black Duke was too cruel. Had she been in love with Quinn, as she had honestly believed she might have been at one time, thrusting his brother forward as witness would have been beyond low. And if Quinn had shared those feelings, it would have wounded him deeply as well.

But obviously, he did not. Otherwise he would

not have accepted a role in Rogan's elaborate wedding ruse. And yet, he had.

"Lady Upperton, will you stand as witness as well?" Rogan's tone was level and serious.

Oh, he was a master.

"Dear?" Faded blue eyes stared up at Mary. Lady Upperton separated her from Rogan and led her several feet away. "You know I believe he is the one for you. He is your heart's match. But first, I need to hear that you no longer have feelings for Lord Wetherly."

Mary was stunned by the question. "No, I don't. As I stand here this night, I wonder if I was ever really in love with him, or if I was merely in love with the idea of him."

"What does your heart tell you?"

Mary lowered her head. "The latter. That I never truly loved him. I only thought I did."

Lady Upperton beamed back at her. "Then, I will stand for you, dear gel," she exclaimed for everyone in the Turkish room to hear. Then, in a blink, the old woman gave Mary a tug back toward the gentlemen.

"Lady Upperton, please wait—," Mary sputtered, but before she could finish her thought, Rogan reached for her and brought her to his side.

"Darling," his voice was low, almost mocking, "you are not having second thoughts?"

He was so sure of himself. So sure that she would turn and scamper off like a frightened hare. She straightened her spine. "Not at all." Mary looked straight ahead and focused her gaze on the supposed vicar. "I am ready."

Rogan took her hands in his, and the ceremony began.

The wedding was not but a haze, a disturbing blend of sacred words and utter folly. *It isn't real*, she reminded herself as Rogan slipped a golden ring onto her finger and settled it over her knuckle.

Just as Mr. Archer uttered the final admonition, "What God has joined, let no man put asunder," Mary glanced up to see Lord Lotharian and her sisters standing in the doorway, mouths fully agape.

She could not go through with this. She couldn't. She conceded. Rogan had won.

Mary turned to Mr. Archer, meaning to ask him to stop this farce, but it was too late.

". . . declare you man and wife."

She looked up at Rogan and saw that he was already gazing down at her . . . as if in a daze.

Her stomach clenched. Something felt very wrong. Very wrong, indeed.

From the edge of her vision, she could see her sisters and the elderly lord rushing into the room, but her gaze remained locked with Rogan's.

He released her hands, and she felt his fingers slide around her waist. He cupped her chin with his other hand and tilted her face upward.

"You have won, my dear. You are a duchess and will live the rest of life in luxury and comfort."

His mouth came down on hers then, and he kissed her mouth hard before pulling away.

It wasn't at all like before.

Didn't move her mind and body to wish for other things, for more.

This kiss was punishment.

When he pulled away, Mary stood there, blinking, confused, and feeling hurt for some reason.

The next moments were a blur of shaking hands and congratulatory kisses.

Suddenly, a pen was slipped into her hand and guided toward a book of ruled and numbered vellum pages.

"That's right. Sign your full name, dear," Lady Upperton urged. "Good, good. Now, here too."

The last slip of paper Mary signed was whisked away, and Lady Upperton and Lord Wetherly bent, in turn, to ink their names on the sheet as well.

"Congratulations. May I be the first to address you as Your Grace?" Mr. Archer said as he bowed before her. "It was my honor to be of service."

He, too, signed the paper and handed it to Rogan, then, with the vellum register under his arm, abruptly left the Turkish room.

"Mary?" Anne laid her hand on Mary's cheek. "What is wrong with you? You seem all afluster."

Mary stared into her sister's eyes. "Something is very wrong. This is not what was supposed to happen."

"What do you mean?" Anne asked softly, as if trying to keep her calm.

"In the saloon, I saw Rogan slip Mr. Archer a bag of coins. This was all a ruse."

She looked at Elizabeth then, who was shaking her head.

Mary heard a soft whimper escape her lips. "The vicar wasn't real," she whispered.

Lord Lotharian moved near. "Dear gel, I have known Mr. Archer for many years. Met him when we were young and he was assisting his uncle at our parish church."

"Then . . . he's truly a vicar?" Stunned, Mary stared down at the ring on her finger. "But this was just a game of wits. It wasn't a real wedding. It could not have been."

Rogan had come up behind her. "I know it was a game to you, but not to me. I was dazzled by your beauty and tender touch. I did not see that *I* was your real target in your quest for title and coin."

Lord Lotharian shoved the duke back from Mary. "How dare you! How dare you make such an accusation. I assure you, this woman possesses a large dowry, more than enough to see her marry well, and she is of the noblest blood. The absolute noblest. Truth to tell, Blackstone, she has no need for your *paltry* title."

Mary shook her head. "No, my lord. All of this must stop." But Lotharian's eyes were flashing wildly.

Rogan did not seem to pay her any heed. "She is the daughter of a country physician, Lotharian."

"No, she was *raised* by a physician in Cornwall.

But in fact, she, and her sisters, are the true daughters of the Prince Regent himself."

Rogan reached past Lotharian and caught Mary's arm. He hauled her to him. "What nonsense is this?"

"It is the truth." Lotharian reached inside his coat and produced the Kashmir shawl. "And I have proof!"

Rogan stared down at Mary, waiting for her to answer him. "Is this true, Mary?" he demanded as he shook her slightly.

"I-I don't know. I tell you, I don't know," she replied.

Was this possible? Rogan wondered.

Or had the lot of them escaped from Bedlam?

Rogan looked at the old man shaking a stained red cloth in the air.

At Mary's copper-haired sister mouthing the word "princesses" again and again.

At the old woman running her tiny fingers along the edge of the shawl with reverence.

Oh, yes. They were all *mad*.

He looked down at Mary, peered into her golden eyes, which were frantically searching his. "Is it true, Mary?" he asked her. "You must know."

"Until tonight, I didn't believe it possible," she reluctantly admitted. "It was just a crazy story . . . a story of three royal babes, left for dead and handed over to my father in Lady Jersey's shawl."

"You said until tonight," Rogan prompted.

"Yes. It was just a story, beyond belief, until we found the shawl hidden amongst my father's belongings—that shawl—and matched it beyond a doubt to one Lady Jersey wore in the portrait hanging in the Harrington gallery."

Rogan's eyes went wide. "Still, even if that did belong to Lady Jersey, it does not prove—"

"You're right, it doesn't." She reached up and gently touched his shoulder. "Whether or not my sisters and I were those babes, if they ever even existed, it doesn't matter. What does matter is that you and I have made a very large mistake this eve. Please, Rogan, let us find Mr. Archer before it is too late. Let us admit our error and hope that he can find it in his heart to forget this union ever happened. We made a mistake."

"A mistake," he absently repeated.

He had to think. Make some sense of this, but the din of the room made thought quite impossible.

There was only one thing to do. He took Mary's hand, and, before anyone could stop him, he rushed her from the Turkish room and down the grand staircase.

When they reached the landing, he whirled her to face him.

"It was a mistake, Rogan," she repeated. "A grand mistake. I thought this whole evening, from your proposal of marriage to our wedding, was naught but folly. I thought you toyed with me, and so I played along, hoping to best you."

"And I thought you had bested me. That you sacrificed your body, your maidenhood, for my name and plump pockets."

"We must reverse this travesty. We must! You didn't truly want to marry me. Nor I you. We were both so certain that the other meant to take advantage that we blundered into a marriage neither of us truly wanted."

"Mary, at this moment you are a duchess. Do you know what you are saying?"

"I do." She ran her hand tenderly down his arm. "Let us find the vicar. Perhaps it is not too late to undo what we have done this night."

My God. He had misjudged her.

Terribly misjudged this kind, beautiful, young woman.

She'd never wanted his money. She wasn't an opportunist like Quinn's guinea-hungry mother.

She was just an innocent.

How could he have not seen the truth, when it should have been so clear to him all along?

Rogan pulled her to him, and without a thought as to what possessed him, he kissed her mouth.

When he released her, he could see that he'd startled her. "I-I apologize. I am just so relieved that we finally know the truth about each other."

"As I am." She smiled up at him. "Now, shall we find the vicar? If we remain married much longer and word escapes that you did the honorable thing by me, your reputation as the Black Duke will be polished up beyond repair."

Rogan threw back his head and laughed. "Well, we cannot have that, can we?"

"Indeed, we cannot."

Rogan grasped her hand, and together they raced up the grand staircase and into the Saloon Theatre.

Chapter 16

～⚬⚬～

The carriage lurched to a stop before the Royle sisters' Berkeley Square town house, and, without waiting for the tiger or coachman, Rogan leapt out of the vehicle and handed Mary down.

"Hurry. A change or two of clothing, and whatever else you might need for the journey." Rogan practically chased her to the door. "If we leave right away and drive the horses hard, we might catch the vicar well before he and his sister reach Gretna Green."

"Do you really believe we can catch him up?"

"I do, if we hurry. Could save ourselves a few days of travel."

"I'll just be a few minutes." Mary rushed inside

and up the staircase to her chamber, calling frantically for Cherie.

She could never have imagined such a predicament as she now found herself in.

She thought that when she and Rogan had returned to the Saloon Theatre, they had had a fair chance to convince the vicar of their mistake and persuade him to destroy the license and pretend that the wedding had never occurred.

It might have taken a generous donation to the church, but they at least had had a chance, since only a few minutes had passed.

Such was no longer the situation.

When they'd reentered the Saloon Theatre and inquired about the whereabouts of the vicar, they'd promptly been informed by Lord Lotharian that Mr. Archer had gone.

From what Mary could gather, the vicar's sister had rushed into the saloon only moments before, upset and agitated, her eyes full of tears because her headstrong daughter had run off to Gretna Green with the household's handsome young footman.

The vicar quit the Heroes' Fete at once, and now he and his sister were in desperate pursuit of the runaway young couple.

In just a few minutes, Rogan and Mary would be in pursuit of him as well.

Mary opened a handkerchief and scooped into its middle a boar's hair brush, horn comb, a clutch of hairpins, and a few small pots and bottles from her dressing table. She tied the handkerchief into a small bundle and whirled around to call again for Cherie.

But the maid was already behind her, pulling the half-packed portmanteau from beneath the tester bed, where it had been left when Mary had thought to return to the country.

Cherie opened the case, then hurried to the clothespress and returned with two chemises, pantaloons, and stockings. She plucked the toiletries from Mary's hand, settled those inside, then belted the portmanteau closed.

She turned her dark, questioning eyes up to Mary.

Mary sighed. "The duke and I were married this evening." She held out her hand and showed the maid the golden ring encircling her finger.

Cherie smiled brightly and nodded her head excitedly.

"No, I am not happy. It was a mistake. Neither of us wanted this, and so we are leaving to find the vicar and see this farce of a marriage put to an end before it is too late."

Cherie reached out and ran her tiny index finger over the golden wedding ring. The maid lifted the ringed hand and laid it atop Mary's heart.

Mary looked from the ring glittering on her finger to Cherie's intense, chocolate-brown eyes.

Her throat suddenly felt raw. She made to lower her hand to her side, but the little maid pressed it back to her heart.

"No. It was a *mistake*."

Cherie did not remove her gaze from Mary.

"I am not in love with him."

Mary tried to reach past Cherie to grab the leather-wrapped handle of the portmanteau, but the maid caught her arms and held her still.

She took up Mary's hand and, for the third time, set it atop her heart.

Mary's eyes began to burn. "It doesn't matter what I feel anyway, Cherie. Even if I did love him," she said, her voice shaking, "our joining was not meant to be. To him, I am naught but a country miss, far beneath his notice."

The maid lifted her tiny hand to Mary's cheek. It was all that was needed to send a tear plummeting down her face.

Mary grabbed the portmanteau and turned for the door. She stopped before taking a single step.

Rogan's huge form darkened the entire doorway.

Without an invitation, he walked straight into her chamber, which was quite shocking to Mary, but then, he was her husband.

Lud, her *husband*.

At least for a few more hours. Or days. Certainly not for weeks.

He took the portmanteau from her. "Is there anything else you need for the journey? We must away."

Mary's gaze flitted about the bedchamber until it lit on her father's book of maladies. She snatched it up, in the event a headache on her wedding night just didn't suffice. "Just this."

Then, as if she felt she might never come home again, Mary pulled petite Cherie into her arms and hugged her good-bye.

More than an hour had passed, neither of them speaking, when Mary realized they had not collected Rogan's clothing from his home on Portman Square.

The silence bothered her like an insect buzzing around her head. When she could endure it no more, she decided to mention his oversight. "You haven't any change of clothing."

As if her voice was an affront to the hush of the cabin, he turned his face from the window, and his gaze impaled her.

"I do *not* consider you beneath my notice." His words were precisely spoken, as though he'd practiced them countless times.

She dropped her eyes beneath his unyielding gaze. He had heard her when she'd been talking to Cherie. *Oh, my God.*

"At the very least, you might need nightclothes," she added, hoping to redirect the uneasy conversation.

"I do not wear nightclothes." There was such a sharp edge to his voice that she flinched.

"Oh." She lifted her eyes and turned her gaze out the window, suddenly anxious to escape his overwhelming presence. "Nor do I," she muttered, hoping to shatter the tension between them. But she heard no laugh, no muted chuckle. Nothing.

"Mary, look at me," Rogan finally said. He reached across the aisle and grasped her hand. *"Look at me . . . please."*

His touch forced her attention.

She did as he asked and looked up. A burst of bronze within his dark brown eyes seemed to glow in the light of the carriage lantern.

But what she saw there in his eyes was not at all what she had expected. There was no shadow of anger residing there, only naked regret.

Tenderly, he ran his thumb along her bare hand. "I was wrong, Mary. I erred in my every thought about you, my every presumption, my every prejudice. I should have listened to what my heart told me. But I didn't."

He leaned his head back and gazed at the ceiling. "For years, I have shielded myself, and of late even my brother, from the pain of giving my affection, my heart, to someone who did not care for me but rather for my title and my position."

Rogan lifted his head from the rest and looked at her, his eyes dark and liquid. "I doubted everyone's motives, no matter the situation, distrusted every woman."

Mary felt her heart clench at the emotion in his words, in his eyes. She rose and sat down next to him. Hesitantly, she reached up and rested her hand comfortingly on his shoulder. "Who hurt you? Who did this to you?"

He stiffened then and shrugged her hand from his coat. "No one hurt me. I learned a valuable lesson, that's all." He set his elbows on his knees and cradled his head in his hands.

Mary was very still and silent. She wanted to comfort him.

She stretched out her arm and touched his shoulder again. "Who did this to you?" she repeated.

Rogan turned his head and looked at her. "She didn't hurt me. She hurt my father. She pretended to love him, pretended to love me. But shortly after they married, she showed herself for who she truly was. Her affection, her kindness, her love—it was all an act. She only wanted his money. That's all she ever wanted."

"Your stepmother?" she asked hesitantly.

Rogan nodded and turned away to look out the window at the rolling countryside. "She hurt him, hurt him badly."

"She hurt you, too."

His head snapped around, and he stared at her. "Did you not hear what I said? She hurt my father."

"She hurt you, too. She made you distrustful. Made you afraid of opening your heart to a woman."

He didn't reply. He remained silent, neither agreeing with or denying what she'd said.

Raising her arm higher, she slid her hand gently across his temple and eased her fingers through his thick, black hair, around to the back of his head and slowly down his neck and back. His eyes closed, and she heard a soft sigh slip from his mouth.

Leaning closer, until her body was pressed against his, she pushed her fingers upward from the nape of his neck through his hair again. As she did this, she moved her mouth to his cheekbone and kissed him softly.

His eyelids fluttered open, as if she'd surprised him. He turned and wrapped his arms around her.

Mary slid her arms about his waist in response, lifting her lips and pressing them to his warm mouth.

When she broke the seal of their lips, slowly, ever so slowly, Rogan exhaled softly. "Mary."

She drew her knees onto the seat cushion and balanced herself against him. Her face was above his now, and he tilted his up to hers.

She touched her lips to his forehead. She felt his breath on her throat and heard him murmur something unintelligible.

Rogan closed his eyes as she trailed moist kisses over his eyelid, and over his cheek and down to his beard-roughened chin, before kissing his mouth once more.

"Mary." Her name floated atop his heated breath. "I-I . . ."

His chin rubbed against the sensitive skin of her own as the passion of their kisses grew more fervent.

"I-I . . ." He pulled back just enough to look into her eyes, his gaze stoking the growing fire within her. "I *can't*," he finally managed.

He grasped her waist and moved her away from him. "We can't, unless we put an end to our pursuit of Mr. Archer."

Mary blinked, feeling suddenly light-headed. "What are you saying?"

He looked into her eyes. "We . . . we could remain husband and wife."

What? "Remain married? Are you mad?" Mary straightened her back, and her gaze darted around the carriage cabin in her disbelief. "You *must be*. That is the only explanation for what you are suggesting."

"Are you forgetting that I ruined you—in this very carriage, no less? And would have lain with you again had we not separated just now?"

"Yes, I must remind myself to avoid riding in carriages with you in the future." She flicked up an eyebrow.

"I am serious, Mary."

"I hardly feel damaged, so unless you announced our . . . encounter to the *ton*, no one will know, and I shall not suffer in the least," she retorted quickly, drowning out the pounding of her heart.

"I have wronged you, therefore I think it only fair to you that we remain married."

Mary's eyelids raised up, and she shook rigid hands in the air. "Are *you* forgetting that you do not want to be married to me?" She sighed with exasperation, and yet the backs of her eyes began to sting.

"Are you so certain of that?" Rogan's gaze searched her face, as if delving inside her, looking for her answer.

The tenderness in his expression and his words surprised her and inexplicably propelled Mary to her feet.

Pursing her lips, she sucked in a breath in utter astonishment and pressed a hand to the cabin ceiling to brace herself so she wouldn't fall. What a goose she was being standing inside a carriage racing down a pitted, gravel road.

There was nowhere to go. No place to collect her thoughts. No room to craft a pithy reply.

And so she sat back down, folded her hands in her lap, and stared wordlessly out the window.

Remain Rogan's wife. She huffed out a broken breath.

What a preposterous idea.

Chapter 17

The carriage driver had stopped for fresh horses several times during the long night, making it impossible for Mary to sleep for more than a few minutes at a time.

She had tried leaning her head against the leather squabs, but the constant jostling of the carriage as its wheels hit holes in the packed surface of the road—in addition to the fact that whenever she'd opened her eyes Rogan had been watching her—had kept her awake.

By nearly four in the morn, Mary had had enough. She begged Rogan to temporarily stop their chase in Baldock to rest and take their breakfast.

To her surprise, he did not resist the idea at all

but rather proclaimed it a wonderful suggestion.

The only problem with the notion was that The White Horse Inn was completely filled. In fact, had Rogan not had sufficient coin to bribe another guest, who had risen early to catch a mail coach, to relinquish his room to them, there would not have been a room at all.

As it was, Rogan informed her that they would have to share a bed.

Mary was far too tired to argue, so she tucked the book of maladies and remedies under her arm, just in case she suddenly had need of either, and followed the glow of the candle the innkeeper had given Rogan up the dark staircase and into a small bedchamber.

Rogan settled the chamber lamp on a night table beside the bed and immediately began to remove his clothing.

"Um, Rogan." Her words came out thin and strangled. "I know you do not see a need for bed-clothes, but might you wear something to bed? I realize that we are husband and wife, but with any good fortune at all, tomorrow we shall no longer be so joined."

"Very well, my darling," Rogan laughed. "You needn't fear. I shall remain clothed." He glanced at the book of maladies cradled in her arms. "And though this is our wedding night, you are safe from any advances in this bed."

"Oh, I know that," she replied with feigned in-nocence. She set the book down and slid beneath the coverlet. "This is a bed. Not a *carriage*, after all."

Rogan laughed and climbed into bed beside her.

She didn't know when it had happened, or why, but there was an ease between them. A comfort she had not noticed before. But she felt it now and could not deny it.

Within minutes, though she was lying in a narrow bed with the one man who made her heart beat like a fresh team at full gallop, to her surprise, Mary felt herself falling asleep.

Three hours later, the sun streamed through the threadbare curtain stretched across the window.

Mary stood in the sunlight and held a hand mirror before her face. She grimaced into the looking glass. "*Red.* It's completely red."

Rogan rubbed his eyes as he awoke, and blinked up at her. "What is red?"

"This." She whirled and pointed at her chin. "Your Grace, I take back my words. I am damaged. Just look at what you've done."

He propped himself up on his elbow and squinted up at her. "How on earth did that happen?" Then his eyes widened and he rubbed the coarse black stubble upon his own chin. "*Oh.*"

"Your beard. It obviously scraped my chin when you were kissing me last night in the carriage."

"I beg your pardon, darling, but I believe I was attempting to stop *you* from kissing me."

"Not when *this* happened." Mary held the mirror up again and peered into it with a sigh. "I remember quite clearly."

"As do I." Rogan smiled wickedly and climbed out of bed. He approached her, then lowered his mouth and placed a chaste kiss upon her reddened chin.

She smiled, then playfully shook her finger at him. "Back away, Blackstone. My chin is already quite red enough."

Rogan tucked in his shirt, then caught her hand holding the mirror and raised it up before him so he could tie his neckcloth properly.

Or, at least as well as a gentleman unaccustomed to dressing himself could possibly do.

He had just finished when Mary caught the scent of frying rashers. Her stomach growled. "Shall we take breakfast before boarding the carriage?"

"Absolutely." There was a glint of humor in his tone. "I shall need all the strength I can muster if I am to spend another day in the carriage with you."

With a grin playing at her lips, Mary picked up her book, cape, and reticule, and watched Rogan as he shrugged his coat over his broad shoulders and picked up her valise.

She sighed quietly, willing away the wicked

thoughts burgeoning in her mind. Such a gloriously formed man.

Rogan opened the door for Mary. As she turned her head to look at him when she passed through the doorway, her preoccupation with him hardly went unnoticed.

Mary walked straight into a gentleman who had picked that moment to pass their room.

"Oh, I do beg your pardon, madam," he began, as he backed out of Mary's path.

"The fault was mine, sir," she interrupted. "Please do forgive m-me—" Mary felt the blood siphon from her face. "Mr. Archer!"

"Good morn, Vicar," Rogan said, perfectly poised and bursting with confidence. "Just the gentleman we had hoped to see this day."

Rogan stepped in front of Mary, who, it seemed, could not draw forth another word.

"Saints be praised, Your Grace!" The vicar hurriedly bowed. "What splendid coincidence, meeting you and Her Grace on the road." He glanced at Mary and belatedly bowed to her.

"Not a coincidence at all. We tracked you through the night, inquiring whenever we stopped for fresh horses as to whether you'd passed that way or not."

"Did you now?" The vicar glanced nervously behind him, down the passage.

"You are crushing your hat, sir," Mary noted.

And so he was. Mr. Archer was wringing his hat as tightly as if it had been soaked all night in a washtub. His face glowed like a beacon, and a sprinkling of sweat dotted his forehead.

A heavy woman, nearly twice the weight of the vicar, shuffled up the passage toward them. "I'm coming. I'm coming, my dear."

Rogan swept her with a curious gaze.

When the woman reached the vicar, she gave him a nudge. "Thank you for waiting for me." She gave Rogan an appreciative glance but paid no attention to Mary. "Won't you introduce me to your friend, Archie?"

The vicar could not quite hide the apprehension in his eyes. "Your Grace, Your Grace," he nodded his head to both Rogan and Mary, "may I present my sister, Heloise."

"Oh, that's rich," the woman chuckled. "Yes, I am his sister." The neckline of her frock was fashioned daringly low and barely covered her breasts. Hardly appropriate for a vicar's sister.

Rogan felt Mary's hand on his shoulder, and he turned to see her eyes clouded with suspicion. *"Sister?"* she mouthed.

No, Rogan didn't believe it either. But Mr. Archer's true reason for traveling to Scotland was not his concern. "Dear sir, may we join you in the dining room? We urgently need to speak with you."

The vicar grew visibly more agitated. "Oh, yes, well . . . we are in a dreadful hurry."

"Sir, a great wrong has been done." It was then that Rogan noticed the vicar's unseemly garb. His coat was rich-blue kerseymere, and the waistcoat beneath, why, he'd be deuced if it wasn't constructed of fine jonquil yellow silk embroidered with a line of hearts and diamonds.

Hardly the somber attire of a man of the Church of England.

Rogan drew his eyebrows close and studied Mr. Archer.

The vicar managed a tremulous smile. He glanced across at Mary, as if searching for a respite from Rogan's concentrated notice. "Dear me, Your Grace, have you been injured on the journey?"

"Injured?" Mary repeated.

"He means your chin, Sweeting. It's all scraped up and hot." The vicar's sister tapped her own with the tip of her index finger. Then she grinned and looked at Mr. Archer. "No, she hasn't been hurt, dear brother." She turned her notice back to Mary. "Have you, Your Grace?"

Mary looked mortified.

Rogan stepped between her and the offending woman. "Mr. Archer," he said more sternly than he intended, "I will speak with you."

The vicar expelled a loud sigh. He dropped his hat to the wood plank floor and pressed the heels of his hands to his eyes and began to groan.

"Mr. Archer."

"Very well, I knew this would happen. I did." He

lowered his hands and scooped his rumpled felt hat from the floor. "Come with me. I have everything in my case." He turned and started back down the passage.

Rogan looked at the woman, who started off instead in the direction of the staircase.

"Your business doesn't concern me," she called back to them. "I am famished and can smell the rashers and buttered toast from here."

"This way, Your Grace," the vicar said resignedly as he gestured to the door at the end of the passage. "I know what you've come for."

Rogan slipped his arm protectively around Mary's waist and led her to the vicar's chamber.

When they entered through the open door, Mr. Archer was rummaging through a leather case. He withdrew a sheet of paper and handed it to Rogan.

"Here's the license. I'd burn that if I were you." He returned to the case and extracted a leather volume from it.

Muttering to himself all the while, Mr. Archer flipped through the lined and numbered pages until he found the one containing their entry. He took a small knife to the book and made to cut the page from the register.

"You can't do that," Mary gasped. "Destruction of a register is punishable by death!"

"Ah, learned woman." Mr. Archer delivered the vellum page to Rogan. "And yes, you are correct.

Had this been an actual register of a license of marriage, I could have been hanged." He snapped the book in his hand closed. "But as it is, it's only my household accounts register."

"I-I do not understand." Mary turned and searched Rogan's eyes for an answer.

As Rogan fought to retain his composure and tamp down his raging urge to tear Mr. Archer limb from limb, he told Mary the insane truth of the matter. "It seems our Mr. Archer here is not truly a vicar."

"Then we"—Mary's voice broke almost painfully—". . . we were never married."

Rogan's gaze shot to her eyes the moment he heard the regret and pain she had not been able to strain from her words.

She should have been happy, jubilant, joyous that she and Rogan had not been wed after all. But she felt none of these things.

Instead, she felt hollow. Tears trembled on her lashes. "I-I need to sit down."

Rogan helped her to the plank chair near the doorway. Then he turned on Mr. Archer. "How did this happen? Who arranged for this?"

He grabbed the false vicar by the throat and slammed him against the wall. "Tell me *now*."

Mr. Archer's eyes bulged in their sockets, and a smothered whimper burst from his open mouth.

"Rogan, no!" Mary cried. "Please, let him speak."

Rogan yanked back his hand as quickly as if he'd been burned.

Hastening his hands to his throat, Mr. Archer slid down the wall and sat on the floor, legs spread. "I-I told Lotharian it was madness. But he was sure it would w-work." He looked across the room at Mary then. "And, judging by the lady's pink chin, well, he might have been right."

Rogan took a step forward. "What do you mean? You'd best explain yourself, Archer."

The duke was a formidable man, but seething with barely-restrained anger, as he was now, he was clearly terrifying the man trembling on the floor.

"I owed Lotharian a good deal of money. C-couldn't pay him off. So when he approached me at the fete with a proposition that would wipe my slate, well, I could not refuse."

"What was his proposition?" Rogan's face was a scowling mask of rage. "What was it?"

"He needed someone to pose as a vicar. To perform a false wedding . . . if everything went as planned. He knew I could do it. I had studied at my uncle's side—he was a clergyman—as a young man, until . . . well, until my true nature exposed itself. I lost some parish tithings . . . to my weakness, gambling. Well that was the end of my training, such that it was."

Mary came to her feet and came to stand beside Rogan. She slipped her hand around his balled fist and caressed it, easing the tension he held there until he relaxed his fingers and interlaced them with hers. "Why did Lotharian wish to arrange this false wedding? What possible reason could he have?"

"You mustn't know Lotharian well." Archer exhaled. "He is a gambler of the first rank. He cannot lose. He can read a person so well that he can predict his actions in any given situation. And he predicted yours, Miss Royle, as well as yours, Your Grace."

"What was his prediction?" Rogan's hand tightened around Mary's.

"He knew you wore blinders. You were so damned angry with each other that you could not imagine the possibility that your perceptions of one another were completely wrong. That your passionate dislike of each other masked true passion itself. That you were meant to be together."

Mary felt heat rising into her cheeks. She could not look up at Rogan, though she was longing to know if he felt as she did.

Lotharian had been right. Wicked man that he evidently was, he'd guessed correctly.

"But why the wedding? By Lotharian's measure of our natures, Miss Royle and I would have realized our so-called passion eventually."

"I don't know. You must quiz him on that. All I know is that the false wedding was not so important as your pursuit of me on the Great North Road."

"I don't understand. The value of our pursuit

was that we learned we were never married," Mary retorted.

"No, the time you spent together, alone, united in purpose, was the value Lotharian envisioned. Time enough to see the other clearly. Time to realize that love is not only possible but . . . *inevitable*."

She heard Rogan's breath hitch in his throat. She didn't know what to say or do.

They both stood silently for several moments before Rogan started for the doorway, pulling Mary along with him.

"We're heading back to London. *Now*."

The carriage tore down the road, sending clouds of earth spiraling out behind it.

Mary sat rigid and still in the corner. "You didn't know either." Her words were merely an observation, but Rogan seemed to hear them as a question.

"I should think that quite evident. Had you not prevented it, I might have pounded Archer senseless."

"It wasn't his fault."

"No, it was Lotharian's, and I will remember that fact." He exhaled a long breath, then inclined himself forward to look into her eyes. "I am sorry for all of this, Mary."

"You are sorry?" She regarded him quizzically. "You are in no way to blame for this."

"None of this would have happened had I restrained myself." There was something flickering in his eyes, and she knew he had more to say. "Had I not been so taken with you that night, allowed my passion to overtake my logic, perhaps I would not have been willing to do anything to make you mine."

Mary sat mutely and stared at him.

"Lotharian was right, at least about my feelings for you. I never hated you. I *desired* you. I did from the moment I first saw you . . . in the garden. I just could not admit it to myself."

Hearing his words, her heart fluttered wildly in her chest. "I never hated you either. I . . ." Mary could not admit anything else.

In truth, she knew that what had happened in the carriage had been her fault. *Her* desires, *her* passions, *her* wanton dreams come to life by her own doings.

But it was all too much to confess.

And so she sought to lighten the conversation. "However, I did think you to be a wicked rake."

For a moment, his eyes brightened. "And you were not wrong." But then his gaze became serious again. "But I am no longer that man."

Mary considered him for a moment. "No, I don't think that you are."

Rogan reached out and placed a hand on her arm. "So there is no reason we should not marry."

"Except one."

Rogan furrowed his eyebrows. "What is that?"

"*Love.*"

* * *

Mary's sisters were not at home when she arrived at Berkeley Square that evening. She was bone-weary and drained, and so the solitude suited her very well.

Mrs. Polkshank served her a cold dinner in her bedchamber. Though she'd barely eaten all day, she only picked at it.

When Mary was finished eating, she sank into the steaming bath Cherie had drawn for her.

Raising her left hand from the soapy water, she watched the liquid slowly trickle down her fingers and over the gold ring Rogan had placed there.

She tugged on the ring. She'd have to give it back to Rogan in the morning. She tried twisting it, but her fingers had swelled in the hot water and the ring would not be removed.

A raw and primitive sadness washed over her.

She would have agreed to marry Rogan when he'd asked in the carriage. Would not have needed to think at all about it.

All he'd had to say was that he loved her.

But he hadn't.

The aching in her heart evolved into a sick, painful gnawing.

A sob overtook her, and she allowed herself to weep aloud, rocking back and forth in the hip-bath.

Cherie rushed into the chamber, wrapped a towel around Mary, and led her toward bed.

When Cherie doused the candles, Mary curled to her side, pulled the coverlet high around her, and buried her face in her pillow.

Then something occurred to her, and she sat straight up in bed.

Rogan had not confessed his love for her.

"But nor have I."

Chapter 18

When Mary descended the staircase very early the next morning, she had no intention of sitting down to breakfast with her sisters.

She had a mission. Arguably the most important of her life.

Nevertheless, she had planned to quickly stop by the dining room. She needed a swipe of butter. The stubborn wedding ring still would not slide off her swollen finger.

The sun had risen only an hour past, time enough for Mary to see to her morning ministrations and dress. Even with Cherie's nimble fingers assisting, she'd taken much longer than usual to prepare her toilette.

Her hair had to be perfect, her clothing neatly

ironed. She'd fastened a triple strand of creamy pearls, a gift from her father long ago, around her neck.

It was important to her that she look her best when she pressed the wedding ring back into Rogan's hand. Because her true purpose for seeing Rogan was not to return his property but to confess the depth of her feelings for him.

To tell him that she loved him.

She trembled just considering that moment. What would she do and say if he did not reply in the manner she hoped?

Lud, what if he just said "Thank you" and nothing more?

Either way, she had to return the ring. If she was lucky, she would soon see the ring on her finger again when he admitted his love for her.

If not . . . well, the ring had never truly been hers anyway.

Because of the early hour, and her sisters' late night, Mary did not peek into the dining room before entering for a bit of butter. This proved to be a mistake.

"There you are!" Elizabeth exclaimed. She leapt from her chair and rushed over to Mary. "Mrs. Polkshank told us you had come home."

"And that you practically collapsed last night." Anne had a concerned look in her eyes when she hugged Mary.

Mary drew a deep breath and expelled it.

She had hoped to avoid telling her sisters until

after she'd called on Rogan that the wedding had been naught but a hoax.

She had her mission to perform first, after all, and she knew any mention of that would not sit well with her sisters, or rather one sister in particular. A young lady visiting a bachelor, well, it was simply against the rules of propriety, as Anne certainly would remind her.

"I must tell you something. Something horrid," Mary began.

Before she could say another word, Elizabeth interrupted her. "That the wedding was a sham arranged by Lotharian?"

Mary was dumbfounded. "W-why, yes. How did you know?"

"Lady Upperton told us everything," Elizabeth admitted. "She is furious with Lotharian."

"She thought she recognized the vicar during the ceremony, then belatedly realized that she knew him from one of Lady Carsington's faro parties," Anne added. "When she approached Lotharian about it, he confessed his scheme, though he still believed it had been the right thing to do."

"He said that had he not acted quickly . . ." Elizabeth paused, her gaze tracking the slow progress of the butler as he headed toward Mary with a large tea tray mounded with cards and the *Morning Post*. "As I was saying . . . had he not acted quickly, you and the duke would never realize that you belonged together."

"Your Grace," MacTavish said, "some cards have arrived for you."

"Please, just set them on the table if you will." Just then, it struck Mary just how the butler had addressed her. "MacTavish, why did you address me as 'Your Grace'?"

Anne narrowed her eyes at him. "Were you perhaps listening to our conversation?"

The butler shook his head. "No, miss. I happened to notice the *on-dit* column in the newspaper this morning." He opened the newspaper and tapped a column on the front page. "There it is."

Elizabeth snatched up the newspaper and read the heavily inked head of the column. *"Miss Royle Weds Duke in Surprise Ceremony."* She looked up at Mary. "Was there . . . perhaps *another* surprise ceremony?"

Mary shook her head slowly, then sank down into the nearest chair at the table.

Anne slapped her hands to her cheeks. "Oh, no. Mary, your name will be ruined once it is known that the wedding was false. Our names will be ruined. No one will desire a connection to the Royle family!"

Just then, there was a hard knock upon the front door.

The sisters exchanged a circle of worried glances, then as one, they called out to the butler, who had already disappeared into the passage headed for the entry hall. "Don't answer it!"

"Too late," came Rogan's rich voice from the doorway of the dining room.

Mary looked up at him in disbelief. *"Rogan."*

"May we speak privately?" he asked. In his hand was a copy of the *Gazette*.

Mary set her palms on the surface of the table and pushed up. "We can talk in the parlor." She glanced up into his warm brown eyes as she passed him, gesturing for him to follow. "This way, please."

Rogan thrummed his fingers atop the folded newspaper he'd balanced atop his knee. "Mary, I don't know how anyone learned of the ceremony at the Argyle Rooms. But there is nothing we can do about the column now. By now, everyone of consequence has read of our *wedding*."

Frustrated, he leaned his head backward, but the settee had been constructed with tiny misses in mind and was consequently too short for him. This only added to his annoyance.

"We could ask for a retraction."

"That would only bring more scrutiny and interest in our situation." He leaned across to Mary and took her hand. "No, I fear we have but one course to avoid the ruin of both our family names—we must marry."

"I beg your pardon."

"I am sorry, but we must, and we must do so quickly and quietly."

Mary's eyes were as round and golden as the sun as she stared up at him. She nodded dutifully. "If there . . . is nothing else we can do."

Suddenly, Rogan's heart felt very heavy. He had hoped she would be somehow happier about the prospect of sharing their lives together. "There is nothing else," he finally replied.

"Very well." Her eyes glistened with unshed tears.

Was his offer so terrible that it made her cry? Rogan swallowed hard and came quickly to his feet. "I shall instruct my solicitor to go to Doctor's Commons and secure another special license the very instant the archbishop's office opens on Monday morning. Meanwhile, I shall find a minister. Do you have a preference?"

She smiled meekly. "Anyone but Mr. Archer will do." Then, as if something had just broached her mind, she took hold of the wedding ring on her left hand and tried desperately to twist it off. "It won't come off. I'm sorry, Rogan, but I've tried, but now my finger is swollen. It is as if it wants to remain there forever."

"And so it shall," Rogan replied softly. "I shall send the carriage at three this afternoon. Is that sufficient time for you?"

Mary rose and followed him toward the passage. "Time enough for what?"

"Why, to pack your belongings."

"Why would I do that?" she asked, her eyes growing wider.

"Until we are truly married, if our families' names are to be spared, we must give all appearances that we already are husband and wife."

Then, so there would be no misunderstandings, Rogan spoke very plainly to her. "Mary, you must remove yourself to my house. Into my bedchamber."

"Your bedchamber!" she sputtered and slapped her palm to her forehead. "You are not serious."

"Servants talk, and since we do not know the source of the column's information, we cannot afford to take any unnecessary chances."

Mary just stared at him.

"So, three o'clock then?"

"Y-yes." Mary rubbed her fingers to her temples. "I will be ready."

A harsh sun beat down on London, sending crowds to Hyde Park to sit beneath the trees near the Serpentine and savor what breezes were to be had.

On most any other day at three o'clock, this is where Mary would have been.

But not today.

Today she sat beside the braced-open parlor windows fanning herself as she awaited Rogan's carriage to take her, and what few belongings she owned, to Portman Square.

Cherie plumped a pillow and eased it behind Aunt Prudence's back, then she removed the empty cordial glass from her hand. She started to leave the room, then seemed to change her mind, for she rushed over to Mary and squeezed her hand. The young maid's eyes were threaded with red, as though she'd been crying.

"Do not be sad, Cherie. We shall see each other quite often, I promise." Mary set her fan in her lap and patted the top of the maid's hand.

Cherie shook her head frantically. She poked her chest with her index finger.

"I-I do not understand. What are you trying to tell me?"

The maid slipped her hand away. She rushed from the room, then returned two minutes later and handed Mary a scrap of foolscap with something written on it.

Mary held it to the light shining through the window.

Lord Lotharian sent me to watch over you.

What was this? Mary turned her gaze upon Cherie.

"You were sent here to spy on me . ... and my sisters, for Lotharian?"

"I told you she was a spy," Mrs. Polkshank said as she entered the parlor and settled a tea tray on the table beside Aunt Prudence. "Ask if she's French. I bet she is."

"Mrs. Polkshank, please summon my sisters," Mary said. "I should like to speak with Cherie privately, if you don't mind."

"Yes, Miss Royle." Mrs. Polkshank walked into

the passage, glancing over her shoulder as she moved.

Suddenly Mary realized she had seen Cherie once before. "Zeus! You served tea the day my sisters and I visited the Old Rakes Club."

Cherie nodded, then lowered her gaze to the floor.

"And you have been reporting to Lotharian all of this time?"

The maid shook her head furiously. She raised a single finger in the air.

"Once. You reported to him once." Mary nodded thoughtfully. "One time. What did you tell him?"

Cherie slowly reached out her finger and touched the wedding ring Rogan had given Mary, then she lifted that hand and placed it atop Mary's heart.

"You told him . . . that I loved the duke?" Cherie didn't truly answer, but Mary could see it on her face.

This was how Lotharian knew her feelings. Likely how he read the true nature of people as well. He spied.

He was a gambler, gamester, and a good one, apparently. He knew that to win, one must leave as little to chance as possible.

The elfish little maid suddenly grew very still, as though she had heard something.

And then Mary heard it too. She turned her notice toward the passage. One of her sisters was descending the stairs.

Mary turned back to Cherie. "That's all you told him?"

Cherie mouthed word "yes."

"Do you wish to stay on here, with my sisters?"

"Yes."

"Then this must remain between us. And you must promise to never again share what goes on in this house with anyone. Do you understand?"

Cherie nodded and smiled, then hurried through the parlor door.

Just then, Mary noticed that Aunt Prudence was peering at her through half-open eyes.

"Aunt Prudence, were you listening to me?"

"You would be surprised at how much I hear when others think me asleep." The old woman smiled mischievously. "But do not fret, Mary. I am inclined to forget whatever secrets I uncover before I next blink. So carry on."

The moment Elizabeth entered the room, Aunt Prudence snapped her lids closed again, but her smile lingered.

Elizabeth was carrying a valise filled with Mary's dressing table articles. She set it down beside the lone chest Mary was to take with her to her soon-to-be-husband's home.

"I cannot believe you are really leaving us," Elizabeth said as she crossed the room to Mary and took her hand. "How will we get along without you?"

Mary forced a small laugh. "Dear, you won't

have to get along without me. We can visit each other every day if you like."

"Promise you will. I daresay Anne will spend every penny set aside for our household account within one month. Two at the most."

Mary's laugh was genuine this time. "Mrs. Polkshank is very thrifty, so I seriously doubt you will have anything to fret over."

"When is the wedding? Have you heard anything more?"

"No, and I doubt I shall until the special license has been secured." Mary squeezed Elizabeth's hand as she folded her fan in her lap. "But I promise you, Sister, you will be the very first to know."

Mary released Elizabeth's hand as a soft, humid breeze blew through the window. Mary leaned against the chair back and closed her eyes as it blew across her cheeks. "Were I at home this night, I swear I would sleep in the courtyard for the cool night air."

"Instead, you will be sleeping with a duke," Anne said from the parlor doorway.

Mary's eyelids snapped open and she sat up. "There is naught I can do about that, Anne. Would you prefer it if I stayed here and risked word slipping out that Blackstone and I were never legally wed?"

"No. I know you were only thinking of me and Elizabeth when you agreed to the duke's solution." Anne lowered her gaze to the Turkish carpet. "I hope you can forgive me. I just cannot stop fretting over the fact that you will no longer be here."

"Oh, Anne. It was bound to happen someday. It just happened that circumstances required that it be today."

The clop of horses' hooves echoed against the row of houses as Rogan's gleaming town carriage entered Berkeley Square and drew to a halt before the Royle sisters' home.

Mary peered out the window, and with a sigh came to her feet. Her stomach was tied in tight knots as she saw Rogan and a footman walk up the short steps to the house. The door knocker sounded, setting Mary into panicky motion, hurrying past both her sisters to the door.

Mary opened the door for Rogan and the footman, then immediately turned back to her sisters and hugged them both. "Every day. Remember, we can see each other every single day."

"And we must, for we have yet to locate Lady Jersey," Elizabeth reminded Mary, as if this might be just the incentive to lure her home again. "We must confront her about the Kashmir shawl."

"Lady Jersey?" Rogan asked.

Heat rushed into Mary's cheeks as her gaze met his. "I told you, it matters naught."

"It does!" Elizabeth countered. "The Kashmir shawl Lotharian held in the Turkish room belonged to Lady Jersey. We are sure of it, for she is wearing it in her portrait hanging in the Harrington gallery."

Rogan blinked in surprise. "I remember that painting. I must admit, this mystery of yours, Mary, is quite intriguing." Rogan's tone was firm and even, not mocking at all. "Are you certain that the shawl you possess is the very same one?"

Mary drew a breath, punctuated by several tiny gasps. Too much was happening now. She did not wish to discuss this with Rogan, with anyone, just now. "I believe so."

"It *is*." Anne's conviction was clear; Mary only wished she could share her sister's unflinching belief. "There is no need to conceal anything from Blackstone any longer. He is to be your husband."

Rogan flashed a pleased smile in Anne's direction. "Thank you, Miss Anne." He lowered his voice to a confidential tone. "But remember, for all of our sakes"—he glanced at the footman removing Mary's chest from the parlor—"we are already married."

The duke snared Mary's gaze and gestured toward the door. She kissed Aunt Prudence on her cheek, and each of her sisters. Then, with Rogan's hand guiding her at the elbow, she slowly turned and walked through the door to the carriage.

When the carriage arrived in Portman Square a few minutes later, Mary glimpsed Quinn through that cabin window, caning his way down the front steps to an awaiting carriage.

A liveried footman hoisted a heavy portmanteau

to a muscular coachman standing atop the conveyance to receive it.

Mary turned around in her seat to face Rogan. "Where is he going?"

Rogan leaned forward and peered out the window as the town carriage rolled to a slow stop before the house. He did not reply to Mary but rather flung open the door and stepped down into the road.

"What the hell, Quinn?" Mary overheard Rogan shout as she took the footman's hand and descended the carriage steps to the ground.

Quinn leaned on his cane and rested his other hand on Rogan's shoulder. "To the country. Thought I would stay there for few days to allow you . . . and the duchess . . . time to settle in."

"You need not leave," Rogan said, though to Mary's ear, not too convincingly.

"Ah, but I do. Thought it high time I explore my new property. Survey the land . . . perhaps see what needs to be done in preparation to make the house suitable for a family."

"Are you saying that you and Lady Tidwell—" A single brow lifted as Rogan smiled knowingly at his brother.

"Not yet. But I feel the time will come soon. Might as well be prepared, eh?"

Quinn lifted his hand from Rogan's shoulder and walked to Mary. "Sister," he bowed neatly to her, then pecked her on the cheek.

Mary leaned forward to do the same. "You do realize we are not truly married yet," she whispered in his ear.

"Rogan explained everything this morning," he told her quietly. "I am sorry about the announcement in the *Gazette*."

"It doesn't matter." She leveled her mouth to his ear. "I am not opposed to marrying because I love your brother, and maybe someday he will love me too."

A sudden blush crested her cheeks. She didn't know what had come over her, or why she needed to admit her feelings for Rogan to someone, but she could not help herself.

Quinn's eyes sparkled, and he turned around to look at Rogan, his white teeth gleaming.

"What are you two going on about?" Rogan blinked in bafflement.

Mary's stomach tensed then and did not relax until Quinn grinned and waved a cane at Rogan as he started to climb up into the carriage.

"I shall see you Wednesday morning," Quinn called out to his brother.

Then the footman closed the door and Mary watched the carriage wheels roll forward until the vehicle was no longer in sight.

Rogan waggled his brows at Mary. "Shall we go inside, my darling?"

A smile flickered on her lips as she took his arm and walked up the three steps to the threshold.

The footman passed by and opened the door for them.

Rogan paused and glanced her way most mischievously, then he suddenly scooped her up in his arms and stepped into the house.

"Welcome to your new home, my duchess."

Chapter 19

⌢⌣⌢

The balance of the day passed more quickly than Mary could have imagined.

Sitting at a Pembroke table before one of her bedchamber windows, Mary stared out at the flame-colored sunset above the town houses of Portman Square.

Every room of the house was elegantly appointed with vibrantly colored, rich fabrics and unusual artwork. There were a number of pieces of over-sized furniture, which, Rogan was quick to explain, had been specially designed to accommodate his extraordinary height.

The scale of his furniture would take some getting used to. She first realized it when, after being

301

introduced to the household staff, she sat upon the large sofa in the drawing room.

To her surprise, her slippers dangled a few inches from the floor, and she felt a bit like the diminutive Lady Upperton.

She glanced across the bedchamber at the enormous bedstead situated between the windows. It was huge and solidly-built, much like Rogan himself.

To her horror, she suddenly found herself imagining Rogan lifting her in his arms, his body naked—as he had admitted that he did not care for nightclothes—his muscles taut and hard as he carried her to the bed, gazing at her with a wicked, rakish look in his eyes.

How long until their wedding night?

Mary grinned at the thought as she opened the valise Elizabeth had packed for her and emptied the bottles, pins, and pots onto her makeshift dressing table. She unfolded a lace-edged handkerchief and dabbed the beads of moisture at her temples.

"It's quite warm inside the house, isn't it?"

Mary turned to see that Rogan was standing in the doorway, watching her.

"If you are finished, why don't you join me for refreshments in the courtyard? There is a breeze passing through the greenery in the garden."

"Sounds lovely." She smiled at him. "I shall join you in a moment."

When she could hear Rogan's footfall descending the staircase, Mary lifted the hand mirror from the table and peered into it.

Blast! It was as she feared. Her cheeks were as red as the sunset.

She glanced out the window and saw that much of the color had already drained from the sky.

The facades of the houses across the square were sheathed in thin veils of gray, but the alleyways between them were as black as a pot of ink.

Mary exhaled in relief.

At least her flaming cheeks would not be so obvious in the growing dimness.

She ran her fingers over her face. Or so she hoped.

When Mary came downstairs, the house, which had been teeming with scurrying maids and busy footmen, all afternoon, seemed quite deserted.

As she walked down the shadowed passage, she poked her head into each room she passed. But there was no one.

The house was dark inside. Not a single candle lit Mary's path to the French windows leading to the outside.

"Rogan?" she called nervously. She pressed down the latch and stepped into the courtyard.

Crickets chirped in the night, and the air was lightly scented with lilac and roses. But Rogan was not there, either.

"Please, Rogan, answer me. Are you here?"

"This way, my darling."

She whirled toward the sound of his deep voice and squinted her eyes to peer into the lush garden beyond.

There, a single lantern flickered in the distance. A beacon in the darkness.

She walked down a path of crushed oyster shells, deeper into the lush garden, ever closer to the light.

He had to be near now, just on the other side of a large walnut tree.

She stepped from the path, and coils of ivy twined around her ankles. "Rogan?" Resting her hand on the rough trunk, she peered around the tree. But the light was suddenly gone.

The moon was just beginning to rise, and a soft blue light cut through the branches of the walnut tree.

Just ahead, she glimpsed something moving in a small clearing. "Rogan, is that you?"

She hurried for the swath of grass she'd seen, and when she reached it, she stilled and held her breath to listen.

Where was he?

Large, calloused hands suddenly smoothed over her shoulders from behind, and she sighed with pleasure.

"Ah, there's my goddess," he whispered to her. "My garden statue."

His mouth was moist upon her ear, his breath,

hot against the skin of her throat. "I wonder, will the moonlight bring my statue to life as it did once before?"

"*Rogan.*" Mary closed her eyes and leaned back against him, reveling in the closeness of her body to his.

"Perhaps a kiss might prompt her forth. I shall try it." He turned her around to face him. Slowly, he slid his hands down to grasp her waist and pull her to him.

"No, we can't . . . the servants." She brought her hands up and pressed against his chest. "We should not—"

"They are gone." He smiled. "Sent them all to the special victory performance at Astley's Amphitheatre, which means they won't be back until very, very late."

She gave a whimper because an unmarried miss should do just that, but her empty protest was drowned as his lips pressed down upon her mouth.

She wanted him so much. She arched her body against him as she gave in to his sweet kiss.

He lifted his lips from hers, only a breath apart, and whispered to her. "I need you, Mary. Need you in my life. I am only sorry that I didn't realize it before—"

"Before we were ceremoniously *not* wed?" Mary tilted her head up and smiled at him, then touched her lips to his as she trailed her fingers sensuously over the muscles of his stomach.

God above, she should not do this. Kissing him, touching him, as she was, would lead her down a path of no return.

But tonight, she didn't care.

Rogan was to be her husband.

This time, there would be no questions.

And so she gave in to the passions she had suppressed for so long. Willingly. Eagerly.

With nimble fingers, she caught the billow of his lawn shirt and tugged it free, then eased her palms beneath it and over his smooth skin.

He shivered with pleasure at her touch and pulled her roughly up against his body.

Fortunately, she guessed, because of the heat of the night, he wore no neckcloth, and his shirt was open at his throat.

She nibbled along the long column of his neck, tasted the saltiness as she kissed the pulse beating through his skin. But her hands, her arms, still craved the feel of his body.

She wanted more. She wanted all of him.

Abruptly, she pulled back and yanked his shirt upward.

A primitive glint shone excitedly in Rogan's eyes. He slipped his arms free and whisked the lawn shirt over his shoulders, casting it off his body.

He gazed hungrily at Mary's white linen gown, and her breath came faster.

A sudden breeze blew through her tumbling hair, smoothing her gown against her aroused body.

The coolness of the breeze blowing on her warm skin hardened her nipples.

Rogan's gaze instantly focused on the two hard buds pressing against her thin gown. His fingers traced the curve of one breast, then he palmed its fullness, rubbing his thumb over her erect nipple.

Mary gasped as his heated touch and her own wanton thoughts drove her arousal to the edge. She turned her head up and stared up at him.

"I need you, too," she whispered.

He cupped one hand to the small of her back and with the other eased down the capped shoulders of her gown. And then her chemise, pushing both down about her waist.

Instinctively, she crossed her arms over her breasts, covering them.

Raising his hand, he stroked her cheek as he gazed deeply into her eyes. "You needn't fear me." His fingers slowly played their way down her throat, then moved lower, until they lightly pushed her arms away. His fingers slid over the soft skin of her breast.

She closed her eyes at the sensation. "I don't fear you," she said softly, her words barely riding a breath. "I want you."

His breath hitched in his throat as she spoke those simple words.

"Oh, Mary." Her name, wrapped in his heated breath, washed over her throat. His moist lips followed the same path and pressed against her skin there.

She let her head fall backward, and her hair fell loose from its pins, sending the dark locks of her long hair cascading down her spine.

His hand, which had been pressed so firmly into the small of her back, slid upward and cupped the curve behind her neck. He pulled her head forward, her face upward to his, and he kissed her hungrily.

As he moved his mouth over hers, he removed his hand from her breast and suddenly swung it down behind her knees, lifting her into his arms before gently laying her out on the grass beneath him.

He stood over her, studying her body through those dark, smoldering eyes of his.

She was panting now with her need. She reached a pleading hand through the air to him.

As he came down on his knees beside her, she slipped her hand around his neck and pulled him down atop of her. She touched her lips to his, then slipped her tongue into his mouth.

He was as hard as the deuced stone under his left knee.

It would take an act of the Church and Crown to restrain himself now.

Mary arched against him, pulled him, with both hands, harder against her.

Her willingness, her desire for him and her passion were not in question. She wanted him as badly as he wanted her.

Now.

He rolled beside her, and as he fed on her mouth, he gathered up the layers of her gown and underpinnings and shoved them up to her waist. Baring her to his hands.

She sighed as he cupped his hand behind her knee and dragged it toward him, parting her legs to his touch.

He ran his hand slowly up between her creamy thighs, higher and higher until he felt the humid warmth of her beneath his palm.

As he raked his fingers through the downiness he found there, she pressed her mound firmly against his hand.

She felt hot and wet, and he slipped his index finger between her cleft and circled the small bud there.

Mary's eyes went wide. She stiffened and feebly grabbed at his wrist, trying to pull him from her. *"Rogan."*

He angled his shoulder against her arm and pushed her hand away as he touched his lips to her mouth, as his fingers continued to explore her wetness.

He thrust two fingers inside her and felt her muscles contract around them as he moved them in and out.

Mary squirmed, whimpering in frustration. She bucked against him. "Rogan, *please.*" Her arm caught his shoulder, and she pulled hard, trying with all her might to move him fully atop her.

He knew she wanted to feel his weight. Wanted to feel him inside her.

Her desire was his undoing.

He withdrew his wet fingers and leaned back from her, releasing the two buttons that restrained him. His erection sprang forth.

Her gaze fell upon him, and her eyes widened for several moments. Then she calmed and raised her hand.

He expected her to reach out to him, but instead, she curled her fingers around his hardness and stroked him firmly as he moved between her knees.

He gasped a breath of surprise. "Where did you learn that maneuver, from that book you've been carrying around with you?"

Mary smiled wickedly up at him. "Well, of course. It's all about river sickness, dysentery, and seeping infections—oh, and of course how to seduce a duke."

"Say anything about how best to seduce a goddess?"

"Not a word."

"Then I fear I shall have to learn through a lot of trial and error." He cast her a wicked grin, then peered down at the porcelain, satiny skin of her thighs. He nudged them farther apart, wanting to sheath himself deep inside her that very instant.

Abruptly, his gaze shifted to her face. Her expression was that of an innocent, and he remembered that despite her passionate nature, she was inexperienced in the ways of making love.

But then, though he had lain with too many women to remember, so was he.

Until this night, he had never been with a woman he loved.

And he truly did love her.

The backs of his eyes began to sting with the naked realization of his feelings for her. For the first time in his life, he felt what it meant to be in love.

Love.

The Black Duke was in love.

And, as his eyes met hers, he knew, with every fiber and sinew of his being, that she loved him too.

"Rogan, I want you," she gasped, sliding her fingers faster against him as she guided him between her legs. "I don't want to wait."

Damn it all. Not like this.

Not like last time, her first time.

He had to do this slowly, gently, even though his bollocks already tightened in anticipation.

He watched her face intently as he touched her with one finger where she was most sensitive. He felt her thighs tighten against his knees as she reflexively sought to close her legs.

Once again, he touched her softly. His finger circled the bit of flesh, gradually pressing harder, moving faster.

Mary's eyes closed. She turned her head to the side and bit down into her full lower lip.

Yes, this is what he wanted for her. And more. Much more.

His finger circled faster, as he slowly rose up on his knees and leaned back, then lowered his mouth between her quivering legs.

She gasped and reached down to his head as if to pull him away to stop him. Her fingers entwined in his hair as he lapped at her.

He eased his fingers into the tightness of her, and she moaned and instinctively pressed him harder against her. He slowly drove his fingers into her depths, making her writhe with mindless pleasure as he flicked his slick tongue against her.

"Rogan, please. *Please.* No more. I want *you.*" Her voice was husky with want.

Eager to oblige, he pushed up on his hands. He had grown almost painfully hard, and he throbbed with his own need for her.

He bent his elbows and pressed a kiss to her belly. She wrapped her hands around his neck and led him higher, letting him kiss her ribs.

Higher still to suckle her breasts. And then, she brought him to her mouth.

He pressed a hand down in the grass beside her shoulder and supported his weight as he reached down with his other hand and positioned his hardness between her folds.

Rogan stroked her with his firm, plum-shaped tip, wetting it with her essence. Then he lifted her bottom and slid into her.

She sighed, and her eyes widened as her body accepted him slowly, but surely.

He paused, feeling her muscles tighten around him as he sank deeper into her. He squeezed his eyes closed and fought the incredible urge to take her hard, take her fast.

Mary raised her hips. She wanted to feel him deeper inside of her. Rogan groaned and thrust into her, slowly, steadily.

She slipped her hands under his arms, wrapped them around his back and squeezed him tight.

Harder. Faster. Deeper.

In a move that surprised him, Mary raised her knee and hooked her leg around his back. She jerked her leg hard and buried him deep within her.

Her muscles cinched around him. He could wait no longer.

Rising up on his hands, he slammed into the searing heat of her. Tiny whimpers of pleasure fell from her mouth as he pumped her again and again.

She cried out his name, and his body tensed and released.

He kissed her, and as he settled his head in the crook of her neck, he thought he heard her say something . . . but no, she could not have said that.

It would be too much to hope.

But she kissed his ear and whispered again.

"I love you, Rogan."

Chapter 20

The next morning, Mary awoke to find herself alone in the giant's bed. Or rather, her soon-to-be husband's bed. She smiled in her bliss.

Maybe someday soon they would actually use a bed for something other than sleeping. But until then, there were always gardens and carriages. Mary chuckled to herself.

They were as good as married already anyway.

Why, they'd had a ceremony, albeit an illegal one, attended by family and friends. The marriage had already been consummated. And she had the ring.

Smiling, Mary held up her left hand to look at it. But the ring wasn't there.

Blast!

A tremor raced through her, and she sprang from the bed and tore back the sheets and coverlet.

She shook the pillows and tossed them on the floor while she searched the mattress.

Oh, God, she couldn't find it anywhere! How could it have come off? She'd tugged on it for two days, and it would not be removed.

Why now, when she would need it at any time?

Then it struck her. *The garden.* It must have slipped off in the grass last night.

Clad only in her chemise, Mary raced down the staircase, down the center passage, and into the bright courtyard.

"Good morning, darling." Rogan sat beside another gentleman before a paper-strewn iron table in the center of the courtyard. "This is Mr. Lawson, my solicitor."

Suddenly all too aware of her state of undress, she crossed her arms over her chest, then nodded her head and gave an embarrassed smile to the solicitor. "Good morning." She moved her bare feet slowly backward, retracing her steps to the French windows leading back into the house. When her heel stubbed the threshold, she reached her hand behind her and felt for the door latch.

"Mary, is there something that you require?" Rogan asked politely.

She depressed the handle, and the door opened behind her. "No, no. 'Twas nothing really. I just . . . wanted to know if you were at home, nothing more." She started to duck in through the door when she heard Rogan's voice again.

"Mary."

She held the door in front of her barely dressed form and peered around the French window at him. "Yes?"

Rogan had an amused smile on his face. "I received a note of response from the rector of Marylebone Parish. The wedding will be here, late Wednesday evening. Does that suit you?"

"Late on Wednesday?" Forgetting herself, she stepped from behind the shield of the door.

"Best not to alert the neighbors that the newly-wedded couple is getting married *again*."

"Oh, quite right. Yes, Wednesday suits me perfectly." Then, without another word, she hurried back inside the house and to the bedchamber to dress.

She fumbled through the crystal bottles of scents and powders on the Pembroke table. She searched through every seam of the dress she'd worn the night before.

Nothing.

At least the wedding was not tomorrow. She had until Wednesday night to find the ring.

Mary dressed quickly, but her fretting about the ring set her pacing back and forth across the bed-chamber.

Finally, she decided that she had tarried long enough in finishing her toilette.

There was no use circling the room like a caged beast. The ring was not to be found in the bedchamber.

Rogan and his solicitor might already have quit the courtyard by now, leaving her free to conduct a proper, and most thorough, search of the garden.

Whirling around, she hurried from the bedchamber, crept through the passage, and tiptoed down the shadowy staircase.

She supposed she could admit the ring's loss, but Rogan had been so sweet declaring that the ring would not come off because it was meant to stay there forever.

No, if she couldn't locate it, she would just have to buy another. It shouldn't be too hard to locate another simple gold ring. Any jeweler on Bond Street should have them available, shouldn't they?

Then it suddenly struck her.

I am supposed to be a married woman.

If the ring was not on her finger, she could not possibly leave this house! If she did, and was noticed, rumors might spread—and the truth of Lotharian's hoax of a wedding might surface.

All of their plans to secretly wed would be for naught!

No, no, no. She needed her sisters' help to find

the ring right away. She'd just send a missive to them and ask them to call as soon as they were available.

Mary hurried downstairs and had only walked halfway along the passage when she heard Rogan's deep voice coming from the direction of the courtyard.

She turned and went into the study for some paper and ink with which to write a note to summon her sisters to her.

Near the front window was a large, mahogany secretaire-bookcase, edged in satinwood with gleaming lion's head brass pulls.

She grasped the two rings on the front drawer and pulled it open. Inside were numerous legal documents, letters, and . . . at last, a sheet of foolscap paper.

Snatching it up, Mary closed the drawer, then turned the key that opened the glassed bookshelves on the upper half of the secretaire. She withdrew a pot of ink and a pen.

She hurried with her takings to a rosewood writing table and sat down to pen her message.

"Oh, perdition!" Mary stared down at the foolscap. She hadn't noticed that the reverse side had already been used.

Standing, she was about to return the scribbled page back to the secretaire's drawer when she noticed her name written upon the sheet.

She walked to the window and tipped the page to the morning light.

Country Miss wins Duke's Heart
A Royle Wedding

Both of these were crossed through. Evidently not the winning selection. *That* was written below and underlined three times.

Miss Royle Weds
Duke in Surprise Wedding

As Mary read the writing below and recognized it as the column she'd read in the newspaper—the column that had necessitated another wedding, a legal wedding—her mood veered into black anger.

Rogan had written the column and had dispatched it to be placed prominently in the newspaper. *He* had done it!

She slapped the paper to the writing table. But why? Why would he do such a thing?

Bah! Did it really matter?

No, it didn't.

He was manipulating her, again.

Nothing was sacred to him. Everything was naught but a game of chess.

She turned and ran to the bedchamber and snatched up her father's book of maladies and remedies. Everything else she left behind as she stormed from the house, slamming the front door behind her.

She didn't know or care what society would say about her or him and the sham of a wedding. At this moment, she didn't care.

All she knew was that she was never coming back.

How lucky for her that she had lost the wedding ring.

Had she not, she might never have known what Rogan had done with absolutely no regard for her or her sisters.

Swinging her arms angrily as she walked, Mary barged across the square in the direction of Oxford Street, on her way home to Berkeley Square.

After Mr. Lawson left the courtyard, Rogan lingered a while longer. Everything about this day seemed sweeter—the air, the sun . . . his life.

With a smile curving his lips, he strolled down the shell path into the garden, tilting his face toward the warm sunlight.

He veered off the crunching pathway, stepped through the clinging ivy, and passed the walnut tree, until he reached the clearing.

He nodded to himself. This was the place.

The very place where Mary had confessed her love for him.

And it would be the place where he would do the same before God and family.

This was the spot where they would marry.

Just then, something caught his eye. Something glittering and winking at him through the soft green blades of grass. He knelt down and picked up a circlet of gold.

Mary's ring.

It must have slipped off last night whilst they'd . . . *made love.*

Rogan rose and rubbed the gold ring on his coat, polishing it.

Then it occurred to him. When Mary had run into the courtyard in a state of undress, her face stricken, it had been because she had just realized that the ring had slipped from her finger.

Rogan grinned. Even now, she was probably tearing the bedchamber apart looking for it. Turning on his boot heel, Rogan headed back for the house.

The bedchamber was in shambles, as he had predicted. Pillows, sheeting, and the coverlet were thrown on the floor. Even the mattress had been turned on the bedstead. He chuckled, imagining what a sight she must have been in her panicked search.

Supposing she must be searching other rooms for the ring, he walked down the stairs. But he did not find her in the drawing room.

Nor in the library, nor the breakfast or dining rooms.

He headed down the passage for the study and poked his head through the doorway. "Mary, are you in here?"

Rogan started to turn away, when from the corner of his eye he noticed something out of place.

He entered the room and crossed to the writing table. He picked up a sheet of foolscap he found next to a pot of ink and a pen.

Though the writing utensils had not been there the evening before, he noticed immediately that the scrawl on the paper was in Quinn's own hand.

Raising the document to his eyes, he began to read.

He had barely begun when, to his astonishment, he realized what he held in his hand.

And what Mary had found.

"Bloody hell."

Chapter 21

⁓⦿⦿⁓

Cavendish Square

"**M**ary is hurt. She, even her sisters, will not see me, will not take my cards, nor my messages." Rogan raised his eyes from the hat in his hands to Lady Upperton's round face. "I need your help. She will listen to you."

"Dear boy, she will listen to you as well," the old woman told him. "You only need to give her a true reason."

"What more reason is there than I love Mary and want to spend my life with her?"

"Do you now, Blackstone?"

"I do."

"Have you told Mary this?"

323

"No . . . not specifically." Rogan turned his hat in his hands and thought about her question. "She knows how I feel about her. I am sure of it."

Lady Upperton huffed at that. "Never underestimate the power of words, Blackstone. Sometimes, when we most need to hear them, words can be stronger than deeds."

Rogan thought about what Lady Upperton said. And it was true. When Mary had whispered, "I love you" into his ear, his heart had swelled.

He hadn't known then how much he'd needed to hear those three simple words. It seemed he'd been waiting his entire life to hear "I love you."

"I shall speak with Lotharian. We will assist you, Blackstone." Lady Upperton raised her hand before Rogan could argue the wisdom of her suggestion. "Now, now, do not interrupt. Lotharian needs to redeem himself. He wishes to see you and our Mary together almost as much as yourself."

The little woman scooted to the end of the settee and pulled a lever, which shot forth a footstool. "You said that the rector is able to officiate on Wednesday, is that correct?"

"Indeed. Ten in the evening."

She stepped onto the footstool, then to the floor. Rogan took her elbow and walked alongside her into the entry hall.

"Do not change your plans," she told him as they reached the front door and the footman opened it.

"But how will—"

"No, no. No more chatter for now." She patted his arm. "Wait for my message on the morrow. There *will* be a wedding." Her crimson-painted lips curved upward. "You will see. Trust the purity of Mary's heart. She will not let you down."

It was Wednesday.

And this night Mary would have become the Duchess of Blackstone.

Instead, she remained inside the house, curtains drawn, the knocker removed from the front door as though the family was not at home.

When Mary heard the door open, she rose from the window seat in the parlor and walked to meet her sisters, who had gone to Portman Square to collect her belongings from Rogan.

Only they had returned very quickly.

When Mary walked into the entry hall, she saw that Elizabeth and Anne were not alone.

Quinn's cane clicked on the marble floor as he stepped toward her, his hand outstretched.

"Miss Royle," he said, his voice quavering slightly. "We must speak. *Please.*"

Mary's gaze shot to Anne's.

"We had only just arrived when Lord Wetherly's carriage drew up before the house. He had come from his country house to help his brother prepare for the wedding."

"But your sisters told me that there would not

be a wedding today. And I fear the fault is mine." Quinn's gaze crawled along the floor before he gathered the courage to meet Mary's.

"Your fault? How can that be?" Mary asked. When Quinn did not immediately reply, she gestured for him to follow her into the parlor.

When Elizabeth made to join them, Mary turned back to her. "Would you two please put my belongings in my bedchamber?" she asked, hoping to glean a few private moments hearing what Quinn had to tell her without her sisters listening to every word.

"Oh, we did not collect your belongings. And we do apologize for not doing so." Elizabeth nervously glanced at Anne for support.

"Quinn was certain that what he had to tell you would repair the misunderstanding between you and the duke." Anne took a step backward. "So I told Elizabeth that we should just return home and leave your belongings. It was the wisest course of action, for there may yet be a wedding this eve after all."

Mary pinned Anne with a heated gaze, but she said nothing and walked into the parlor with Lord Wetherly.

Mary offered him a chair, but he appeared more than a little on edge, admitting to her that he preferred to stand.

"I-I thought you knew," he stammered.

"I don't understand, Lord Wetherly."

"I apologized. And you accepted it." He peered at her through squinted, confused eyes.

Mary set her hands on her knees and leaned forward. "Please, Quinn, speak plainly. I do not recall any apology. What could you have done that might warrant one?"

"Truly, you do not know?"

Mary shook her head brusquely, hoping that Quinn would hurry along with his confession.

"I was so happy for my brother. So joyous that he had found a woman so worthy of his heart." He swallowed hard and took a deep breath. "I wanted to share my brother's happiness with everyone, but so few knew of the ceremony. So I submitted the column recounting your wedding at the Argyle Rooms."

Mary shot to her feet. "*You*? But I found it with Rogan's papers in the secretaire."

"I put it there, so later I could compare my wording with the *on-dit* column when the news of the wedding was published. Surely you are aware of the columnists' penchant for embellishment. I wanted to be sure they reported everything correctly. It was important to me."

"Then Rogan never saw the draft or knew of the column before it was published?"

"No, he didn't." Quinn shrugged sheepishly. "I was reading the very column I had supplied to the editors at the newspaper when Rogan came down the stairs to break his fast. I had been out the night before and hadn't realized that he had come home."

Mary's head began to ache. She didn't want to hear any more, but she knew she must.

"When Rogan told me that the wedding had been Lotharian's lark, I could not speak. Rogan took the newspaper from the table and began to read it. He was headed for the door before I could confess my error. As he was leaving, he told me he would be bringing you back with him. I knew he would marry you and the cart would be set to rights again."

"Why didn't you tell him? Or tell me?"

"Rogan was so happy. Oh, he tried not to let on, but I could see it. I have never seen a man whose heart was so full. I couldn't tell him. And the article really didn't matter at that point anyway. You and he were going to be married."

Mary's eyebrows inched toward her nose. "Wait a moment. You did mention the column to me." She raised a finger in the air as she dug deep into her memory to recall the words. "You apologized for the column." She looked at Quinn. "But I thought you meant that the release of the column was regrettable. Not that you wrote it!"

Quinn coughed an uneasy half laugh. "I suppose on some level I knew you misunderstood. I only hoped that you would realize that I had supplied the information for the column when you read it and saw that my name alone was left out."

Mary shook her head. "I was too shaken by the

consequences of the column to notice," she said under her breath.

She turned and walked nearly blindly into the entry hall, where she snatched her straw bonnet from a hook on the wall.

Quinn followed close behind. "I am sorry, Miss Royle. You cannot know how much."

Mary opened the front door and started down the steps.

Quinn's cane clicked behind her.

"I have to speak with Rogan. I have to apologize for doubting him—" she began.

"Let me take you to Portman Square," Quinn said. "'Tis the least I can do."

Before Mary could accept, she heard MacTavish calling her name from the open door.

"Miss Royle!" He raised a folded square of vellum in his hand. "This came for you while you were in the parlor with Lord Wetherly."

"I shall read it when I return," she replied curtly.

"It is from the duke, Miss Royle. His footman bade me tell you it was very important."

Mary spun around, raced up the stairs, and took the missive. She broke the red wax wafer and unfolded the letter. Her eyes skimmed over the short note.

She looked to Quinn. "He has gone to Cavendish Square. Can you take me there to meet him?"

"It would be my honor, Miss Royle."

* * *

Mary and Quinn were led into Lady Upperton's library, where the portly old woman and Lord Lotharian sat waiting.

Mary glanced about the room. Rogan was not there. She lifted the short letter in her hand to show Lady Upperton and Lotharian. "I-I was under the impression that Blackstone would be here."

"Oh, and he shall." Lotharian rose and walked over to reach out his hand to her.

Mary took a step backward.

"My dear, you might be quite miffed at me now, but I vow, in one hour's time, you will be kissing my cheek."

"I doubt that very much, my lord. The past few days have been the most miserable of my life."

"But how were your nights, my dear?" he asked, casting a loathsome, rakish wink at her.

Mary looked past the ancient rake and spoke instead to Lady Upperton. "I beg your pardon, Lady Upperton, but if Rogan is not here, then where is he? It is important that I speak with him immediately."

"I am here."

Mary spun around to see Rogan entering the room with a gray-haired older woman on his arm.

The woman held herself most regally, and Mary was sure she recognized her from somewhere. Just where, though, she couldn't recall.

Lord Lotharian and Lady Upperton approached the woman and began to speak with her. But

Mary's eyes were fixed on Rogan, and she paid the woman no heed.

Rogan released the lady's arm and politely left her side to come to Mary. "Mary, I must speak with you."

Lady Upperton turned and snared both of them by the arm. "There will be time, all the time in the world, for the two of you to speak. But right now, it is time that we hear from Lady Jersey."

"Lady Jersey?" Mary sputtered. She stared hard at the woman. Yes, it was she. The woman from the portrait in the Harrington gallery.

Only now she was older. Her hair gray, not chestnut. Her skin pale, rather than vibrant. "Lady Jersey! B-but, how?"

Graciously, Lady Jersey allowed Lord Lotharian to escort her to the settee, and she sat down.

She raised her eyes to Mary and gazed at her as if assessing her. "I knew the late Duke of Blackstone quite well. His son, here, asked me to come to speak with you about a Kashmir shawl of mine that you might have found."

Mary's eyes went wide. "Yes, we did find a shawl amongst my father's belongings after he died."

Lady Jersey raised her thin brows. "I do not believe I know you, gel."

A jolt rushed through Mary as it occurred to her that if the Old Rakes' story was true, this woman would have preferred her and her sisters . . . *dead.*

Lady Upperton quickly made the requisite introductions.

When appropriate, Mary curtsied hesitantly, for her bones felt as though they had been replaced with ice.

"Miss Royle?" Lady Jersey narrowed her eyes. "Your name is somehow familiar to me, though your face is not. Have we met before? At the theater, or a rout, perhaps?"

"No, my lady. Perhaps you met my father and know his name? For a time, he was the personal physician to the Prince of Wales."

Mary watched for a flicker, anything that might belie the story of her and her sisters' births.

But there was nothing.

"I do not recall him specifically, no." Lady Jersey's tone remained even. How odd that she could speak through her teeth without moving her mouth but the smallest amount. "The Prince maintains the services of a number of physicians. Both in years past, and now."

Lotharian brought forth the shawl, likely realizing, as Mary did, that Lady Jersey's patience with them was waning. "This is the Kashmir shawl the duke mentioned," he said. "It has been noted that you were wearing one of the very same design in the portrait now hanging in the Harrington gallery. Is the shawl yours?"

Lady Jersey leaned forward and peered at the shawl. "It appears to be one of the several Kashmir shawls I owned."

Lady Upperton's eyes were flashing. "Lady Jersey, the shawl is badly stained . . . with what appears to be dried blood. Can you tell us how that came to be and how Mr. Royle might have come into possession of your shawl?"

An uncomfortable smile spread over Lady Jersey's mouth. "There is only one instance I recall when my clothing might have become stained."

She flicked the shawl with the edge of her reticule, turning it over on the tea table before her. Then she looked up at Lady Upperton and laughed.

"I should not say, but since this particular shawl seems to hold great interest for your party, I will tell you. It happened many years ago. The Prince of Wales was feverish and could not be consoled after Mrs. Fitzherbert left him for a term. The physicians had no choice. He had to be bled."

Mary swallowed deeply and listened.

"I was a close friend of his at the time, so I sat with him to ease his nerves whilst a physician opened his arm. He jerked, though, and blood began to spurt rather than trickle. The physician, needing to act quickly, snatched my shawl from my shoulders and tied it around the Prince's arm to slow the bloodletting."

"And the shawl?" Rogan prodded. "What became of it?"

Lady Jersey stood up. "I never saw the shawl again. Nor did I care to. I had others." She looked up at Rogan. "Now, if there is nothing else, Blackstone, I should like to be returned to my lodgings, please."

Rogan bowed, then turned to his brother. An exchange of glances was all it took for Quinn to take Lady Jersey's arm and escort her outside to his waiting carriage.

"Well, I am sorry her report was not more encouraging, Miss Royle," Lotharian sighed loudly.

"It changes nothing for me. It is not my past that interests me . . . but rather, my future." She allowed her gaze to touch Rogan's face. "Though my sisters might be rather disappointed." Mary looked at Lady Upperton and smiled. "But our stay in London is not finished, and, I daresay, with Elizabeth and Anne poking about, there will be other clues."

"Mrs. Fitzherbert still lives," Rogan broke in. "I could approach her for you and your sisters."

"Thank you, but no." Mary turned, and her gaze locked with Rogan's. "My sisters and I agreed that we would never approach such an esteemed woman with our story—without irrefutable evidence. We have nothing." After speaking, she allowed her gaze to linger.

Lady Upperton saw the intimate exchange of glances. "Lotharian, might I speak with you in the passage for a moment?"

"What, whatever for—"

"I have been having a problem with rodents. Come this way." With amazing speed, the old woman took Lotharian's arm and led him out of the library and into the passage.

Mary's eyes flooded as she peered up at Rogan. "I am so sorry, my love. I should have trusted you."

Her voice shook with deep regret, and she could not stop the torrent of tears that began coursing down her cheeks. "I am so sorry—"

Rogan set his fingers over her lips to quiet her. "Shhh. Say nothing more. Please, just listen."

Mary nodded mutely.

Rogan cradled her face in his hands and peered down into her watery eyes as he dabbed away the tears on her cheeks with the pads of his thumbs. "I love you, Mary. With all my heart and all that I am, I love you."

He bent and pressed his lips to hers, and she melted into his arms.

When he lifted his mouth from her lips, he smiled down at her. "I cannot make you a princess, but if you will have me this night, a duchess you will be."

Rogan reached into his waistcoat pocket and withdrew a gold wedding ring. He held it before her eyes. "If you love me, as I love you, say you will, Mary. Say you will be my wife."

"I will." Mary's eyes misted as she gazed up at Rogan, but then took on a glimmer. "I still get to wear a tiara, right?"

Portman Square, that evening

The moon shone like a lantern upon the grassy clearing of the garden where the three women stood, their skin smooth and white as marble in the blue glow of the light.

Their snowy gowns draped gracefully from their shoulders, and they were tied with crossed ribbons of ivory silk. The looked like goddesses from another time and place.

One, in particular.

Rogan smiled with pride as he gazed down at Mary, standing at his side. Her sisters dutifully stood to her left, his own brother to his right.

The air was filled with the soft, sweet perfume of newly planted crimson-budded roses, and their scattered petals made a lush velvet carpet for the wedding party.

Tears of joy streaked down Lady Upperton's face, cutting wet tracks in her heavily powdered face. Lord Lotharian was beside her, smiling most confidently. However, his gaze seemed to alight on the small leather pouches of wagered coins both Gallantine and Lilywhite held in their hands at the ready in the event that the couple actually married as he'd predicted.

The rector prompted Mary's reply.

"I will," she replied. She turned her gaze to Rogan's then, and her smile broadened.

Rogan squeezed her hand. He'd never felt so blissfully happy. Never before had his heart felt so full.

Never had he been so completely in love.

"I love you," Rogan whispered to her as he slipped the ring of gold over her knuckle and pressed it down to the base of her finger. "And I will, forever."

"I love you too, and shall, forever," she echoed.

A warm glow spread through Rogan just then.

He knew the ring would never come off her finger again, because this time nothing could come between them.

They would truly be together . . . forever.

Epilogue

～⊙⊙～

Mary leaned against the tufted leather cushion inside the carriage and tilted the pages of her father's book of maladies and remedies to the light breaking through the window.

"You can't mean to read *that* book during the entire journey to Blackstone Hall." Rogan snatched the volume from her hands.

"I cannot stop wondering why my father included this book, of all of the other medical texts in his library, in the document box. Elizabeth is certain there is a clue or some other important information in this book that might assist us in learning the identity of our true parents. My father scrawled so many little notes, underlined segments. There has to be something here. I am just missing it."

"I thought that book was about how to seduce a duke."

"Mmm, you remembered that, did you?" Mary grinned back at him. "Well, I studied that particular chapter. Have it memorized, in fact."

"Have you, now?" One corner of Rogan's mouth slipped upward, and he flashed that rakish smile of his. "And what does that chapter suggest?"

"Oh, it's quite simple, really." Mary reached up, drew the shade down over the window, and turned her most seductive smile upon him. "Just find a carriage."

A footman, liveried in deepest blue satin, stood just outside the circular glow of the candle upon the writing desk.

He was nearly invisible to Lady Jersey as she dipped her pen into a crystal pot of ink and moved it across the page, but she knew he was there. He was waiting to deliver the all-important missive she was hurriedly writing.

She sprinkled sand on the words, then tapped the page on the desk before folding and sealing it with a dollop of red wax. She pressed her ring into the drying wafer, then turned and handed the missive to the footman.

"Take it to her. Hurry. She must know."

He bowed and disappeared beyond the reach of light.

Lady Jersey leaned her elbows on the desk. The

granules of sand bit into her thin skin as she rested her head in her trembling hands and closed her eyes.

God help me.

The babies lived.

They lived.

The adventures of
Kathryn Caskie's
Royle Sisters

continues when we all learn...

How To Engage an Earl

Coming in June 2007

from Avon Books